PRAISE FOR *THE LAST MAN*

"Goodman writes crisp, confident prose, giving us a novel as compelling as the incredible true story it's based on. *The Last Man* blends thrilling, cinematic set pieces with convincing character work that explores the nature of crime and rehabilitation. Fans of historical fiction should list Goodman among their 'must-buy' authors." **(James Wade, two-time Spur Award-winning author of *Beasts of the Earth*)**

"*The Last Man* seizes the reader on page one and doesn't let go. Goodman has deftly brought his characters to life…. Smooth, engrossing, entertaining reading, from start to finish." **(Lone Star Literary Life)**

"Goodman's debut novel is a remarkable accomplishment. Through gripping action scenes and slow-burn character studies, Goodman delivers an authentic Texas story that will keep readers turning the pages. At its core, though, *The Last Man* is more than the tale of a botched heist. It is a haunting exploration of man's inherent brokenness and the longing for redemption and liberation." **(Eileen Flynn, Austin American-Statesman staff writer and editor 2007-2020, and University of Texas adjunct journalism professor 2007-2019)**

"If you're from Texas and a history buff, you may have heard about the Santa Claus Bank Robbery, but I guarantee you haven't heard the story told like this. Goodman mixes fact and fiction in an irresistible blend of storytelling and action that will have you turning pages until the very end. Do not miss this fabulous Texas tale!" **(Kathleen Y'Barbo, Publishers Weekly bestselling author of *The Black Midnight* and the *Bayou Nouvelle* series)**

"Goodman's research and meticulous attention to detail places the reader at the scene of the robbery and the aftermath, including the court proceedings, jail, and prison life. Most important, though, is the saving transformation of 'the last man'—a success story that all correctional professionals like me hope for, strive for, pray for, and love to see." **(David Stacks –Director of the Texas Prison Museum and Retired Warden of the Texas Department of Criminal Justice)**

"*The Last Man* is a fascinating story and told very well! It has just the right amount of detail and a smooth balance of dialogue and description to keep the reader thoroughly engaged from beginning to end. Plus, the life lessons to be learned are abundant." **(David Hardage, Executive Director for Texas Baptists 2012 to 2022)**

THE
LAST
MAN

*Based
on a
true
story*

THE
LAST
MAN

THOMAS
GOODMAN

A NOVEL OF THE 1927 SANTA CLAUS BANK ROBBERY

Copyright ©2023 by Thomas Goodman

Published by
Mainsail Books
Austin, Texas

Edited by: Michelle Hope
Cover design by: Clarissa Yeo, Yocla Designs
Interior layout by: Veronica Yager, YellowStudios

Publisher's Cataloging-in-Publication Data
provided by Five Rainbows Cataloging Services

Names: Goodman, Thomas, 1961- author.
Title: The last man : a novel of the 1927 Santa Claus bank robbery / Thomas Goodman.
Description: Austin, TX : Mainsail Books, 2023.
Identifiers: LCCN 2023904220 (print) | ISBN 979-8-9877508-3-4 (hardcover) | ISBN 979-8-9877508-0-3 (paperback) | ISBN 979-8-9877508-1-0 (ebook) | ISBN 979-8-9877508-2-7 (audiobook)
Subjects: LCSH: Bank robberies--Fiction. | Death--Fiction. | Texas--Fiction. | Historical fiction. | Christian fiction. | BISAC: FICTION / Historical / 20th Century / General. | FICTION / Christian / Historical. | FICTION / Crime. | FICTION / Westerns. | GSAFD: Historical fiction. | Christian fiction.
Classification: LCC PS3607.O53 L37 2023 (print) | LCC PS3607.O53 (ebook) | DDC 813/.6--dc23.

Paperback ISBN: 979-8-9877508-0-3
Hardcover ISBN: 979-8-9877508-3-4
Ebook ISBN: 979-8-9877508-1-0
Audiobook ISBN: 979-8-9877508-2-7
Library of Congress Control Number: 2023904220

First edition.

The reader may ask how to tell fact from fiction. A rough guide: anything that seems particularly unlikely is probably true.

—Hilary Mantel

EL PASO, TEXAS, 1931

The man stood in the midnight shadows for a long time and studied the empty bridge that led into Juárez. Light spilled from the customs booth closest to him on the American side of the river. Two hundred yards away, a bare incandescent bulb glowed in a booth on the Mexican side.

Slow and casual, he told himself, and approached the bridge. He turned up his collar as if to block the chill wind, but mostly to keep his face hidden from the customs officer sitting behind the glass of the stateside cubicle. He kept moving. He wasn't required to stop on this side.

He was halfway across the Rio Grande when headlamps from a car behind him lit up the bridge. In the beams, his silhouette stretched and wavered toward the Mexican customs booth. Brakes whined faintly as the motor rig slowed to his pace, but he continued walking and kept his face forward. The car advanced into his sidelong view. Lamps like chrome cones rested on wide fenders that curved gracefully down to become running boards. A gold star was painted on the side, encircled with the words "City of El Paso Police Department."

He sighed and his shoulders slumped. It was going to come to an end sometime anyway, the other three being dead and all.

1

CISCO, TEXAS, 1927

Louis Davis hefted the borrowed pistol again. The weight still surprised him. The steel barrel and cylinder were cold in the December morning, but the longer he held the wood-trimmed grip, the more it warmed in his palm. It felt alive. He felt alive.

He knew the two men in the front seat of the sedan didn't want him in the heist. They had never said it, but he knew. They wanted someone like them. Hard. Experienced in this kind of thing. Louis didn't qualify. Back in Wichita Falls, he had a factory job and a wife and three small children. What he didn't have was money. Or excitement. The man next to Louis in the back seat had persuaded the others to bring him along.

Louis swayed left and right with the motion of the car, synchronous with the rocking movements of the other three. He would prove that they had made a good decision to include him. He raised the gun in front of him, imagining what it would be like to point the weapon at someone. The factory worker pretended to fire it, and he mimed the pistol kicking back on him.

HENRY HELMS SAT beside Louis, amused at the simulated pistol fire. His brother-in-law could use a little adventure in his life. He had loaned Louis one of his own handguns for the job, and all the man would need to do with the weapon was look threatening. Like Louis, Henry had a wife and kids back in Wichita Falls. For their sake, he had tried to find work after his release from Huntsville on an armed robbery charge. No one would hire him, but he had been unable to muster the enthusiasm to show up for some square john job, anyway. Nothing had stirred his blood until he heard the plans for this heist, and as the car reached the outskirts of Cisco, his senses began that familiar sharpening.

BEHIND THE WHEEL, Bobby Hill slowed the sedan as he passed the city limits sign, and he began the downshift.

Find the gear. Release the clutch. Feel the teeth engage.

He smiled at the smooth execution. The Buick Bobby drove was a beauty. It was painted the midnight blue of a deep lake, and the enclosed cabin and the suspension it rode on were luxurious. The owner was a Wichita Falls oilman who liked to keep it parked in front of his house for everyone to see. Even without moonlight, Bobby had no trouble finding the key under the floor mat. The Master Six beneath the hood wasn't the fastest engine ever built, but it was plenty powerful to outrun most cars if it came to a chase.

Bobby was nineteen, unmarried, and if there was one thing he had learned in his brief life, it was that cars were easier to figure out than people. Especially the people in the back seat. He didn't like Louis for this job—too green. And he didn't like Henry for anything—too self-interested. But the man who sat beside him had decided on them all, and he had never let Bobby down since they'd met in Huntsville. So, here he was.

NEXT TO BOBBY, twenty-four-year-old Marshall Ratliff rolled down the front passenger window. He rested his elbow on the frame and smiled as the car passed landmarks familiar to him. This was his town, and the heist was his plan.

Marshall had no family in Cisco anymore. His mother had sold her café and moved to Fort Worth, his brother was in prison again, and his wife had divorced him and taken their two small boys away while he was in Huntsville. That's where he had met Henry and Bobby. Still, plenty of people would recognize him here. He had planned for this. He raised a white Santa beard to his face and tied the string behind his head.

Marshall nudged Bobby and pointed. "Let me off at this next block. I'll walk down Main to the bank while you get the car set."

He got out and tucked his pistol into the waist of his trousers. As the car pulled away, he arranged the folded potato sack over his gut. It would serve as padding for his costume and then as a bag for the bank's money. Just as he closed the festive red Santa coat and buckled the wide black belt around his middle, someone behind him called out.

"Well, it's been a while since I've last seen you."

He whirled. It was George Carmichael, a police officer who had jailed him on several occasions for transporting illegal booze. Marshall was at a loss for what to say, but the policeman grinned and said, "Merry Christmas, Santa."

The officer had not recognized him. The fake beard and Santa costume had worked. Marshall attempted a mock-grandfatherly voice. "Merry Christmas to you, my boy."

Carmichael poked Marshall in the gut, just missing the gun in the waistband. "Today's December 23, Santa. You ain't got but two days to fatten up." He chuckled and walked on.

Marshall let out a quiet sigh but kept an edgy eye on the officer until Carmichael turned right at the next corner and strolled toward the police station. Marshall continued straight on Main.

BOBBY EASED THE sedan up the wide alleyway between Garner's Department Store on the left and the First National Bank on the right. Marshall had instructed him to pull forward until the front bumper reached the sidewalk so no one could block them in. He turned the key, and the engine shuddered to a stop and began to tick as it cooled.

IN THE BACK seat, Louis observed how Henry checked the chambers on his pistol and stowed it in his waistband. He did the same thing with his borrowed handgun. Finding nothing else of Henry to imitate, Louis went over Marshall's instructions in his mind again. After Marshall entered the front door, they were to follow in after him. None of them would be recognized in Cisco except Marshall, so no bandanas. Marshall said if they had masks as they entered the bank, it would alert anyone in the street that a robbery was underway. He had assured them they wouldn't be in the lobby long enough for anyone to be able to describe their features later.

Louis was to enter last and lock the lobby door. He only needed to point his pistol at the customers and look like he meant to shoot anyone who got out of line. That's what Henry had told him, anyway. After Marshall emptied the safe and the cash drawers, they'd all escape out the alleyway door in the bookkeeping room. They'd be in the car and out of town in three minutes.

IN THE FRONT seat, Bobby drummed his fingers on the wheel as he waited for Marshall to appear. On a cable pole in front of the bank, the corner of a poster fluttered in the breeze. He squinted at it, and then stopped fidgeting. The corner that had come loose curled over part of the printing, but he saw enough of it to know what it announced.

Wanted. Dead Bank Robbers.

Just two months ago, the Texas Bankers Association had promised a five-thousand-dollar payout for anyone who killed a bandit—and "not one cent," they added, for the capture of a live one. Five thousand dollars was twice a year's pay for a working man. The bankers' incentive had generated considerable interest. And controversy. A deputy sheriff was on trial for convincing four drunk laborers to stand near the bank in Stanton and then shooting them in hopes of claiming the money.

When Marshall first laid out his plans, Bobby had raised a concern about the reward. But Marshall just clapped Bobby on the shoulder and laughed. He declared that with a wheelman like him, they'd be far away before anyone outside the bank could respond.

Commotion from his left took Bobby's mind off the poster. On the sidewalk in front of the Buick, Marshall appeared in his Santa suit and fake white beard.

Children surrounded him like a cloud of fleas on a dog.

MARSHALL HERDED THE children forward, trying to respond to their questions in a hearty voice. "No, Santa don't have no candy . . . Well, now, you'll have to wait till Christmas morning to find out what I'm bringing you . . . Sure, Santa knows where you live."

He then straightened his back and put his hands on his hips. "Run on, now. Santa's got work to do." As the children reluctantly dispersed, he nodded at the men in the car and entered the bank.

Inside, he blinked a moment until his eyes adjusted. It was as he remembered. No more than thirty feet wide and less than a hundred feet deep. The cashier's office and a cage for two tellers ran along the south wall to his left. The office was separated from the bank lobby by a four-foot-high wall that met the teller cage. To his right, a white marble countertop was mounted along the north wall for customers to complete their forms. A door straight ahead of Marshall led into a back room for bookkeepers, and that room contained their escape door to the alley.

There were four men in the lobby. All of them would have recognized Marshall without the Santa Claus disguise. There was Marion Olson in his three-piece suit. He was enrolled up north at Harvard but must have come home for the holidays. Olson was chatting with Alex Spears, the bank's cashier. He still wore the same round owl-eyed glasses that Marshall remembered. Spears had provided bail after Marshall's arrest for the Valera bank job, along with a lecture on how Marshall's mother didn't deserve that kind of heartbreak. Only one of the two stations in the teller cage was occupied. Mr. Jewell Poe was taking a deposit from Oscar Cliett, a local grocer who had not bothered to remove his store apron.

Four men. Perfect.

Spears grinned at him. "Good afternoon, Santa."

Marshall opened his mouth to respond to Spears's greeting, but he was distracted by the creak of hinges. The door from the back room opened, and two little girls walked into the lobby. They gaped in surprise at the Santa Claus and grinned at each other in excitement.

He peered at the shorter one, trying to figure out why she looked so familiar.

Spears tried his greeting again. "So, Santa, are you here to make last-minute payroll for your elves?"

"Uh-huh," Marshall mumbled, trying to muffle his voice under the fake beard.

The front door opened behind him, and when he turned around, it wasn't his men. A mother and her daughter had come in. The child walked straight toward him, holding out what looked to be a Christmas wish list in her hand.

The lobby was getting too crowded. And those two kids coming from the back room meant there had to be people in there, too. Maybe the robbery wasn't such a good idea.

The lobby door rattled as Henry, Bobby, and Louis entered.

Alex Spears nodded at them. "Afternoon, boys."

Henry left the greeting unreturned and walked to the customer side of the teller cage. As he walked, he pulled a pistol from his belt and pointed it at the grocer and the teller.

"Hands up."

The little girl who had come into the bank with her mother screamed, and she gripped Santa by the arm, huddling behind him for protection.

Marshall couldn't stop things now if he wanted to.

2

DEATH TRAP

Marshall yanked himself from the child's grip and pulled out his pistol. He gestured at the woman and the girls and said to Henry, "Corral them in the back room." He turned to Bobby. "And get these men out of view of the front door."

He entered the teller cage and pointed his revolver at Poe while he sifted in the counter drawer. He expected a pistol to be stashed there, and there was. He stuffed it into the wide black belt that wrapped around the Santa coat.

He gestured to Poe. "Open the safe."

"It's on a time lock."

Marshall hadn't anticipated this. He raised his gun to Poe's chest. "You think I don't know about your other safe upstairs? Let's go." They exited the teller cage through a door in the back wall and began to climb a flight of wooden stairs.

WHEN MARSHALL DISAPPEARED, Henry stopped shuffling the woman and the three girls toward the back room. He assessed things in the lobby.

Seeing Louis frozen inside the front door watching the robbery unfold, Henry snapped at him. "Hey, ain't you locked that door yet? Do it."

His brother-in-law's hands shook as he locked the front door.

Henry continued, "And get Apron Man over with the others." Henry didn't know any of these people by name. Apron Man and Owl-Eyes and Three-Piece-Suit Boy.

Louis leveled his borrowed gun at the grocer, and gave Henry an uncertain look, as if he wanted confirmation that he was doing it right.

Henry scowled at his brother-in-law. Waving his gun at Apron Man, he said, "Go over there with him." The grocer joined the two other men that Bobby already had against the wall. Louis stood next to Bobby and imitated how he held his gun on the men.

A door slammed, and Henry turned around to find two of his hostages had disappeared into the back room. The two little girls were still there, but the mother and her daughter were gone.

"Get out of my way!" Henry swept the two girls aside, and his pistol struck one of them. She howled and bent over, holding her head where Henry had hit her. He stumbled past the girls and tried to open the door to the back room. It was locked. He raised a leg and slammed his boot heel above the knob. The jamb splintered and the door swung away from him. He didn't find the mother and daughter. Instead, there was a man and a woman he hadn't seen before. The bank's bookkeepers, maybe. They were at the exit and pushing open a screen door.

Henry gestured at them with his pistol. "Back inside."

The man and woman raised their hands and returned to stand by their desks. In two steps, Henry was at the screen door, and he pushed it open. To his left, the mother was running down the alley, pulling her child with her. He raised his pistol at them and hesitated, and the two escaped around the corner behind the department store. He muttered a curse and reentered the bank.

MARSHALL WAS HALFWAY up the stairs when Poe stumbled in front of him. He prodded the bank teller in the back with the barrel of his pistol.

"Keep climbing."

At the top of the stairs, they stood before an ordinary closet door with a sturdy padlock. Poe removed the lock and stepped inside, groping upward until he found a string and pulled it. A bare light bulb flared and swung on its wire, sending swaying shadows across deep wooden shelves. Marshall removed the burlap sack that had been padding his middle and gave it to Poe.

"Fill it."

Banded bills and security papers were stacked on the shelves, and Poe swept them into the sack. Marshall grabbed the bag and hurried the man down the stairs. Bobby and Louis still had their men lined against the wall. Marshall cocked his head toward the back room and said, "Come on."

Henry's voice called out from the bookkeeping room: "Is he back yet?"

"I'm here."

Henry appeared in the doorway. "We've got trouble."

Marshall waved Bobby and Louis toward the back room, and they rushed their hostages out of the lobby, gathering the two little girls as they went. The two bookkeepers that Henry had discovered in the back room were known to Marshall. Vance Littleton and Freda Stroebel. They would have recognized him, too, but they only stared in confusion at the Santa Claus with a gun.

It was crowded with eleven people in the room, but two were missing, and Marshall's eyes narrowed. "Where's that woman and her girl?"

Henry waved his gun at the back door. "They locked me out and got away."

Marshall didn't have enough time to shout at Henry's incompetence. He pointed to Bobby. "Start the car."

Bobby pushed through the crowded room and peered out the back door. "Hey, we got a badge with a shotgun hiding behind a cable pole out front."

Marshall gestured at Henry to join Bobby at the door. "Lay down some fire for him."

BOBBY EASED OPEN the screen door. As Henry stood in the doorway and fired over him at the officer, Bobby scrambled in a hunch toward the sedan. He was halfway to the car when a crack sounded from behind, and he felt a dozen sharp pricks in the back of his head and neck. He spun. Four men were coming up the alley about twenty yards away. Bobby raised his automatic and fired a few unsteady shots at them as he stumbled back into the bank.

Wincing as he held the back of his neck, he said, "Coming up from our left, we got four men with firearms. Two wearing badges and two guys in postal uniforms." Bobby raised his palm in front of him and checked for blood. "One of them got off a round. Stings like bees."

Marshall called out to Bobby over the heads of the hostages. "There's a post office behind the bank. One of the clerks has him a dove-hunting rifle, I guess. You get any of them?"

"Scared them off a bit."

Henry stood at the screen door and fired two more shots toward the front of the alley. "Well, this one ain't been scared off yet," he said, and fired again.

LOUIS NUDGED MARSHALL and pointed to the front windows in the lobby. "There's a bunch of men with rifles in the street, and they're coming toward the bank."

Marshall pushed him into the lobby. "Fend 'em off." Louis pointed the gun at one of the men outside, put pressure on the trigger, and hesitated. He figured all he needed to do was scare them from raiding the front door. He raised the barrel to the ceiling and fired. The powerful recoil from Henry's pistol surprised him.

Out on the street, the men ducked at the sound, but they didn't run away. One raised his rifle. Louis saw it jerk against the man's shoulder. The glass door pane shattered, and he felt a thump in his gut forceful enough to send him stumbling backward. The hostages parted as Louis fell against them, and he sat down heavily on the floor at Henry's feet. He gripped his middle, and blood began to ooze between his fingers.

Louis stared up in dazed confusion at his brother-in-law. "I . . . I think I'm hit."

HENRY'S FACE HARDENED into an angry frown, and he kicked open the screen door. He pulled a second pistol from his waistband and stepped out, bracing the door with his left leg. With one weapon, he fired at the men to his left, and with the other, he fired at the officer behind the cable pole. The four men to his left ducked for cover, but the man at the front of the alley was a big target. One of Henry's bullets hammered the man's left shoulder, and he abandoned the pole and took up a position at the corner of the department store.

Henry stepped back inside the bank and let the door slap against the frame. "Everybody's coming to claim that reward," he shouted to Marshall. "You've boxed us in a death trap here."

MARSHALL PUSHED HIS way through the hostages to get a look at what Henry was seeing. In the alley to his left, Officer Carmichael hid with another policeman Marshall did not recognize. They crouched behind wooden crates with the two postmen. To his right, the uniformed man peering from the corner of the department store was the chief of police everyone called "Uncle Bit" Bedford.

Marshall supposed the woman who escaped with her child had run to the police station. It was just a block away. No use in arguing with Henry over that now. He glanced around the room, thinking.

Hostages. They'd all be safe behind hostages. He gestured at Spears and Olson and waved them toward Henry. "You two. Go with him."

HENRY NUDGED LOUIS with his foot. His brother-in-law looked up, his eyes glassy and unfocused. His cheek was smeared where he had swiped at the blood welling from his mouth.

"I'm coming back for you," Henry said. "You hear me?"

Louis nodded drunkenly.

Henry prodded Owl-Eyes and Three-Piece Suit Boy with his pistol and said, "Let's go."

When the trio shuffled out the door, they met a volley of whistling bullets.

WATCHING FROM INSIDE the bank, Marshall gaped in disbelief. He had never been in a firefight before. In the past, he only had to point his gun and shout threats to make people do what he wanted. Now Henry and his hostages were buckling under a fusillade of incoming lead. Spears took a glancing blow to his jaw and collapsed against the outside wall, his owl-eyed glasses askew. A blast hit Olson in the thigh, shredding the fabric of the Harvard student's fine three-piece suit. When Henry returned fire up and down the alley, Marshall watched in horror as Officer Carmichael's head snapped back in a red spray. The policeman who had wished him a Merry Christmas on the street just ten minutes ago arced backward, landing hard with his arms and legs outstretched.

When Henry leaned against the wall to reload, Marshall grabbed the bookkeeper Freda Stroebel and the grocer Oscar Cliett. He entered the alley, hoping he looked like one of the hostages—a Santa Claus with a sack flung over his shoulder scrambling from the bank with a grocer in an apron and a young woman in a skirt. The firing stopped and Marshall made it to the car. But while he was occupied with opening the front door and tossing in the sack, Strobel and Cliett made a break for the back of Garner's store. Marshall shouted for Cliett to stop and fired at him. It was a warning shot to the ground, but the bullet found the grocer's heel. Cliett howled in agony and fell forward, but he continued to crawl until he was behind cover. At the shot, Stroebel screamed and flattened herself to the ground in surrender. The fallen officer lay next to her, a pool of blood surrounding his head.

Marshall swung around in time to see Chief Bedford step from the front corner of the department store. Together they raised their weapons and fired. Each staggered back, and after an effort to remain standing, they dropped to their knees. Marshall gripped his shredded leg, his nerves a raging fire. That wasn't just birdshot that had struck him.

Chief Bedford had been hit in the right shoulder, but he raised his rifle again and pulled the trigger. Marshall braced for the blast, but nothing happened. The lawman threw the weapon aside and reached for the pistol in his holster.

From behind Marshall, gunfire cracked in rapid succession, and Bedford jerked stiffly. When the firing stopped, the lawman slumped to the sidewalk and did not move. Before Marshall could look back to see who had brought down the police chief, movement in the street caught his eye. A man ran to Chief Bedford, picked up his unfired pistol, and dashed to the corner of the department store. He shoved the pistol around the corner and fired blindly from side to side.

Marshall ducked and turned away from the shots. Henry and Spears and Olson were still out in the alley, and all three hunched down and covered their heads with their arms as the bullets whistled around the narrow space. Spears and Olson shouted at the man to stop, but he sprayed the rounds until the hammer fell on empty chambers.

BOBBY STOOD AT the bank's alley door behind the last two bank employees as the spray of bullets ricocheted around them. Brick chips peppered one of the hostages in the face. He lunged back, shouting to Bobby, "It's useless to try to escape."

When the rapid gunfire ended, Bobby said, "Get on with it."

One of the hostages gripped each side of the doorframe with his hands to stall his entrance into the alley. Bobby shoved the barrel of his gun into the man's kidney and ordered him to move. The two hostages shuffled out the door with Bobby in between them. Stumbling over each other's feet, the three lurched awkwardly to the car.

When he reached the driver's door, his hostages broke for the front corner of the department store. Reflexively, Bobby pointed his gun at one of the men. A shot from the street made Bobby duck into the car, and the men escaped. Bullets struck the windshield as Bobby hunched behind the dash and tried to get the car started. He fumbled with the ignition and gear shift and foot pedals until the engine cranked to life.

IN THE MIDDLE of the alley, Marshall struggled to his feet. Blood from the wound above his left knee deepened the red felt of his festive costume.

He waved at Henry. "Come on!"

Henry continued to fire up and down the alley as he moved back toward the screen door. "I'm getting Louis."

Marshall shouted, "Leave him and come on!" But Henry disappeared into the bank.

A shot from the street whistled past Marshall's head, and he flinched. He needed shields. The grocer Cliett had disappeared. Freda Strobel still lay weeping on the ground next to Officer Carmichael, but she was too far away to grab. The wounded hostages Henry had abandoned were near at hand, though. Marshall hobbled back to Spears and Olson on the ground next to the bank door.

He pulled Olson by the collar of his coat. "Get up."

Marshall pulled him toward the car, and both stumbled against each other from their wounded legs. When he remembered Spears, he turned around in time to see the cashier rounding the corner behind the bank. Angry, no longer interested in sending warnings, Marshall aimed for his head, but the bullet went high, and Spears escaped.

Marshall yelled at Olson over the incoming fire that crisscrossed the alley. "Open the door."

The college student obeyed, and Marshall shoved him into the back seat. Marshall opened the front door and dropped heavily into the seat, hunching with Bobby behind the dash for protection. He fired off a few rounds at the men in the street, and when he twisted back, the seat behind him was empty and the door on the other side stood open. Olson had escaped.

Inside the bank, Henry found Louis still sitting on the floor. He reached down for the wounded man and raised him until they were both standing.

"Put your arm around my neck."

Louis flopped an arm around his shoulder.

Henry took a step toward the door, but a tiny, muffled whimper stopped him. He bent down and looked under the bookkeeping table. Huddled there were the two girls he had earlier pushed out of the way to get into the back room.

He straightened and kicked a leg of the desk. "Get out from there."

The girls crawled out and stood trembling as they held each other. With his right arm draped around the two children and his left arm around Louis's back, he shuffled out the door.

The firing stopped.

IN THE CAR, Marshall's ears rang in the sudden lull. The sharp-sweet smell of burned gunpowder hung thick in the alley as thin blue streaks of smoke dissipated. The sight of the girls had shut down the gunfire completely.

Marshall let out a raspy laugh as he yanked one of the girls into the front seat with him. "Come sit on Santa's lap."

She seemed so familiar, but he didn't have time to follow the thought. He sat her on his uninjured right leg and slammed the door. Draping an arm over the girl, he shot at the gunmen in the street, who did not return fire.

HENRY OPENED THE back door of the car, pushed Louis across the bench, and shoved in the other girl. Bobby put the car in gear, and it jolted forward while Henry was still crawling in. When they careened to the right, the left door swung open, and the girl in the back seat screamed as she and Louis rolled toward the opening. Henry grabbed Louis's flailing right arm and kept him in the cabin. The car straightened onto Main Street, and Henry reached over Louis and slammed the door shut. Louis's body slumped into an unconscious heap, and the little girl between them moaned miserably.

More men ran into positions along the street, and they fired at the car. The men who had stopped shooting at the gang when the girls appeared were now waving and shouting to the newcomers about the children in the car. But the shots continued, and Henry tried to keep them at bay by returning fire.

When he stopped to reload, he kicked a box on the floorboard toward his little hostage. "Quit that wailing and throw these out the window."

The girl's moans fell to hiccupping whimpers as she reached into the box. She raised a few roofing nails with a trembling hand.

Henry flicked his wrist to snap the loaded cylinder into place. "Toss them out the window," he told the girl. "Like this." And he scattered a handful of nails behind the Buick. The girl delicately reached over the bloody and unconscious form of Louis to toss her little handful of nails out the window. Henry and the girl continued to spread the nails until the road was jammed with stalled cars. The other pursuers slowed to make a wide pass around the stranded vehicles and the path of nails.

MARSHALL LET OUT a brief, triumphant laugh at the sight. None of them were patrol cars, and they'd give up soon enough. He shook the spent shells from the chambers of his revolver and reloaded with rounds from his bandoleer. A few more miles and they would abandon the stolen sedan, leave the girls behind, and vanish. He patted the dash. "You got us a good one here, Bobby. That straight-six engine 'll outrun them all."

Bobby kept his eyes on the road. "We got to get another one."

"I know it. They'll have a report out on this one. Get us to the next town and we'll find us another."

Bobby tapped the gas gauge on the dash. "No, I mean we got to get another one now."

Henry punched the front seat. "Your boy done run us out of gas."

Bobby shot a guilty look at Marshall. "With all that shooting, they must of knocked a hole in the gas tank, is all."

Marshall didn't remember getting gas at any of their stops along the long ride down from Wichita Falls. But he didn't respond to either of them. He gestured forward with a nod of his head and said, "There's your next car."

An Oldsmobile touring car was heading toward them. Bobby turned slightly into the oncoming lane and hit the brakes. Marshall put the girl in his lap next to Bobby and struggled out the car door, sending electric shocks of pain up his leg. With the sack of stolen money over his shoulder and his gun hidden behind his back, he limped into the path of the oncoming car.

A teenage boy was behind the wheel. He pulled the Oldsmobile to a stop and cranked down the window as Marshall approached. The boy grinned at the Santa character, and said to the man sitting next to him, "Daddy, Santa come early this year."

Marshall took his gun from behind his back and pointed it at the boy and his father. "Get out."

The two climbed from the front seat with hands raised.

Henry and Bobby ran to either side of the Oldsmobile.

HENRY GESTURED WITH his gun at the woman on his side of the car and ordered her out. The father took a step toward him. "That's my wife and her mother." When Henry raised a pistol to his chest, the man froze and said, "You—you can have the car. Just don't hurt my family." His wife emerged from the back with her hands raised, and she edged past Henry to join her husband.

BOBBY WAVED HIS gun to get the old woman to climb out of the back seat. She stared at him, frozen, wide-eyed, breathing rapidly. He stuffed his pistol into his belt and reached into the car to lift the woman into his arms. Gunfire popped like firecrackers from the pursuers still three blocks away. A headlight on the family car shattered, and on impulse, Bobby whirled to get himself between the gunfire and the old woman. He cradled her head in his left arm and shuffled sideways toward the roadside as bullets whistled around him.

He felt a sudden painful thump in the back of the arm shielding the woman's head, and Bobby sunk to his knees with a stuttering grunt of agony. He inspected his left triceps. Blood was spreading through shredded cloth above the elbow. He rose and carried the old woman to the roadside, where he eased her to the ground. Staggering back to the family's Oldsmobile, he fired unsteadily up the road.

HENRY RETURNED TO the Buick sedan and patted Louis's face. "Wake up, now. You got to wake up."

Louis lolled his head toward Henry and offered his arms. Henry pulled him from the car and braced him up. "You two," he said to the girls. "Walk ahead of us." Together the four made it to the Oldsmobile.

Bobby cradled his wounded arm and told Henry, "I ain't fit to drive."

Henry nodded. He directed the girls to get in the back, and he shoved Louis in after them, where the man slumped against the seat and did not move. Marshall opened the back door on the other side, tossed his sack on the floorboard, and climbed in. Bobby jumped in the front seat on the passenger side.

Henry reached for the key, but it wasn't in the ignition. He shouted at the family on the roadside, "Where's your boy run off to with the key?" The man and his wife were tending to the old woman, but the boy was nowhere to be seen.

Pellets from a shotgun thudded against the windshield, sending veiny cracks running through the glass.

"Get back to the other car," Marshall said, and threw his door open. He shuffled forward with the girls in front of him as shields.

Henry reached for Louis.

"Leave him," Marshall shouted. "I'll wager he's dead, and we will be, too, if you don't drive us out of here."

Henry hesitated over the unmoving body. Blood bloomed, wet and shiny, across Louis's shirt at the gut. He looked done for.

Marshall waved him toward the Buick. "You're the only one who can drive us."

Bullets struck the ground near Henry's feet with muffled thuds. He backed away from his brother-in-law and ran to their original getaway car. Marshall directed one of the girls to sit between Henry and himself, and he placed the other child in the back next to Bobby. Henry cranked the engine and pulled away.

MARSHALL TRIED TO hold his wounded leg up from the bumping seat. He scanned for familiar landmarks and then suddenly slapped the dash. "Turn here." When it looked like Henry would miss it, Marshall shouted, "Here!"

Henry took the left turn onto a gravel road at full speed, and the sedan slid sideways toward the bar ditch. But he regained control and began working up the gears again. Marshall adjusted the side mirror to monitor the pursuing cars. The lead vehicle miscalculated the sharpness of the turn, too, but wasn't so lucky. It slid into the ditch and slammed onto its side, and the spokes fluttered as the front wheel spun uselessly in the air. The rest of the pursuers passed the wrecked car and continued the chase.

The sedan vibrated rabidly on the dirt road, and shards of broken glass wobbled loose and fell into the cabin, raising fresh outbursts of weeping from the girls.

"Pipe down!" Henry shouted at the girls, and then he scowled at Marshall. "You got to tell me sooner if you want me to take a new road."

Marshall ignored him. After a wide rightward bend, he pointed ahead. "Take this one."

When Henry took it, Marshall glanced again at the side mirror and guessed the cars were about two hundred yards behind. It was hard to tell how many vehicles were in the group. It had to be five or six, considering the cloud of dust they raised. The oilman's Buick that Bobby had found was pulling farther away from them.

As they crested a rise and dropped below it, they were hidden for a moment from the posse. Marshall pointed to a road that crossed the bar ditch to their right. "Take this. It'll get us over to the Rising Star highway."

"And a gas station?"

"Well, we'll just go as long as we can."

Henry turned. When the motorcar passed over a cattle guard with a low, vibrating hum, Marshall frowned at his own mistake. The tires ran along a double track of shallow sand and solid rock. Tall, thin stalks of winter-brown prairie grass rose between the tracks. It was a rancher's feed road and likely to peter out in a field. The stony lane gave them one advantage, though. They were no longer kicking up a cloud of dust for the posse to follow, and a thicket of scrub oak and brambles to their right hid them from the road they had abandoned.

HENRY PRESSED FORWARD for a half mile without any sign of their pursuers. Other than the rhythm of the engine, the only sound was the raspy swish of grass under the floorboard of the sedan. When the road entered a place where the brush and trees were denser, the whispers of grass under the car gave way to scraping and thumping as they passed over saplings and low cacti. Branches screeched against the sedan as Henry pushed it forward as far as he could into the brush.

He shut off the engine and gave Marshall an annoyed scowl. "Now what?"

Marshall put his hand on the door handle to leave, but then he turned and searched around the Buick with quickening motions.

Between his feet.

Underneath his seat.

Behind the girl next to him.

He turned around and scanned the floorboard in the back.

Bobby's eyes followed in the direction Marshall was searching. "What is it?"

Henry banged his hands on the steering wheel and glared at Marshall. "You went and left the money behind in the other car with Louis, didn't you?"

Marshall swore loudly and shoved the door against the brush until he had it open wide enough to slide out. He went to the back of the car and stood with his hands on his hips as he stared in the direction they had come. Henry and Bobby joined him.

Henry spoke in a low voice. "What about them girls?"

"We'll leave them here and head out on foot."

Henry leaned in close and flicked the long, white whiskers still hiding Marshall's identity. "They've had a good long look at me and the boy."

MARSHALL PRESSED HIS lips together and returned to the sedan. He opened the back door where a duffel lay on the floorboard, and he inspected the food and weapons and extra ammunition stuffed inside. Closing the bag, he hoisted it on his shoulder and regarded the girls. One sat in the front seat and one sat in the back.

He said, "You girls lie down now."

Slowly, they stretched out in the seats on their stomachs, staring uncertainly at him.

"Now put your head down and cover your eyes."

When they obeyed, Marshall tugged at his Santa beard. Blood had already coagulated where a bullet grazed him on the jaw, and the whiskers were matted to the wound. He gave the beard a sharp yank. As it ripped off the scab, he grunted in pain.

The girls raised their heads at the sound, and one opened her mouth in surprise.

Laverne Comer.

Five years earlier, Marshall had sat in his mother's café with the little girl while their parents took care of some paper-signing. His mother was selling the café to the Comers, and nineteen-year-old Marshall had sat Laverne in his lap, entertaining her with card tricks while the two waited. That was a lifetime ago, before his marriage, before the Valera robbery, before the jail time.

He raised the bloodstained Santa beard over his face. "I told you to keep your head down."

He was unwilling to point his weapon at Laverne and the other girl, but he brandished it for emphasis. "Do it now."

Both girls dropped their heads into folded arms.

Marshall darted a glance at Henry, who was staring into the cabin from the other side of the sedan. He tossed his bloody Santa beard by the car and began picking his way through the brush. When he looked back,

Bobby was following him, his left arm cradled in his right. But Henry was still at the car, frowning at the girls.

"Come on," Marshall repeated. "They can't be far behind."

3

REFLECTION

Louis coughed weakly, sending up fresh blood to join the trickle that ran from the corner of his mouth down his cheek. He heard someone say, "Hey, he's coming to," and then the sound of a car door opening.

A man chuckled. "Lookee here. They left the loot behind."

Louis rolled his head to the right and tried to get his eyes in focus. Someone was gathering up banded stacks of bills from the floorboard and stuffing them back into the potato sack that Marshall had carried from the bank.

The door next to him opened, and someone shook his shoulder, sending shocks of pain up from his gut. Louis turned his head, wincing, and squinted at a uniformed man.

"What's your name?" the lawman demanded.

This one must have just arrived because a man behind the officer began to explain things. How Louis had ended up in the Oldsmobile. How others were in pursuit of the bandits.

Louis grew uneasy as a large crowd closed in around the car. Most had weapons.

The policeman returned his attention to Louis. "You tell me now. Who was with you?"

Louis's head flopped back on the seat, and he shook it twice from side to side. He smacked his lips and swallowed.

The officer shut the door. "Right now, he's not going to be much help, I don't guess. Let's get him to the hospital."

The car started up and pulled away, and the crowd noise faded. A bump through a pothole made Louis wince. He reached for his stomach and felt the squish of blood-soaked clothing.

BOBBY HEARD A voice as if echoing up from a deep well. "Bobby. Get up, Bobby. We've got to keep moving." He opened his eyes, and Marshall swam into view above him.

Bobby looked around, confused. They were under a stand of live oak. "What happened?"

"Keep it down!" Henry whispered fiercely.

Marshall spoke in a low voice. "You fainted." He raised Bobby to a sitting position. "That arm's a mess, but I've snugged it up a bit. It won't be bleeding on you so bad now."

Bobby squinted down at his arm. It was wrapped with strips of cloth Marshall had torn from the Santa coat. Bobby's own jacket lay nearby, shredded above the elbow and still wet with his blood.

Henry stared at Bobby, coldly assessing him. He said to Marshall, "We can't stay here no longer. They'll be out with the hounds. If the boy ain't fit to walk, I say we leave him."

Marshall helped Bobby to his feet and held both his shoulders as though he expected him to drop again.

Bobby nodded. "I can go on."

Marshall released him and began to make his way through the dense oak shinnery. Bobby took a couple of careful steps to make sure he could trust his legs, and Henry brushed by him with a dismissive frown. Bobby picked up the pace and tried to shake the fog from his head.

Louis lay in the hospital bed with a wide white bandage around his middle. Two deputies questioned him.

"Mister, they left you behind. Abandoned you. You don't owe them a thing."

The other deputy joined in. "Here you are protecting *them* when they didn't figure *you* was important enough to protect."

Louis rested a hand over the bandaged wound and stared at the ceiling.

"We got two lawmen in this hospital hanging on for dear life," the first deputy added. "You ain't helping yourself by staying silent."

The door swung open and voices in the hallway spilled into his room. A large crowd of officers outside his door talked to each other while a thin blue haze of tobacco smoke floated above them.

A man entered the room and closed the door behind him. "Anything?"

"No, Sheriff."

Louis returned his gaze to the ceiling. The county sheriff approached Louis's bed. "Listen, we've got lawmen coming in from all over. You hear them out there in the hall, don't you?" Unlike the deputies, his voice was gentle. "We didn't catch your friends today, but we will. Protecting them won't do you any good, see?" The sheriff took off his Stetson and eased down on the edge of Louis's bed. "Listen. What you need to think about now is how to get back to your family as soon as you can. You got a family, I expect."

At the mention of family, a lump formed in Louis's throat. He took his eyes off the ceiling and regarded the sheriff. The man's wire-rim glasses and blond hair gave his face a kinder appearance than the men who had been interrogating him.

Louis spoke for the first time since his capture. "Would someone go let my wife know I'm here? My name's Louis Davis and I live in Wichita Falls. I want to see my wife."

"Sure, sure," the sheriff said in a reassuring tone while one of his deputies wrote down the information. "We'll call up to Wichita Falls and let your missus know where you are."

"I ain't got a phone. I got a sister outside of Cisco in the oil camps in Moran. Cathleen Fox. She'll go get my Sue."

"We'll get someone out to your sister's place, then." The sheriff pulled a cigarette pack from his pocket. He offered one to Louis. "Want one? They're ready-rolled."

He shook his head. "I don't smoke."

"You don't?" The sheriff gave Louis an amiable smile as he lifted a cigarette from the pack and tapped the end on his knee. "Every man needs at least one vice. If it ain't tobacco, what's yours, Louis?" He lit the cigarette and waved the match to put out the flame.

"Don't got none, I guess." He gave the sheriff a small, weak grin at the irony.

"What do you do up in Wichita Falls, Louis?"

"Been at the glass factory for six years now."

"Got any kids?"

"A boy and a girl, and a new baby girl."

"I'm sure they can't wait for Christmas."

Christmas. Marshall said they'd all be home for Christmas.

The sheriff put his hand on Louis's leg. "Louis, I ain't going to lie to you. You're in tall trouble. You probably won't see those three kiddos this Christmas. But, Louis, there ain't no reason why you have to take the blame for everything that happened today. If you cooperate, I can assure you you'll be back with that family soon."

The hubbub from the hallway rose as the door opened, distracting both Louis and the sheriff. An officer entered, closed the door behind him, and whispered something to one of the deputies.

The sheriff returned his attention back to Louis. "Louis, tell me who was with you. I figure you didn't organize this robbery. Let the guys who are responsible take the blame."

But the interruption from the hallway had broken the spell, and Louis frowned. He figured this sheriff didn't care about him any more than his deputies did. He was just using kindness, where the others had used threats. Louis returned his gaze to the ceiling and remained silent.

One of the deputies stepped toward his bed. "Well, let me tell you, Louis Davis, you had better talk." He spoke to the sheriff while keeping his eyes on Louis. "Sheriff, I just got word that Uncle Bit didn't make it."

The sheriff stood from the bed. "Chief Bedford's dead?"

The deputy spoke to Louis while pointing to a uniformed man stationed in the corner. "Listen here. We posted that guard to keep you from getting *out*. But now that man will have to keep the good citizens of this town from getting *in*. Uncle Bit was loved around here. If you don't start talking, maybe we'll just back off and let them string you up."

Louis's eyes widened in panic. "I didn't kill nobody!" he wailed. Then he tried to calm himself as he made his plea to the sheriff. "Mister, I only shot once, and that was at the ceiling in the bank. I didn't want no one to rush the front of the bank and get killed. You check my gun. There ain't but one bullet fired."

The deputy asked, "Who shot the lawmen?"

Louis's mind flashed back to the bookkeeping room where he was sitting on the floor, stunned at the wet red spot spreading across his shirt. Henry was at the screen door firing to the front and the back of the alley.

He shook his head. "I don't know."

"Well, let's start with who was with you."

"I want to see my Sue."

The deputy kicked a bedpost at the foot of the bed. "If you don't start talking, the only thing you're going to see is a mob with a long rope."

"I . . . ," he began. His resolve to stay silent was melting. "I was with a guy named Henry—" He stopped. He might not be a real gangster, but he didn't have to be a rat, either. His patient, steady gaze at the ceiling returned. "I was with a guy named Henry Crocket. John Williams was with us, too. And Fred McCheney."

The deputy wrote down the names. "They got families in Wichita Falls like you?"

"I don't know nothing about their families." He coughed, and then winced as he covered his stomach with his hands.

"Are they planning any other jobs?"

"That's all I know." He coughed again, grimacing at what it did to his middle.

After another ten minutes, the sheriff and his deputies gave up their questioning and left for the night.

IN THE MORNING, Louis was attempting some small bites of toast for breakfast when he heard a timid knock. His sister, Cathleen Fox, stuck her head in the door with an uncertain expression. The guard who sat in the corner nodded at her and returned to reading his newspaper.

Louis lifted his hand to his sister in a weak wave. "Merry Christmas Eve."

She gave him a melancholy smile in response to this family tradition. As children, the first of them to shout the greeting got to open one present a day early.

"Are you . . . ," she started, but her voice trailed off.

He grinned. "Aw, I'll be walking out of here soon, you'll see." But his hand went to the bandages at his stomach. It was the third wrapping the nurses had tried, but this one was stained red, too.

"Louis," she said, and stopped. She began again. "They tell me you was in a bank robbery. They tell me a lawman's dead and another one might soon be."

"I didn't shoot no one."

She slid a chair close to the bed and sat. "You ain't never done nothing like this." The guard in the corner didn't seem to be paying attention, but Cathleen leaned forward and lowered her voice. "Did he talk you into this?"

Louis knew she meant Henry, and he didn't reply.

"Of course he did," Cathleen said, and there was a long silence. Then she sighed and shook her head. "This ain't the Louis I know a-lying in this bed."

He shrugged slightly. "I needed the money. I was in debt."

"You didn't have to resort to this. I could had loaned you and Sue some money."

At his wife's name, his eyes welled with tears, and he swallowed at the lump in his throat. He extended his hand to his sister, and she placed her hand in his. "Please go get my Sue. Tell her I'm sorry and I want to see her."

Cathleen squeezed his hand. "I will. I'll go back to Moran first to tell Sam where I'm headed. But then I'll drive straight up to Wichita Falls today."

"I'm tired now. But I'm glad you come. I don't guess I expected none of what happened. I sure didn't want it."

Cathleen stood, and the guard gave her a solemn nod before returning to his paper. She gave a last worried wave to Louis and left.

Louis continued to stare at the door his sister had closed behind her. "Them officers in the hallway last night are gone."

The guard kept his eyes on the article he was reading. "Tracking down your gang."

His gang.

He let out a regretful sigh.

THE THREE FUGITIVES spent the Saturday after the robbery hiding in a thicket near the highway. In the late afternoon, bloodhounds bayed a couple of miles away. The men prepared to shoot it out with the trackers, but darkness fell without incident, and Henry took Bobby in search of a car. They returned with a Ford, and Henry told them he was driving them to the Moran oil field camps, about twenty miles northwest. Most of it was abandoned after the region's oil boom had played out. But Sam and Cathleen Fox still had a cabin there, and they were family. Sam was the brother of Henry's wife, and Cathleen was Louis's sister.

Henry led Marshall and Bobby through the woods behind the cabin. He knocked quietly at the back door. After a moment, the flame of an oil lamp floated through the kitchen and the door opened.

"I figured you'd turn up," Sam Fox said with disapproval.

Henry didn't wait for an invitation from his wife's brother. He pushed past Sam and entered the house, and Marshall and Bobby followed. It was shortly after midnight on Sunday, Christmas morning.

Henry scanned the small cabin. "Cathleen in bed?"

The frown had not left Sam's face. "The Law come out early Saturday. Told us Louis had been shot in a bank robbery and was in the hospital. Cathleen went to see him."

"In the hospital? We thought he was dead." Henry glared at Marshall and opened his mouth to complain about abandoning Louis. But he changed his mind and turned back to Sam. "Get Cathleen out of bed. I want to talk to her."

"She's gone up to Wichita Falls to get Sue."

"Did Louis say anything to the Law about us?"

Sam dismissed him with a wave. "Her brother probably won't make it, and that's all you care about? What'd you get him into, Henry?"

Henry ignored the accusation. "We need food." He went to the pantry without asking.

"We need bandages," Marshall added as he unwound the bloody strips of cloth from Bobby's arm.

Sam didn't make a move to help as he continued to stare at Henry. "They tell me you took two little girls hostage."

Henry stopped rummaging around in the pantry. "They ain't been found yet? We left them in the car."

"They've been found. Cried hysterically all the way back to their mommas, I was told." Sam shook his head. "My God, Henry. You have a girl their age."

"There wasn't a scratch on those girls. No thanks to all them church deacons shooting at us."

Sam huffed in resignation and opened a kitchen cabinet. He pulled out tweezers, ointment, and a roll of gauze, and Marshall drew the bullet from Bobby's arm and dressed the wound.

Bobby worked his arm to test the firmness of the fresh bandaging. He pointed to Marshall's leg. "What about you? Want me to draw that buckshot out?"

"No. We can't stay any longer. I have stood it this far, and I will stand it now to the end, I guess."

Henry found a can of soup, a few oranges, some jerky, and half a loaf of bread. He gathered it into a bag and left the house without a further word. Marshall thanked Sam, and he and Bobby followed Henry into the night.

THE NURSE PUT the back of her hand on Louis's forehead and frowned. She pushed a thermometer into his mouth and held his wrist to check the pulse. After a moment, she pulled out the thermometer and squinted at it. "Your fever's up again. And there is still too much blood in the bedpan."

She raised the cover over his lunch plate. "You didn't touch your lunch. You want I should take this away?"

He nodded once, his eyes on the foot of the bed.

She picked up the tray and stopped.

He gave her a defensive look. "What?"

"You just don't seem the type."

His eyes returned to the foot of the bed. She shook her head and carried his lunch away.

Louis wondered what kind of Christmas dinner Sue and the children were having. She probably had the tree all trimmed with the decorations she had saved from their fourteen Christmases together. He hoped Sue would come soon. He hoped Sue would come.

A scrape and a thump at the window startled him. A face peered through the dusty window. The face belonged to a man in a business suit who cupped his hands on either side of his eyes to stare into the room. After a moment, the man turned to talk to someone, but Louis couldn't hear what he said.

From the right, another face appeared. This face belonged to a burly man, who bobbed his head around the windowpane and squinted to get a clear view into the room.

He remembered what the deputy had said about letting the mob string him up, and he grew uneasy.

The burly man stepped away, and another person took his place from the right. This time, it was an old woman who clutched her purse with both hands at her chest. A moment later, she was replaced by yet another woman, who turned to the woman who had left and issued some complaint that Louis still could not hear. It must have had something to do with the dust on the window, because the woman swept the pane with her handkerchief in an unsuccessful attempt to remove the grime.

When she was replaced by a man to her right, it dawned on Louis that the people were part of a line outside his window. People were filing by on Christmas Day to get a glimpse of a real live bank robber. He was a freak in a carnival sideshow.

He raised a hand to get the guard's attention. "Hey, mister. Can you close my curtains so all those people will quit looking in here?"

The guard made no move to stand, but he put down his newspaper and assessed the activity outside. "Naw," he said finally. "They cain't be seeing much through that window, anyhow, considering the dust and the sun. They're only seeing their own reflection."

A man in overalls squinted in the window. Louis chuckled softly. "What're you trying to see?" he asked, though he knew the man in the window was unable to hear him.

The man left and a woman peeked in.

"Didn't you hear the officer?"

An old man with a gray beard took her place.

"You cain't see nothing but yourself, you know."

Louis propped up on his elbows with effort as the next person stood at the window. "Hello." He gave a sardonic wave. "It don't do no good looking in here."

Another filed by, and Louis shrugged his shoulders at the man and said, "All you can see is yourself."

Louis cackled, which sent him into a wheezing cough. He fell back on his bed in agony, gripping his stomach. The guard shook his head and returned to his paper. Louis picked up his hands. Fresh blood spread through the bandages. He closed his eyes and breathed rhythmically to draw down the pain.

By sundown Christmas Day, Louis Davis was dead.

4

MANHUNT

Henry cranked the car and drove from the thicket where they had been hiding throughout Christmas Day. Under darkness, he returned to the road. He tried to bear north toward Wichita Falls while avoiding the state highway, but the meandering back roads disoriented him. Marshall offered his own guesses of where to turn or what roads to take, but when Marshall and Bobby nodded off, Henry was left to pick out the route himself. Little more could be seen than the ten yards of gravel road that the headlights illuminated for him. It gave him the hypnotic sensation that he was on a great conveyor belt that rolled toward him and under the car. He was beginning to fall under the spell of the motor's monotonous chug, and he fought to keep his eyes open.

Motion from his right startled him. The headlights caught a jackrabbit as it leapt in front of the car. Instead of crossing the road to the other side, the hare hopped rapidly forward. Henry turned the steering wheel slightly left and right to keep the hare in the center of the headlight beams, and he accelerated toward the leaping figure. As he bore down on the desperate animal, Henry raised up to see over the hood, and waited to feel the thump of the body under the tires.

The hare darted to the left out of the light, and Henry realized his mistake too late. He tried to swerve back into the lane, but the tires slipped off the road and the machine dropped sharply down into the bar ditch and lurched to a stop.

Marshall cursed.

Henry muttered, "I fell asleep along with the two of you." He shut off the engine and the lights.

The three men climbed out uninjured. They walked around the car, but even in the dark, it was obvious they weren't going to get it back on the road.

The measured beats of a motor interrupted any thoughts of a next step. Headlights fluttered from their right as a car approached an intersection twenty yards ahead. The three bandits scrambled behind their wrecked machine.

At the intersection, the vehicle braked with a faint whine, and it idled there. A low mumble of voices came from the open windows. The men were discussing which way to go. Finally, the car crept slowly forward into the intersection, and then it accelerated straight without turning.

MARSHALL LET OUT a breath. "That was a close one and to be sure." The three felt their way across the seats and floorboards to gather supplies, and Marshall picked a direction and set out.

After a mile, they spotted a farmhouse. With no sign of a dog to announce their presence, Marshall limped toward the car shed beside the house. Henry and Bobby followed.

The front door of the farmhouse opened, and a man's voice called out. "Carl, you back?"

Marshall couldn't see anything but the man's silhouette behind the screen door. He lurched a step toward him. "We've had a wreck."

The man pushed open the screen door. He was sock-footed, his trousers were on, and an untucked shirt hung on his thin frame. He held a shotgun, the barrel half raised in their direction.

Marshall showed his open hands to the man. "My wife is back in the car. I need to get her to a hospital."

The man lowered his shotgun. "My boy has our conveyance out with a friend or I'd take you myself." The man paused. "Your wife hurt bad?"

"She'll be fine. She can't walk, is all. You got a telephone?" Marshall wasn't interested in calling anyone, but he didn't want the farmer calling anyone, either.

"No. Go up the road to my neighbor's place. He may be able to help. About three miles."

"Thank you, sir. We're sorry to bother you."

"Good luck. Guess it's not too late to still wish you a Merry Christmas."

The three turned and left, but the farmer didn't return inside until they were off his property and on the gravel road.

When Marshall heard the farmhouse door close, he stopped and whispered, "Boys, my leg ain't going to take me three miles. It ain't going to take me one mile more. If that man's waiting for his son to come back with the car, I say we give it a while right here."

They only had to wait half an hour in the shadows before the rhythmic chug of pistons drew closer to them.

As the car slowed to turn into the driveway, Henry ran to the driver's door and pointed a pistol at the farmer's son. "Shove aside."

The young man obeyed, edging away from the pointed gun and into the passenger side. Marshall and Bobby climbed into the back, and Henry slid behind the steering wheel.

At the sound of a screen door slap, Marshall turned. The farmer stood on the porch, raised his shotgun, and fired. Pellets hit the car with a *ting-ting-ting*, and the farmer's son cried out in pain and grabbed his right bicep. Henry sent up gravel in a spattering fan until the wheels found traction, and he raced away.

BOBBY STOOD A few yards behind the kidnapped young man. He held a gun on him as the hostage made water beside a low mesquite.

The young man called back over his shoulder. "You got a name? Mine's Carl Wylie."

"I've got a name," Bobby said, but he didn't offer it.

Carl buttoned his fly and turned around. "You the boys everyone's talking about in town? The ones as robbed the bank in Cisco?"

Bobby didn't say anything and waved his pistol in a signal for Carl to return to the car. Metallic-gray clouds hung overhead, brought in by a freezing norther. Sleet had fallen briefly a few hours earlier and let up, but a biting wind continued to bluster. Bobby wished he still had his overcoat, even if it was torn and bloody. He was glad to return Carl to the sedan.

The car was deep within a cedar stand, and Henry and Marshall dozed in the back. Marshall had instructed Bobby to keep watch through the morning, promising to take over the guard duty at noon.

Carl rubbed his hands together for warmth. "We're about the same age, I expect."

Bobby nodded.

"And we're both winged." Carl gave a slight grin and raised his bandaged right arm.

Bobby said nothing, but he became conscious of his own wounded arm, and he shifted it, trying to find a comfortable position.

"Yours throb?" Carl asked, "Mine sure does."

Henry kicked the front seat but didn't open his eyes. "You two lovebirds can just pipe down."

THE MEN DOZED fitfully, taking turns keeping watch over Carl and the surrounding area. Toward sundown, they were all awake. Marshall told Bobby to see what was left in the bag they had taken from Sam Fox's house. Bobby showed him the two remaining oranges. Marshall nodded, and Bobby peeled them and divided the wedges between himself and Marshall and Henry. None was offered to the captive.

Marshall wiped the sticky juice off his mouth. "By now, everyone'll know what car we're in. We got to find another."

When it was dark, Henry started Carl's car and returned it to the road. Marshall sat in the front with Henry, and Bobby sat in the back with Carl. They crested a low hill, and a small cluster of streetlights winked in the distance.

"That'll be Breckenridge," said Marshall, referring to a town thirty miles northeast of Cisco.

As they approached the outskirts from the west, Marshall directed Henry to pull off the road behind a warehouse. "You two go find us a car. I'll stay here with him."

The eastern sky was lighter by the time Henry and Bobby returned in a dilapidated Model T with no cover. Bobby had a blanket around his shoulders. Henry pulled to a stop beside Carl's car, and Marshall and the hostage got out.

Henry patted the steering wheel. "I tried three cars before I got this old flivver to start. It ain't got a top, but there are some blankets on the seat to keep warm."

Marshall frowned at the roadster's single bench for the three of them. "It'll have to do." He climbed up, and Bobby shifted to the middle as Marshall squeezed in beside him.

Henry put the car in gear, but Marshall reached over Bobby's lap and placed his hand on the steering wheel. He leveled his gaze at Carl. "We're leaving you here. We ain't done nothing to you or your vehicle. That wound's your daddy's doing. You remember that, now."

Carl nodded.

Bobby spoke through chattering teeth. "Give me your overcoat, Carl. Soon enough, you'll be somewhere warm again."

Carl Wylie shrugged out of his coat and handed it over. Bobby stood to give himself room enough to put on the coat. He winced as he worked his wounded left arm through the sleeve. He wrapped the blanket over his head again and lowered himself between Marshall and Henry, shifting against their hips to get down on the single bench.

"Anything else we can do for you, boy?" Henry asked in mock concern.

Marshall waved a hand forward. "Piss on the fire and let's go."

When Henry chose to risk the main highway north, Marshall didn't complain. He couldn't abide the thought of the jarring his leg would take driving over another unpaved side road. As they picked up speed, Marshall tugged down the brim of his hat to keep it from blowing off in the open cab of the roadster.

When they passed a Breckenridge city limits sign a half hour after they had left Carl Wylie in the town that they thought was Breckenridge, Marshall's heart sank. The place they had left their hostage was Cisco. It had been three days since the robbery, and they were no closer to home. He glanced sidelong at Bobby, who was shivering miserably under his blanket. They were hungry and running out of gas and money. Marshall expected Henry and Bobby were waiting for a plan.

"Henry," he said, hoping his voice sounded more confident than he felt. "I figure three men will get someone curious. Drop me here and the two of you go and find some gas."

Henry and Bobby returned a half hour later.

"The last of the money only got the tank half full. But here—" Henry presented three loaves of bread. "We found a delivery truck behind a store."

Marshall stared at him, not sure he wanted to ask about the delivery man.

Henry scowled. "The driver was in the store." He held up a loaf to Marshall. "You want this?"

After the three ate in silence, Henry started the car and wove through side streets until they passed out of town. It was eight in the morning when he turned on the highway heading northeast. Marshall was pleased they hadn't seen any sign of the Law, and they made good time on the open road.

He shouted over the wind whipping around him. "I admire to risk this road till Graham, then spend the day in a field."

Henry nodded.

Bobby had the blanket pulled over his head and cinched under his chin so that only his face was exposed to the biting wind. His chin was lowered to his chest and his teeth were clenched to keep them from chattering.

Marshall nudged him. "Bobby, South Bend is just over that rise ahead. After we cross the river bridge there, we should be able to get ourselves a new machine in Graham. We'll find one with a roof and windows. Maybe even find ourselves something warm to wear and—"

Henry swore and slowed the car, and Marshall turned from Bobby to see what Henry was looking at. They had crested the low rise, and two hundred yards away, police cruisers were parked in a line across the South Bend bridge. Henry made a wide U-turn in the road and began working back up the gears.

Marshall glanced behind. Three cars separated from the blockade, and two lawmen leapt on the running boards of one car as it accelerated toward them. He waved an arm forward. "They've seen us. Make speed!"

He wished they were still in that Buick Bobby had found the night before the robbery. This old machine wasn't going to outrun the cruisers. He pulled his gun from his jacket and turned in the seat, putting his forearms on the bench back and bracing his good knee on the floorboard. He aimed at the motor rig with the lawmen standing on the running boards and fired twice. At the cracks of his pistol, the lawmen crouched, then they raised up and returned fire. Marshall flinched at the firm *thunk* of a bullet hitting the back of his car. He fired again, but the shot went wide. Marshall continued trading shots with the officers, but he couldn't get them to break off their chase.

One of the volleys from the pursuers found the left back tire of their old jalopy, and with each revolution of the tire, the rubber shredded and sloughed off the rim. The car vibrated so violently Marshall couldn't draw a bead on any of the pursuers, but he continued to fire wildly in their direction.

Henry turned sharply to the left onto a dirt road and found himself in acres of derricks abandoned by an oil company after the field had played out. He wove between the structures for cover, but the cars behind him drew closer, and he was running out of open field. The line of trees that bounded the field to his left met a line of trees about a hundred yards in front. One of the police cars broke away to flank him on the right and keep him from circling back to the entrance.

Marshall pointed to a defunct pump jack. The horsehead of its rocker arm drooped low in the down position, resigned to its abandonment. "Get us there and we'll make a stand."

Henry braked hard on the slick clay shelf, and the roadster fishtailed slightly before coming to a stop beside the jack. The three scrambled behind the contraption and fired on the approaching cruisers. The police cars skidded sideways and stopped, and the lawmen ran behind their cars and returned fire.

Behind the pump jack, Marshall reloaded his guns, grimacing at each loud *ping* as bullets ricocheted off the iron of the rocker arm and the gear-wheel. "There's too many to fend off. We can't stay here." He waved his revolver toward the line of trees ten yards away. "Lay down some lead and let's make for the woods."

They ran from behind the derrick, repeatedly firing toward the cars. The lawmen ducked at the sudden volley from the desperate men, but then one officer raised up and fired a blast of buckshot. It ripped into Marshall's left side, shredding the hip above his already wounded leg. He tumbled to the ground. When Bobby reached down to pick him up, Marshall waved him off. "Get going." Bobby hesitated, and then he himself was struck by a blast of the deadly beads, and he jerked backward.

Henry ran past them both, dashing through the gauntlet of gunfire before a whistling spray of buckshot dropped him to his knees five yards from the trees.

In Marshall's swimming vision, Bobby and Henry staggered back up and stumbled into the woods. Then everything went black.

5

THE TEXAN

Henry ran unsteadily on a narrow deer trail deep into the dense brush. When he could go no further, he dropped behind a fallen tree in a small elm motte. Bobby caught up with him, and they both pointed their pistols back the way they'd come. But there was no sign of pursuit, and the insistent pain of Henry's wounds took the foreground in his mind. He rolled over and opened his jacket to inspect the places the buckshot had ripped into him. He lay his head back on the log and closed his eyes, listening to the wind soughing in the treetops.

They had left Louis left behind.

They had left the money behind.

They had no food, and he didn't like the look of his wounds.

He remembered something his wife had told him. "Marshall's smart enough to get you into trouble, Henry, but he ain't smart enough to get you out of it." He sighed and raised himself from the ground. Supposing the lawmen were too experienced to follow them into an ambush, he left the spot. He didn't consult Bobby or tell him to come, but the boy followed. They wandered down a long, gentle slope until they found themselves at the Brazos River.

Los Brazos de Dios. In Huntsville, a Mexican inmate had told him that when Spanish explorers were about to die of thirst, local Indians guided them to the river. From then on, the inmate said, they called it Los Brazos de Dios. The Arms of God.

Henry stepped into the river and sucked in his breath as the chilly water swirled around his legs. "The arms of God could be warmer." He hadn't meant to mutter aloud, and it surprised him when the faint echo of his voice returned off the rocky escarpment across the river.

"What'd you say?"

Henry took another step into the river. "Nothing, boy. Come on. They'll have the dogs out soon enough. We got to throw them off the scent."

They waded knee-deep, making their way upstream. The ambling current pulled at their clothing and the mud sucked at their boots. Each stride was an effort. When they finally stumbled back on the root-woven shore, the sun was low and winking through the oak shinnery.

BOBBY OPENED THE barn door, and the hinges groaned softly. Inside, he and Henry hoped to find jars of fruit or vegetables canned for the winter, but there were only tools. At least there were no plow horses for a farmer to check on. Instead, the barn housed a new Fordson tractor, giving the place a faint smell of oil and gasoline. They hunched down, hugging their knees for warmth, and waited out the night.

The two stayed in the structure through Wednesday, their breath coming out like clouds. They passed the time by looking through cracks in the wooden walls as a drizzling rain turned the fields to mud. Near sundown, Bobby and Henry tried to steal a car from the house near the barn. When the farmer came out brandishing a shotgun, they didn't reach for their weapons to challenge him. They backed away, hands raised, and the farmer let them go. Suspecting the old man would report them, the two left the open fields for the iron-cold Arms of God once again.

HENRY LEAPT INTO the clearing, and turkeys scampered in a thunder of wings. After a short run, one tom slowed to a strutting walk like he was taunting them. Henry reached for his pistol but stopped. He didn't want to draw anyone to the sound. Frustrated, he picked up a stick and threw it after the tom. The turkey skittered away and escaped into the brush.

Bobby stepped into the clearing. "How would we of cooked it, anyhow?"

"Quit your yammering, boy."

Henry scanned the clearing. The turkeys had been foraging under a pecan tree, and he kicked at the nuts on the ground. Most of them were black and rotten, but he found some that looked promising. He selected two, pressed them in his fist to crack them against each other, and picked out the meat.

Bobby joined him in the hunt for more pecans. It was Thursday, six days after the robbery. The rain had stopped, but their wounds and hunger and wet clothing had made sleep impossible. They swayed slightly as they shuffled under the pecan tree, scavenging for the remaining nuts of the season.

THURSDAY AFTERNOON, BOBBY pushed further upstream, his toes numb in his waterlogged boots. The current was up after yesterday's rain, and meandering caramel ribbons ambled past them. Henry often lagged, mumbling to himself, and Bobby finally had to stop and wait for the man.

Henry had nearly caught up to Bobby when he stepped into a section of soft bottom, and his foot sank. He lunged backward, overcorrecting, and sat in water up to his armpits. Bobby reached down to help him up, drenching his own clothing in the process. Their bodies spasmed in the wet fabric that clung to their skin like an icy hug, and a sulfuric smell rose from the decaying sediment Henry had stirred up.

A white egret stood in a shallow inlet and kept a dubious eye on them. They waded forward again, feeling their way back to firmer riverbed, and the bird reluctantly pumped her wings to rise to a high branch. When the egret deemed the men had splashed past far enough upstream, she dropped back into the water.

As Bobby slogged on, he glanced back to see if the bird had found anything to snatch from the water, something he might want to put in his own mouth. But a faint mechanical buzz coming from downstream drew his attention to the tree line. The sound grew louder, approaching them.

"What's that?" Bobby asked, stuttering with the chill.

"You scared of an airplane?" Henry's taunt was raspy and inflected with pain.

At the mocking, Bobby hesitated. Then he said, "You think it's looking for us?"

"It's a mail plane, is all."

"I think it's looking for us. We need to get under that boulder there." Bobby pointed to a rocky outcropping to his right.

They splashed to shore and crouched under the limestone cover. The buzzing engine of the airplane grew into a roar as it passed low over them, tracing the line of the river.

The deafening rattle faded away, and Henry made a move to leave the outcropping, but Bobby took his elbow. Henry scowled at him and opened his mouth to speak, but Bobby put his finger to his lips and pointed up.

Two men's voices came from the ledge above.

"That'll be the Ranger," one of the voices said. "Heard him yesterday say he was going to have the airmail pilot give him a look around."

"Caint be far, can they?"

As the men continued to talk, they didn't sound like lawmen to Bobby. Probably locals out for excitement. Or that reward.

Things got quiet, and Bobby smelled cigarettes. He and Henry had their pistols drawn, swiveling their heads to the right and left for the moment the men climbed down and discovered them.

When the scent of tobacco faded and the talk didn't pick back up, Bobby wondered if the men had left. His legs ached from crouching in one position for so long, and he was about to venture out when movement across the river caught his attention. A doe stepped from the brush. For a moment, she stood stock-still. Her ears pivoted and her flank quivered once, and again. Then she ventured toward the water on delicate legs, picking her way over the stones at the shallow edge. After a couple of feints, she bowed her head to drink.

Crack.

The doe twisted and dropped back on her haunches. She shuddered briefly, struggled up, and limped into the woods.

Laughter came from above the rock ledge. "Never seen someone try to bring down a deer with a pistol before."

The sound of boots scraped as the two men scuttled down from the rock. But they weren't heading to the river in pursuit of the animal they had wounded, and their voices faded as they walked away.

Bobby's racing heart slowed back to a normal rhythm, and then a sob welled out of him, and then another. He tried to stop himself, swiping at the tears fiercely, but self-pity came over him again like a wave, and his shoulders shook with it. He collected himself once more and glanced reluctantly at Henry, expecting to be mocked. But Henry only stared off into the distance, scratching at the dried blood that had crusted on one of his wounds.

They stayed under the ledge throughout the afternoon. Bobby even managed to doze off until moans from Henry awakened him. He put a hand to Henry's forehead. The man was burning with fever. Bobby sat up and sighed. He hugged his knees to his chest for warmth and stared absently at the gurgling river flowing by him, wondering what to do.

IN THE MIDDLE of the night, Bobby woke to Henry mumbling about the town of Graham. The man's teeth chattered as he rambled on about a friend who had promised to meet him in a lodge called the Texas House if things fell apart.

Bobby whispered, "Who is it?"

"It's a friend . . . a friend." Henry's words were thick, as though he were speaking in a dream.

Bobby half hoped it was true, and when Henry crawled out from under the ledge, Bobby followed.

When the two of them stumbled into the Graham town square, Bobby's eyes darted around uneasily. At least it was early. Only one shop was open, a diner. He smelled the aroma of bacon, and tried not to think of how many days it had been since his last real meal.

A bell jangled on the door as a young man stepped from the café.

"Hey," Henry croaked in pain. "Sonny."

The young man turned and regarded the two men in the shadow of the neighboring storefront.

Henry spoke again, his voice only a husky rasp. "We admire to find the Texas House."

"The Texas House?"

"Yeah, a friend told me if I got to Graham, I was to go to the Texas House."

"We ain't got a Texas House."

Bobby dropped his head. This was a delusion of Henry's fevered imagination after all.

The young man from the diner hunched his shoulders against the cold and put his hands in his coat pockets. "Maybe you mean the Texan. We got a lodge called the Texan."

"That's got to be it."

"The Texan'll be four blocks up and then a couple blocks west."

"That'll do. Thanks, sonny."

The young man stared at Bobby and Henry a moment longer, nodded, and crossed the square.

Bobby wondered how good a look the man had gotten of the two of them in the shadows. He apprised Henry. His jacket had splotches of blood, his trousers were torn from running through brambles, and the cuffs were caked with mud. Henry's hair was matted, his face bore a week's stubble, and it was best to stay upwind of him. Of course, Bobby figured he was ripe enough himself.

He pointed to Henry's jacket. "Button up. Your bandoleer's showing."

Henry fumbled thickly with the buttons until he had his coat closed over the belt of bullets.

The two took the sidewalk in front of the diner window, and a man with a badge on his chest sat inside sipping coffee. The lawman was reading his newspaper, and he didn't look up as Bobby hurried Henry past the storefront. Exhausted, they returned to their slow, shuffling steps once they left the square.

THEY HAD JUST reached the front of the lodge house when it happened. Two cars approached from different directions and stopped, facing them. The front doors opened on both sides of each vehicle, and men stepped out and crouched behind the doors, guns drawn. Three of them were lawmen, and the fourth was the young man who had given them directions to the Texan.

One of the officers shouted: "Get those hands up."

Henry took a step back unsteadily and leaned against the picket fence that lined the front yard of the lodging house, his hands half raised in resignation. But Bobby darted away. Behind him, someone shouted and fired a pistol. He turned the corner and tried to keep running, but his burst of energy didn't last, and he fell to his knees. Two lawmen approached him cautiously. While one covered him, the other cleared him of his weapons.

"You're a fool, boy," one of them said. "I could of shot you from ten yards away. Why'd you run?"

Bobby said, "I figured I might as well make it hard for you to claim that reward."

They returned him to the patrol cars, and he squinted up at the front of the lodge house. Was some friend of Henry's really staring down at them between the curtains of a second-floor window, or had the man been imagining things in his fever?

The lawmen laid out the six pistols and five bandoleers they had taken off the bandits and discussed how to divide the souvenirs between them. Bobby and Henry were taken a few blocks to the Young County sheriff's office, where they were questioned and a doctor was called to tend their wounds.

The shotgun blast that hit Bobby at the pump jack had left superficial injuries, but the doctor shook his head throughout his examination of Henry. He pulled buckshot and bullet fragments from Henry's right arm and hip, and a few from his back, and he treated an ugly gash on Henry's collarbone. Several of the wounds were badly infected and his temperature raged. Still, when deputies arrived from Eastland, the county where the Cisco crime had taken place, they overruled the doctor's concerns about transporting Henry. Both captives were to be indicted for armed robbery and murder. The Eastland officials left with Bobby in one patrol car, Henry in another, and two cars in front and behind.

THE CONVOY PULLED up to the Eastland County Jail, and guards escorted Bobby and Henry through the front door into the small office. The jailer stood from his rolltop desk and studied the two captives with a grim frown. Bobby squinted at him, trying to remember his name.

Pack. Pack Kilborn. That was it.

Bobby had been here before. Three years ago, he had been passing through Cisco and had broken into an empty tailor shop and stolen a few suits. He was given two years in the state penitentiary for that. His friendship with Marshall began behind bars because of this briefest encounter with Marshall's hometown.

Nothing much had changed in the jailhouse in the last three years. Same rolltop desk in the office. Same iron stairway that ran steep and narrow up the back wall to the cells on the second floor. Same barred opening in the wall under the stairway for meal trays to be passed from the kitchen. Same doorway to the right that led to the apartment where Pack and his family lived in exchange for doing the jail's cooking and cleaning.

But nothing about Bobby seemed to register on the jailer's face. The man simply received the paperwork the deputies brought with them, and he gestured for them to follow him to the second floor. It took a while for Henry to stagger up the steep steps, and he often stopped to lean against the wall.

The second floor had a cluster of cells to the right of the stairway and another cluster to the left. Pack turned to the left-side cluster, unlocked a door, and spoke into the cell. "Don't guess I need to introduce any of you."

From a bunk in the deep shadows, Marshall stared at them without expression.

VOICES WOKE HENRY, and for a moment, he was confused to find himself lying on the bottom bunk in a prison cell. Then it all came back to him. The firefight in South Bend, the arrest in Graham, and the ride back to Eastland. He wondered how many days he had been here. He squinted at a man with a stethoscope that hung from his neck who talked with a man in a Stetson. Although they were only a few feet from him, their voices seemed to come from far away, and their forms moved in and out of focus.

The man with the stethoscope said, "He should be in the hospital."

The man in the Stetson replied, "We ain't moving him from this cell until his trial."

"Well, in his condition, I doubt he'll see his trial date."

"George Carmichael died yesterday. First the chief and now George. Two officers kilt. None of these men are moving from this prison. He stays here."

Henry closed his eyes and faded back into delirious dreams.

THE FEVER BROKE two days later, and he felt strong enough to take small spoonfuls out of a bowl of hot grits with a little butter and salt.

In the cell next to him, a man read from a newspaper. "They say one of your gang died on Christmas Day," the man said. "This Louis Davis fellow was with you?"

Marshall, Bobby, and Henry had generated considerable interest among the men in the other cells. Reports of the Cisco robbery made the front page daily. Whenever a visitor brought an inmate a newspaper, details of the robbery were read aloud to the others.

Henry lowered his bowl. "What's it say about him?"

"Says here that a deputy told him to name the rest of you or they'd let a mob come in and string him up."

"A mob got to him?"

"No, he died of his wounds."

Marshall was in the same cell as Henry, and he stood at the door, leaning on his forearms through the prison bars. "Threatened to string him up," Marshall repeated. "Louis went and fell for that empty threat?"

"No, it don't seem to have worked." The inmate was still scanning the news report. "Says here he died not a-naming one of you. 'True to the criminal's code,' it says here."

Henry smiled slightly.

Newspaper pages riffled from another cell as a second inmate joined the conversation. "Well, he may not have named anyone, but Marshall, this piece says that you did. Or you named one of them anyway. Right after you was captured." The man squinted down at the article he was referring to. "Says, 'When asked if Henry Helms was one of his companions, he nodded, but when asked if he could name the fourth man in the bandit party, he shook his head.'"

Marshall darted a quick glance at Henry and replied to the reader. "Don't believe everything you read in the newspapers."

A man in another cell said, "Here's one about a woman says she boarded Marshall and Bobby in Wichita Falls." The man read a little further. "Hey, she says she made the Santa suit that you wore, Marshall."

Henry responded to the man, but his eyes bore into Marshall. "Well, don't believe everything you read in the newspapers."

6

THE HIGH-STEPPER

Marshall stood between two uniformed men outside his cell door and buttoned his gray jacket. It was the suit he wore on his wedding day four years ago. His mother had brought it for him to wear for the trial, and it still smelled of mothballs from storage.

The cell door clanged shut behind him, and Marshall turned and smiled at Bobby inside the cell to his right. He raised his cuffed hands and adjusted the knot on his tie.

"How do I look?"

"You look like a man who's going to make it through."

A voice called out from another cell, "Hey, boys, is that a bank robber or a bank president in here with us?"

The other inmates on the hall laughed, and Marshall laughed with them. As the deputies escorted him to the stairs, a voice called from the shadows of the lower bunk of the cell he had left. It was gravelly and hoarse.

"Good luck."

Marshall nodded at Henry, and then descended the stairs.

Deputies attached ankle chains to Marshall before leading him outside. He held his cuffed hands belt high and shuffled with short steps, the iron links rattling on the sidewalk. The January wind made his ears hurt, and when the deputies escorted him into the courtroom, he let out a contented sigh at the warmth. What struck him first was the scent. Wood polish and cologne and laundered clothing. It was refreshing after nearly a month in the stale confines of the jailhouse.

As one of the deputies unlocked his handcuffs, he gave the room a quick scan. About a hundred spectators filled the wooden benches, and another fifty stood around the perimeter walls. Even more were in the hallway, peering through the open door. The hubbub had dropped in volume when he first entered, but now it rose again as the crowd returned to their conversations. A cluster of young women whispered together, eyeing him with what he took to be fascination. He gave them a slight grin and strode to the defendant's table, where his mother already sat. She had requested the court allow her to sit by his side and tend to his needs, as he was still recovering from his wounds. Her hair was pulled back in a bun, and her rimless pince-nez rested on her nose.

"Hello, Momma," he said, and gave her a peck on the cheek before settling down beside her.

She patted his knee and gave him a melancholy smile. "Your suit still fits you good."

He straightened the lapels and cocked his head back at the young women again.

His lawyer worked his way through the crowd toward him. Lee Cearley. Marshall did not know how his mother had secured him. No doubt the attorney had offered her a discount for the notoriety the trial would bring his practice, but she must have had made sacrifices to retain him.

Cearley greeted them and released the leather latches on his briefcase. He pulled out a notepad and a folder and arranged them on the table.

Marshall gestured with his head to the prosecutor's table, where three men sat. "Say, Mr. Cearley, that sure seems like a lot of firepower over there."

Cearley stopped arranging his paperwork and glanced at the prosecution. "Yes, well, the thin one with the bow tie will be the county attorney, Joe Frank Sparks. That's his associate sitting next to him. The third one is the special prosecutor the governor himself sent up from Austin." He sat down behind the table and lowered his voice. "The trials for you and your companions have the attention of the whole state of Texas. That'll light a fire under young Mr. Sparks." Cearley grunted and looked at the prosecutor's table. "Not that the fire wasn't already lit. He'll write his own ticket to the state legislature or even a judgeship if he can get capital convictions for all three of you."

Marshall's mother tightened her grip on the handkerchief she had been twisting in her lap. Cearley's face softened. "Don't worry. We have a good defense for Marshall." He gave her forearm a reassuring squeeze and added, "No one is going to be able to testify they saw Marshall shoot anyone, let alone those two officers."

She nodded, but she didn't let go of the twisted handkerchief.

The formal charge was armed robbery of Alex Spears, the bank's cashier, and the prosecution called Spears to the witness stand first. His face bore a red streak from the bullet wound across his jaw. The prosecutor walked toward the stand, carrying a notepad. "Mr. Spears, do you know the defendant, Marshall Ratliff?"

"I do."

"You helped him out after he was arrested for another armed robbery, didn't you? The one for which Ma Ferguson pardoned him after only two years?"

Low grumbles rose in the gallery at the mention of Governor Ferguson's unpopular pardons.

The defense attorney stood and addressed the judge. "Your Honor, there is absolutely nothing relevant about this for the case before us."

The judge was writing a notation, and he didn't look up as he replied, "Sustained."

Sparks continued. "Describe the events of December 23, 1927."

"Well, about noon, a man in a Santa suit come in the bank—came in the bank." Spears adjusted his owl-eyed glasses. "I greeted him twice before he answered. It was like he was inspecting the place. When his gang came in behind him, the man in the Santa suit went into the teller cage where Jewell was—meaning Mr. Jewell Poe. The Santa, well, he took the automatic pistol we keep stowed there."

The prosecutor walked to his table and took up a pistol. "Witnesses will testify in this courtroom that this is one of the pistols taken off Marshall Ratliff when he was captured at South Bend."

Cearley stood again. "Objection. That has not been established for the record yet."

"Sustained."

Sparks continued. "For now, Mr. Spears, can you simply tell us if this is the pistol that was in the teller cage?"

"It is."

"And the Santa Claus took this pistol himself?"

"Yes."

Spears was asked to describe seeing the Santa Claus disappear to the upstairs vault with the bank's cashier, and how the hostages were led into the deadly alleyway.

When the witness was given to the defense, Cearley stood to cross-examine him. "Mr. Spears, you say you knew Marshall Ratliff."

"Yes."

"You say you heard Santa speak when you greeted him?"

"Yes, I did."

"Did he sound like Marshall Ratliff?"

"I did not recognize the voice."

"Thank you, Mr. Spears. Now, your testimony of what happened in the bank and in the alley was very dramatic. But I want to know if you yourself ever saw the Santa Claus character fire a gun. Did you?"

Spears shook his head.

"I'm sorry, Mr. Spears, for the record?"

"I did not."

Spears was dismissed, and the cashier Jewell Poe was sworn in. The prosecutor had him recount the robbery and the gunfight in the alley. When Poe was shown the potato sack, he said it was the one he was forced to fill with the bank's money. He also confirmed that the bloody beard in evidence was, in fact, the fake beard covering the Santa character's face. But the defense had him admit that he could not identify that it was Marshall who wore the beard in the robbery.

The woman who ran the Wichita Falls boardinghouse where Marshall and Bobby stayed was called to testify. She said the Santa Claus costume Marshall used in the heist had been sewn for her husband to wear at a party. When Marshall had asked to borrow it, he didn't say what he intended to use it for.

After recessing for lunch, the prosecutor called Laverne Comer to the stand.

Marshall shifted uncomfortably. Laverne and her friend were the little girls the gang had used as shields in the getaway.

The fourth grader walked into the courtroom in a pleated plaid skirt and wool stockings, her hair braided into twin ponytails. She looked very small in the witness stand next to the judge's bench. She was asked to recount her ordeal. The prosecutor leaned against the railing of the jury box so that, as she told her story, her face was turned toward him and the jury.

"Now, Miss Laverne," the prosecutor continued in a paternal voice. "That wasn't the *real* Santa Claus in that sedan with you, was it?"

"No, sir," Laverne responded eagerly. "That was a man dressed like Santa Claus."

"How do you know that?" the prosecutor asked in a tone of amused surprise, and he winked at the jury.

"His beard was a fake. He took it right off."

Sparks turned serious. "And you saw his face then, didn't you?"

"Yes, I did."

"Did you recognize him?"

"Yes, sir."

"Is that man here in the courtroom today?"

She pointed at Marshall. "There he is yonder."

When the defense offered no cross-examination of Laverne, the prosecution called the officer who arrested Marshall near South Bend. He described the chase into the abandoned oil field and Marshall's capture.

Sparks asked, "What did you find on the defendant?"

"A double-barreled shotgun, six automatic pistols, three cartridge belts, and a bowie knife."

"It doesn't seem like he was expecting a peaceful afternoon bank robbery, does it?"

The defense attorney objected, and the judge concurred.

The prosecutor held up the pistol he had earlier presented to the banker. "Mr. Alex Spears has testified that this weapon was taken from the bank by a man dressed as Santa Claus. Was this found among the pistols you took off Marshall Ratliff?"

"Yes."

After four days and fifty witnesses, Frank Sparks made his closing argument for the prosecution. He summed up the evidence incriminating Marshall as the ringleader of a robbery that resulted in the death of two officers. He reminded the jury of Marshall's previous incarceration for a bank robbery, and how he had skipped out of jail on a Ma Ferguson pardon after only two years. He demanded the jury return with a death penalty verdict.

In his closing argument, Cearley gestured with an open palm to Marshall's mother, who sat next to Marshall with her arm around him. "This is Jarilla Carter. She is the mother of the accused. She would ask you to spare his life. And you should, since not one witness remembers seeing him firing a gun, let alone firing at the officers who were killed."

The jury was given the case, but when it was evening and they still had not returned a verdict, the judge dismissed them for the night. At noon on the next day, the jury sent word that they were unable to reach a decision. The judge asked them to deliberate a little longer.

Marshall retired with his mother and his attorney to a private chamber beside the courtroom. He flicked cigarette ash into a tray on the table and jutted his head toward the door that led into the courtroom. "What do you make of this delay?"

Cearley had been reading through paperwork on another case he was working on, but he stopped and shrugged. "It's a good sign, I think. There's clearly some argument between the jurymen."

"You saying I might walk?"

"We can't hope for that, I don't think. I imagine they're arguing about giving you a life sentence or"—Cearley glanced at Marshall's mother—"or not."

"I wonder which side'll win."

"History's in your favor. There's been no legal execution from a trial in this county's courtroom before. Only two have even been condemned to die, and their verdicts were overturned by the Appeals Court down in Austin."

"Where are they now?"

"One's serving his term. On good behavior, he could see parole sometime. The other's on the lam."

A blue line of smoke rose from Marshall's cigarette and curled before dissipating into a haze above him. "Well, I'll take either one of them options."

Cearley frowned. "Now, Marshall, I know we're only making small talk here. But you keep in mind I'm an officer of the court. I can't be hearing anything about plans to make a prison break."

Marshall opened his mouth to say something, but his mother patted his arm. He grinned slightly and pulled on his cigarette.

Two hours later, the jury sent word they were ready to report. The packed crowd stood in unison for the entrance of the judge, and the bailiff sat them and called the jury in.

The judge addressed the foreman. "Have you reached a verdict?"

"We have."

"Would the defendant rise?"

Marshall and his attorney stood.

The foreman read from a handwritten note. "We, the jury, find the defendant Marshall Ratliff guilty of the offense as charged in the indictment, and we assess his punishment as confinement in the state penitentiary for ninety-nine years."

The judge gaveled the proceedings to a close, and Marshall sat down. He let out a relieved chuckle as he slapped his hands on the arms of the chair.

Cacophonous noise bounced off the hard surfaces of the courtroom. From the bits of conversation Marshall was able to hear, his triumph over dodging the death penalty wasn't shared by anyone else in the room. He didn't care.

His mother dabbed at her eyes with her twisted handkerchief, and he put an arm around her. "You dry those tears, Momma. I got me a pardon from the lady governor in just two years. There'll be parole for me in no time. You watch."

She shook her head. "You and your brother are going to be the death of me, son."

But he didn't hear her, because several newspapermen leaned over the railing of the gallery to get a statement on the decision. He told them, "This ain't no hill for a high-stepper like me."

It was the line that showed up in every newspaper report the next day.

7

HANGDOG

Henry Helms sat in the deep shadow of his cell bunk and regarded the man the jailer had escorted in. The gray-haired man sat at the visitors' table, crossed his legs, and adjusted the starched crease on the trousers of his black suit. He lay a hand on the Bible he'd brought and idly tapped his fingers on it.

The jailer approached Henry's cell and gestured for him to stand. Henry remained seated a moment longer, then let out a resigned grunt and emerged from the shadows. At the cell door, he extended his hands, and the jailer cuffed him and opened the door and led him to the visitors' table.

The gray-haired man swept his hand to gesture at the surroundings. "I thought you were done with all this."

Henry sighed. "G'morning to you, too, Daddy."

John Helms watched the jailer uncuff one of Henry's wrists and attach the open handcuff to a bar that ran the length of the visitors' table.

"Ten minutes, Reverend," the jailer said to John, and left the room.

The two Helms men stared at each other in silence for a moment. Henry was the first to look away.

"Momma come with you?"

John nodded and spoke in a level tone. "You'll see her at the trial. And I brought Nettie and the kids to sit behind you in court, too."

"Keeping up appearances."

John's eyes narrowed slightly. "Keeping you off death row."

Henry scratched the stubble on his cheek. "Nettie and the kids doing okay?"

"About like you'd expect under the circumstances," John said in a stony voice. He paused, pressing his lips together, and then continued. "I thought things would be different after I convinced the lady governor to pardon you."

"I never asked you to do that."

"You were in for a twenty-year sentence. What would your family have done without you for so long?" John paused. "What are they going to do now?"

ON THE DAY of the trial, guards escorted Henry to the defendant's table, and Henry unbuttoned the coat of his new suit as he took his seat. Next to him sat Lee Cearley, the same attorney representing Marshall. Behind him, in the first row of the gallery, Henry's five children were arranged in order of age.

His father had bought the new suit, his father had enlisted the attorney, and his father had mustered the children. And Henry figured none of it would do him any good.

Joe Frank Sparks began the trial by calling Alex Spears to the stand. The bank's cashier recounted the robbery and identified Henry as one of the robbers. When Spears reached the point in his story where all the hostages were gathered in the back room, the prosecutor interrupted him.

"And where was Henry Helms?"

"He was at the alley door."

"And what was he doing?"

"He was shooting."

Sparks spread his legs and squatted slightly, miming both hands on a pistol. "He had one gun, and he was shooting."

"No, sir. He had a gun in each hand."

The prosecutor straightened up and spread his arms, an imaginary gun in each hand now. "So, he was standing at the door shooting up and down the alleyway."

"Yes, sir."

"Officer George Carmichael was on one side of the alley, and Chief Bedford was on the other?"

Henry slumped back in his chair and crossed his arms. But his lawyer stood and said, "Objection. The witness was not in a position to see who was in the alley at the time."

"Sustained."

The prosecutor adjusted his question. "When these bank robbers forced you into the alley, did you see George Carmichael?"

"Yes."

"Was George Carmichael to your left and Chief Bedford to your right?"

"They were, yes."

"State whether George Carmichael was standing when you saw him."

"No, sir, he was lying on his back."

"Did he have any wounds on his body?"

Cearley stood. "Your Honor, this testimony is only designed to inflame the emotions of the jury, and it is unnecessary to establish the charge this jury is required to consider. Was money taken from Alex Spears against his will by my client or was it not?"

"I will allow the testimony."

The prosecutor repeated the question. "Mr. Spears, when you were forced into the alley and you saw Mr. Carmichael lying on the ground, did he have any wounds on his body?"

"Yes, there were wounds on his body." Spears put his forefinger to his scalp. "On his head right up here somewhere."

At this, some of the men in the jury looked Henry's way, and he lowered his gaze to a small stain on the table as he clenched his jaw.

When it was time for cross, Cearley asked Spears, "Mr. Spears, did you see George Carmichael and Chief Bedford in the alleyway at the time you say my client was doing all this shooting?"

"I saw them when I was pushed into the alley."

"But not at the time you say my client was doing all the shooting."

"No, sir."

"You were still in the bank at that time."

"That is correct."

"In fact, you do not know when Mr. Carmichael arrived on the scene, and you did not see who shot him. Is it possible that the bullet that felled our officer came from one of those guns out on the street?"

Spears frowned and answered doubtfully, "I suppose that's possible."

"There were a lot of citizens out in the street shooting into that alley. Am I correct about that?"

"Yes."

"Trying to get your bank reward."

The prosecutor objected and the judge sustained the complaint.

Cearley walked to the exhibit table and lifted a rifle. "Mr. Spears, I'm curious about this firearm that Chief Bedford had with him. Who supplied him with that weapon?"

"My bank did."

"In fact, your bank gave the police department several high-powered weapons a few weeks before the incident at the First National Bank. Is that correct?"

"Yes."

"Yes, indeed. They were given to the police department at the same time your bank announced that reward for dead robbers."

The defense attorney waited, and finally Spears said, "I suppose it was about the same time, yes."

"So, any reasonable citizen could assume that your bank expected the local police to kill bank robbers with the weapons you gave them."

"I do not think you could say that the police department was given the guns to kill bank robbers. I do not think you could say that was the expectation on the part of my bank."

"But your reward will only be paid for *dead* bank robbers, correct?"

"That is correct."

"And 'not a penny' for a live one?"

"That is the way the poster is worded, yes."

"Mr. Spears, were you aware that men were running from the hardware store with rifles they promised to pay for later, just so they could have a chance at your reward?"

"Someone told—"

Cearley interrupted him. "A few Cisco Loboes football players, even?"

"Well, that's an unfortunate—"

"High school boys."

"I—" Spears began, but then he simply answered, "Yes."

"Mr. Spears, if someone was shooting at you with the intent to kill you, wouldn't you shoot back to save your life?"

The prosecutor objected, the judge sustained it, and Cearley concluded his cross-examination of Spears. The witness was dismissed.

The prosecution called Ellis Oder to the stand.

"Mr. Oder, where were you on December 23 last year?"

"I was in my shop in Cisco. I'm a radio repairman by trade."

"And you heard shooting at the bank."

"Yes, I did. And I come outside to see about the commotion. Down the street, well, there was Uncle Bit firing a shotgun into the alley by the bank."

"Uncle Bit, meaning the chief of police, Mr. Bedford?"

"Yes, sir. There in Cisco, we all called him Uncle Bit—God rest his soul."

"And you decided to investigate the commotion?"

"Well, yes. In hindsight, I don't guess it was very smart of me, but I wanted to see what he was shooting at. I hid at the corner of the Garner store and snuck my head around to get a look."

"And what did you see?"

"Uncle Bit was firing a shotgun at a man dressed as Santa Claus, and the man in the Santa garb was firing a pistol back at him. They both dropped down to their knees. And then a man at the back door of the bank shot Uncle Bit and he fell back."

"The man at the back door of the bank, was he firing a pistol?"

"Two pistols. He had one in each hand."

"And as this man at the back door fired, you saw Chief Bedford fall down?"

"Yes, sir. Fell on his back, he did."

"The man with pistols in each hand, the man who shot our chief of police—is he in this courtroom today?"

The witness pointed to Henry. "Yes, sir, it was Henry Helms, the man at the table over there."

For the defense, Cearley asked, "Mr. Oder, you say you were standing at the corner of Garner's Department Store. There was a lot of shooting going on, wasn't there?"

"Yes, sir."

"You told Mr. Sparks there at the prosecutor's table that when you got to the corner, you just sort of—" Cearley flipped a page of his notepad. "You said, 'I snuck my head around.' Is that the way you put it?"

"I suppose that's what I said, yes."

"That doesn't sound like you had your head around the corner for long, now, did you?"

"I got a long enough look."

"Bullets coming every which way and you stood there with your head exposed to it all."

The witness glared at Cearley. "I know what I saw."

"Well, now, I'm trying to figure out exactly what it was you saw. You say the man dressed as Santa was shooting at Chief Bedford, but you also say some man in the doorway was shooting. And then there were those men in the back of the alleyway. Let's see . . ." He consulted his notepad. "Two post office employees, two police officers, firing away in the direction of the chief. I'm wondering how you can be certain who it was that actually struck down our chief."

"I already told you who it was. It was Henry Helms."

"There were other bandits. The man at the door of the bank, are you sure it wasn't Louis Davis or Robert Hill?"

"No, it wasn't."

"You know what they look like, then."

"I know the man sitting at your table is the man I saw at the door."

"If it really was Henry Helms at that door, maybe he was shooting over the chief, to get him to back away."

Ellis Oder pointed at Henry. "I'm telling you I saw Uncle Bit fall back when that man fired at him."

"All from darting your head into a shooting gallery?"

The prosecutor stood, but before he could object, Cearley withdrew his question. He waved his notepad at the witness like he had tired of him. "Nothing further from this man, Your Honor."

When Ellis Oder was dismissed, the judge recessed court for the day. As the noise of the crowd rose in the gallery, Cearley leaned over to Henry. "Henry, all through the proceedings, you sat there with a hangdog look."

"It don't do no good how I look or how pretty my family dresses up behind me. That Sparks fellow's got it in for me."

Cearley shook his head. "If the jury thinks you've already given up, that's not going to help us a bit."

His father leaned his elbows on the gallery railing. "Your lawyer's right. You got to keep your head up."

Henry let out a cynical grunt as he loosened his tie and opened the top button of his shirt. He nodded at the deputies, and they chained him and escorted him out.

But overnight, Henry considered his lawyer's advice. The next day, he had one of his girls on his knee, and he stroked her hair as the jury entered. When the jurymen sat, Henry took her off his lap and sent her to join her mother in the gallery.

The prosecutor called fourth-grader Emma May Robinson to the stand. She recounted how she and her friend Laverne Comer walked out of the bookkeeping room and found a man dressed as Santa in the lobby, and how three other men came in with guns drawn.

The prosecutor pointed at Henry. "And Mr. Henry Helms was one of those men?"

She glanced at Henry and then looked down at her hands in her lap.

Sparks said, "Don't worry, honey. He can't hurt you. You can look at me as you answer. Was Henry Helms one of the men with guns?"

Emma May kept her head down, but she nodded and said, "Yes, sir."

"Was Mr. Helms very nice?"

"No, sir. He hit me."

"He hit you? You mean he slapped you with his hand?"

"No, sir." She looked up at the prosecutor. "He hit me in the head with his pistol."

A murmur rose in the crowd, and Joe Frank Sparks let it rise and die down before he continued. "This was when he was pushing you and the other hostages into the back room?"

"Yes, sir."

"Now, when you got into the back room, what did you do next, you and your little friend Laverne?"

"Well, it was crowded, and we crawled under a table and hid."

"And all the other people in the room, what happened to them?"

"The men with the guns pushed them into the alley."

"And then you and Laverne were the only ones left, hiding safe under that table?"

"Yes, sir."

"Tell us what happened next."

She pointed toward Henry without looking at him. "He told me and Laverne to get out from under the table."

"For the record, you're pointing at Mr. Henry Helms?"

"Yes, sir."

"And what did he make you do when you crawled out from your safe place under the table?"

"He made us walk in front of him and his friend."

"Into the alley?"

"Yes, sir."

"Where you had been hearing all that shooting and screaming?"

"Yes, sir."

Henry's newborn daughter let out a yowl, and every face in the jury turned to her. Henry followed their gaze back to where his wife soothed the baby. Next to her, his children stared at him with blank expressions. It was no use, he thought, his daddy lining them all up behind him and sitting pretty. Joe Frank Sparks was convincing the jury to pin the death of both officers entirely on him. He put his elbows on the table and dropped his head in resignation.

The prosecution called Carl Wylie to recount his twenty-four hours as a hostage of the bandits, and then lawmen described the gun battle at South Bend and the arrest in Graham. The prosecution rested, and the defense presented no witnesses. The judge called a short recess for the attorneys to arrange their closing arguments. When the trial resumed, Sparks paced to the jury box and rested his hands on the railing.

"Gentlemen of the jury, as you know, there were four men who set out to rob the First National Bank over in Cisco. One died, and Marshall Ratliff, Robert Hill, and Henry Helms each face separate trials for their part in this deadly crime. Other juries are responsible for making the right decision over Marshall Ratliff and Robert Hill, but your job is to make the right decision over Henry Helms. And you have before you the most menacing man from this gang. You have before you the one who was spoiling for a fight. You have before you the one who used his weapons to effect. We lost two officers because of this man. There is no other conclusion than to find Henry Helms guilty. And there is no other justice than to sentence him to death."

Cearley stood and addressed the jury. "The prosecutor's witnesses, one after another, remember seeing our officers lying in the alley, tragically shot. But only one of the witnesses even claimed to see Henry Helms shoot anyone. And can we rely on that witness for accuracy? We cannot. You remember that witness arrived late and could only dart his head around the corner every now and then when he thought maybe he could get away with it. None of the other witnesses could say if Henry Helms was shooting or what he was shooting at. Men were trying to take his life for a pile of reward money. Was he firing over their heads to get them to back away? The witnesses themselves said they supposed that was possible. Lots of bullets crisscrossed the alley that day, from lots of different guns. Could it be that one of our own citizens, eager for that banker's reward, accidentally shot our officers? That's a reasonable thought, and so there's a reasonable doubt about Henry's role in this. And if there's a reasonable doubt, you must *not* send him to the death house."

The judge dismissed the jury to deliberate, and he adjourned the court. The next morning, word came that the jury had reached a decision, and two deputies returned Henry to the defendant's table. While he sat with Cearley and waited for the jury to enter, he watched rain trickle down the windows of the courtroom in meandering streams. Thunder rolled in long rumbles, like the sound of a bowling alley he had once supplied with bootleg bourbon.

The jury entered, and the judge directed the foreman to stand and announce the decision. The foreman cleared his throat. "We declare the accused, Henry Helms, guilty, and he is to be sentenced to death."

When the judge dismissed the jury and adjourned the court, Henry's wife sobbed quietly. But Henry struck a match, held it with a steady hand, and lit a cigarette.

"Well, he poured it on me," he said, in reference to Sparks.

His father leaned forward and put a hand on Henry's shoulder, but he shrugged it off and stood. He offered his wrists to accept the handcuffs.

Cearley said, "Henry, this isn't over. Tomorrow I'll be right back here in this courtroom asking for a new trial. You just be patient."

As the deputies cuffed him, Henry squinted through the smoke of his cigarette. "Yeah?" he said in a raspy and cynical voice. "Well, good luck with that." The deputies escorted him away.

A FEW WEEKS later, Cearley sat with Henry and his father in the visiting area of the jail and explained that the judge had ruled against a new trial.

"Henry, it's frustrating, I know. But I've already expressed our intent to file a claim with the Court of Criminal Appeals down in Austin. That means they won't move you to death row. Normally, you're confined in the jail of the county that heard your case until the Appeals Court has its say. They tell me you're to be sent to the jail in Dallas due to overcrowding here in the Eastland County Jail. But at least it isn't the death house in Huntsville. You should count that as some good news. What's going to happen is that three judges down in Austin will review the case and how the court handled it. Then they'll decide whether to allow a new trial."

Henry stared at a spot over the lawyer's shoulder.

"Be patient over there in Dallas," Cearley continued. "It will take several months before we even find out if they'll take the appeal. If they do, it'll be several months after that before they rule on it."

John patted Henry's forearm. "You hear that, son? You got time. You make good use of that time to come back to God." He slid his Bible across the table to Henry. "Take this."

Henry shoved the Bible away. "Looks like neither one of you has anything I need to hear." He tried to stand, but he had forgotten the handcuff that chained his left arm to the bar fixed on the table. He dropped back down on the bench and shouted, "Guard. Ho, guard, I'm done here."

The jailer walked into the visitation area, unlocked Henry from the table, and returned him to his cell. Henry dropped into his bunk as the door clanked shut. He could hear the voices of his father and lawyer fading as they made their way down the stairway. He lay back on his pillow and put his forearm over his eyes.

8

THE BOY WHO NEVER STOOD A CHANCE

Bobby Hill's legs ached, and he was dizzy with the blood rushing to his head. He was in a line with others, forced to bend at the waist and grab the toes of his shoes while keeping his knees locked in place. The sun blazed on his bent back. Beads of sweat trickled up his face and pattered to the dirt a foot below his head.

A whimper next to him made him turn, where he found an eleven-year-old boy.

Bobby whispered, "Get your hands down. All the way to your toes."

"I can't." The boy's face was beet red. He moaned helplessly as he strained his short, chubby fingers toward the ground. "I'm too fat. I can't."

Bobby kept a grip on his own toes with his left hand and reached out his right to pull the boy's wrist lower. "He's going to see you. Get your hands down."

A man shouted: "Hill! Who told you to release your toes?"

Bobby swept both hands back to his feet. The upside-down form of a big man approached him. He carried a long and thick leather strop.

The man stopped in front of the boy next to Bobby. "New boy's got to learn for hisself. Now grab those toes."

The fat boy squatted slightly to get his fingers to the shoe leather.

"Don't you bend those knees." The man pushed the boy's legs with his boot, and when the knees locked straight, the boy's fingers slipped off his toes. The child grunted as he stretched and wiggled his fingers toward his feet.

The big man, unsatisfied, raised the strop and brought it down on his back.

At the boy's pitiful wail, Bobby jerked and woke up.

He was lying in his bunk in the Eastland County Jail.

He sat up and raked his hands through his hair. He had been a ten-year-old when that incident had taken place at the Gatesville State School for Boys. He and the other wards had been made to line up and "pull toes" many times. The new ones, like the chubby kid, always had the toughest time with it.

Bobby hadn't thought of that boy for years. The child had been caught with a band of boys engaged in a series of petty thefts. After serving a one-year term in Gatesville, he had returned home. Bobby, having no home to take him, stayed in the school until he aged out at sixteen. While most of the boys were serving juvenile sentences, some were just foster wards like Bobby.

His attorney planned to make Bobby's childhood the main point of defense at his trial. It had dredged up a lot of unpleasant memories.

Bobby stood from his bunk and took the two steps to the front of his cell. The visitor bench beyond his cluster of cells was empty. Marshall had huddled with his mother at that bench on many visits. Even Henry accepted the chance to leave his cell and sit there with his father, at least until he could no longer tolerate the old man's alternating lectures and pleas. Now Marshall and Henry were gone, and he had no one to come and sit with him at that empty bench.

A white-haired man approached his cell. "Morning, Bobby."

It was Tom Jones, Pack Kilborn's assistant jailer. Everyone called him "Uncle Tom," even the prisoners.

"Trial's still scheduled to start today, I'm told." The voice was kind and grandfatherly.

"Yes, sir."

"Well, let's get you shaved, then. Turn around."

Bobby knew the drill. He turned his back and presented his wrists for handcuffs. Uncle Tom locked them in place and opened the cell door. All the cells in the cluster faced a small corridor where a deep sink and a single toilet were mounted against a wall. Tom led him into the corridor and sat him on a stool, where he lathered and shaved Bobby. When the razor was put away, Tom released him from the cuffs, and Bobby went to the sink to rinse his face. Stripping to the waist, he lathered soap into his armpits. Goose bumps rose on his skin as he rinsed with the unheated water. He put his one undershirt back on and squinted into a mirror spotted with oxidation while he combed his hair in place.

A dress shirt and suit hung from the cell bars, and he slipped into the outfit and worked the tie into a knot. Unlike the fine-fitting suits Marshall's and Henry's families had supplied them, the one he wore was a little tight, the trouser knees no longer held their shape, and the coat had a shabby shine at the elbows. Still, he thanked the prisoner who had loaned it to him, and he signaled that he was ready to receive the chains for the walk to the courthouse.

Bobby was surprised at the crowd inside. He expected interest in the robbery would have died down by now. Instead, the gallery was overflowing, and spectators who couldn't find seats craned their necks to see inside the open door. Bobby's escorts brought him to the defendant's table and removed his handcuffs. He sat alone and listened to the hubbub from the gallery behind him until his court-appointed attorney appeared. H. L.

Flewellen sat with Bobby and unpacked his briefcase, laying out a note-pad and a folder with Bobby's name on it.

Flewellen leaned toward him and spoke in a low voice. "Bobby, I'm going to ask it one more time before the judge comes in. Are you still set on pleading guilty to armed robbery?"

"I am. I ain't guilty of killing anyone, but there's no use in saying I wasn't there."

Flewellen gestured with his thumb toward the men at the prosecutor's table. "You see the one in the bow tie? That's the county attorney, Joe Frank Sparks." Bobby had heard Henry complain about how Sparks had poured it on him. Flewellen continued. "Next to his associate is an attorney the governor himself sent here. The whole state's watching these trials of you and your companions. Mr. Sparks wants to show the public how he got every one of you on death row. Pleading guilty isn't going to shield you from that sentence if the jury sides with him."

Bobby nodded.

"Well, then, let's convince this jury you don't deserve the chair."

They stood when the judge entered. After the jury filed in, the judge asked for Bobby's formal plea. When Bobby confirmed that he was pleading guilty, the verdict was announced, and the sentencing hearing began.

Sparks stood and walked toward the jury box. "Gentlemen of the jury, Robert Hill pled guilty to the charge of robbery with firearms. We do not need to prove he was involved in this deadly crime. But tomorrow when he gets on the witness stand, I expect he's going to tell you a long sob story of his sorry childhood. When you hear it, keep in mind whether any of that excuses his part in the horror he's charged with. Robert Hill was armed to the teeth when he drove into Cisco. He was behind the wheel of an automobile he himself had stolen. By the time he drove out of town in that same stolen car, two police officers were fatally shot, and numerous citizens suffered from gunshot wounds. I want you to hear from the people who were there. Our own neighbors, even children, terrified for their lives. I want you to keep all of that in mind when Mr. Hill gets up on this stand tomorrow to talk of all his childhood woes. Don't you be drawn in. His crime deserves the death penalty, same as any other man with him."

The fifty witnesses who had testified in the first two trials were scheduled for Bobby's trial, too. When Vance Littleton, one of the bank's bookkeepers, took the stand, Sparks focused his questions on Bobby's role in the robbery.

"Now, Mr. Littleton, who forced you into that deadly alley?"

He pointed to Bobby. "It was that man over there."

"You're referring to Robert Hill."

"Yes, sir. He told me and Mr. Poe to go through the door in front of him."

"He told you? He didn't ask you politely with a please and thank you?"

"No, sir. He was pushing me into the alley when a bullet ricocheted off the bricks right by my head. But he shoved a gun in my back and told me to keep walking out the door, me and Jewell—meaning Mr. Jewell Poe."

"You felt that gun boring into your back."

"Yes, sir."

"You wondered when a bullet was going to come out of that gun and rip through your gut."

"Yes, I did."

"You feared for your life."

"Yes."

"Thank you, Mr. Littleton. Nothing further."

Bobby's lawyer stood. "Mr. Littleton, you said a bullet ricocheted off the wall right next to your head when you stepped into the alley. That must have been very frightening."

"It was."

"Tell me, where did that bullet come from?"

"I don't get your meaning."

Flewellen put his hand on Bobby's shoulder. "Well, Robert here, was he shooting at you?"

"No, sir."

"No, of course not. He was in the bank, and that bullet came from outside." Flewellen walked to the witness stand. "Was it one of his companions out in the alley shooting back at Robert?"

"No, sir."

"Well, who do you suppose it was?"

"I suppose it was one of the citizens out in the street."

"Why do you think someone shot at you?"

"They probably thought I was one of the bank robbers."

"And you feared for your life."

"I did."

"Robert Hill must have been afraid for his life, too, don't you think?"

Sparks rose from the prosecutor's table to object, and Flewellen said, "Withdrawn. Now, Mr. Littleton, when you made it out to the alley, Robert's companions were already out there by that point, weren't they?"

"One of them was lying on the floor inside. He was bleeding from the stomach."

"Yes, but the other two. They were already out in the alley?"

"Yes."

"When you and Mr. Poe walked out into the alley with Robert behind you, you saw Officer George Carmichael."

"Yes, sir."

"He was already shot and lying on the ground?"

"Yes."

"He wasn't moving."

"No, sir."

"And Chief Bedford? You saw him?"

"Yes, sir."

"What was his condition?"

"He was lying on the ground, too. All shot up."

"Not moving?"

"Not moving."

"So, by the time Mr. Hill walked into the alley behind you, the two officers were already shot down."

"Yes."

"Robert could not have been the one to shoot them, is that correct?"

"No, I suppose not."

"In fact, you didn't see this boy shoot down anyone, did you?"

"I saw him shooting."

"But you didn't see him shoot anyone."

"No, sir. I did not."

"Thank you." He nodded at the judge. "That is all, Your Honor."

The prosecution called fourteen-year-old Woody Harris to recount the attempted theft of his family's car. As he had done for the trials for Marshall and Henry, the boy recalled how the Buick sedan cut in front of his path, which made him pull to a stop. He told how a man dressed as Santa Claus emerged from the sedan, approached his family's car, and pulled a gun from behind his back.

The prosecutor said, "Two other men followed the Santa Claus and stood on either side of your daddy's car."

"Yes, sir."

"You're referring to Henry Helms and to that man there, Robert Hill." He pointed to Bobby.

"Yes, sir."

"They had guns drawn."

"Yes, sir. Well, now, Robert there, he tucked his gun away to help my grandmother out of the car. I was hiding, but I saw him carry her to the side of the road to get her away from the shooting. After he got my grandmother to a safe place, he pulled his gun again and shot over the cars coming after them."

A flash of uncertainty crossed the prosecutor's face, and then he regained his resolve. "So, you testify that Mr. Hill participated in the shooting."

Woody replied, "Yes, sir. He was there."

When Bobby's lawyer stood for the cross-examination, he put his hands in his pockets and smiled at the boy. "Woodrow, the men who told you and your family to get out of the car, they did not drive away in it. Why is that?"

"Well, sir, when they told me to get out, I locked the ignition and took the key."

Flewellen raised his eyebrows, impressed. "That was some quick thinking on your part. You are a very clever boy. Now, you told Mr. Sparks there, the prosecutor, you told him that Robert carried your grandmother away from all the gunfire."

"Yes, sir."

"And you said he then drew his gun and shot *over* the cars coming down the road."

"Yes, sir."

"He wasn't shooting *at* them." The attorney mimed a gun pointed level with his shoulder. "You say he was shooting *over* them?" He raised his imaginary gun up at an angle.

"Yes, sir."

"Why would he do that?"

Sparks stood at the prosecutor's table. "Objection, Your Honor. The boy cannot know what was in the mind of Mr. Hill."

The defense attorney raised a finger. "But the young man can testify as to what was in his own mind. So, let me adjust the question. Woodrow, what was in your own mind? What did *you* think Robert was doing?"

"I figured he was warning them, keeping them from getting any closer."

"I figure you are right, Woodrow. Thank you."

THE PROSECUTION CONTINUED to call witnesses throughout the afternoon, but they did not rest their case by the time the judge recessed for the night. The next morning, one of the officers who had captured Bobby and Henry in Graham was called to the stand. Sparks asked him to describe the event.

"We were alerted that two suspicious men were in the Graham square," the lawman said. "They were asking about a lodge house called the Texan. We made our way to the house and saw the men on the street and drew on them. One surrendered and the other one made a run for it."

"The one who tried to run was Mr. Hill?"

"Yes. He did not get more than a block away before he surrendered."

"You searched him for weapons?"

"Yes."

The prosecutor held up a Smith and Wesson .38. "You took this weapon from him?"

"Yes."

He held up a .45. "And this one?"

"Yes."

He held up a Luger semiautomatic. "And this one?"

"That one, too."

Sparks raised two belts of ammunition in each hand, hefting the weight of them for the jury to see. "And these were on Mr. Hill?"

"Both of them, yes, sir."

"You were glad to get a man with this kind of firepower off the street, I suppose."

"I was."

"Thank you. Nothing further, Your Honor."

Bobby's lawyer stood. "When you say my client was running away, was he firing back at you?"

"No, he was not."

"Did he even have a weapon in his hand?"

"He did not."

"Thank you, sir. That is all, Your Honor."

The witness was dismissed, and the prosecution rested. The judge announced that the defense could call their first witness.

Flewellen stood. "I call C. E. King to the stand."

A middle-aged man entered the court, took the oath, and sat.

"Mr. King, you were superintendent of the Gatesville School for Boys in 1916?"

"I was."

"Robert Hill was admitted to your institution that year."

"According to our records, yes."

"He was eight years old."

"Our records show that."

"What crime did he commit to be assigned to the Gatesville reform school?"

"He was not sent to our school for any crime."

A murmur rose from the crowd. Flewellen walked toward the gallery as he addressed his witness. "He committed no crime and yet he was sent to your school?"

"Robert was brought to us when the boy's mother died. The facility was a foster home for a few boys back then."

"But the other boys in the school, they were there for crimes."

"Most of our students had been convicted of crimes, yes."

"Such as?"

"Mostly breaking and entering. Some for assault. A few for armed robbery or arson."

"Serious crimes." Flewellen paused. "Tell me, were the boys separated by age?"

"The dormitories were separated by age."

"But not all the daytime activities?"

"That would have been impossible."

"So, when Robert was admitted for foster care at the tender age of eight, he was mixed in with these other boys, even teenagers? Boys convicted of such serious offenses?"

"We couldn't . . . Yes, yes, he was."

"How was his conduct in his years there?"

"Robert has no reports of poor conduct in our records."

"It was for no crime that he was sent to the Gatesville School, and it was for no crime that he had to remain there."

"That is correct."

The attorney flipped a page of his notes. "Mr. King, while Robert was in the Gatesville School, did anyone visit him?"

"There's no name in the visitor records."

"And he was released from your care at sixteen?"

"At sixteen, yes."

"Did anyone come to receive him upon his release?"

"I do not recall anyone arranging to meet him on his release."

"Thank you, Mr. King. That is all, Your Honor."

The prosecutor stood. "I have no questions for the witness at this time, but I would like the chance to call him back for cross-examination later."

THE COURT RECESSED for lunch, and Bobby was led back to his jail cell. Uncle Tom extended a bowl of stew through the bars, and Bobby took it, but he had no appetite for it. He was thinking about having to take the stand. He didn't know what he dreaded more: facing all those eyes in the courtroom or facing all those memories in his head.

As court resumed, Flewellen called him to the stand. The bailiff presented a Bible, and Bobby rested his left hand on it and raised his right hand. He listened to the bailiff recite the question. "Do you solemnly swear to tell the truth, the whole truth, and nothing but the truth, so help you God?"

"Yes, I . . . yes. So help me God." Bobby felt a streak of sweat trickling down between his shoulder blades.

His attorney began. "Bobby, why were you raised in the Gatesville School for Boys? The jury has already heard you were not there for committing any crime."

"I was an orphan. My father died when I was still a baby. My mother remarried a few years later. When I was eight, she died. It was about this time of year, in February. She had tuberculosis. I remember it was a morning when she died."

"So, your father died, your mother remarried, and then she died. And then your stepfather turned you over to the Gatesville School."

"I never regarded him as my stepfather or a father of any kind to me."

"Your mother's second husband, then. He delivered you to Gatesville."

"Yes."

"Why?"

"He said I was not his and I was not his responsibility."

"This was Bert Hill?"

"Yes."

"He said he did not consider you his responsibility, and yet you carry his surname to this day. Hill. Robert Hill."

"I've carried it ever since I was enrolled with it at Gatesville. I do not remember if he introduced me to the school in that way or if the school put down my name like that. I suppose it was easier for the records."

"Tell us about your experience at the Gatesville School."

"It was hard. We were up before dawn for chores. Farm chores. Milking, or mucking out the stalls, or spreading manure on the garden. Then schoolwork. In the afternoon, we would drill if we were not leased out to farms or mills in the area."

"Drill. You mean like the military?"

"Yes."

"Anyone who couldn't keep up drew some pretty harsh punishments, I've been told."

"Yes."

"Tell us about the punishments."

"Well, sometimes our whole group would have to pull toes for something one boy had done."

"Pull toes. You will have to explain that to us."

"Everyone had to stand in a line and bend at the waist. You had to keep your knees straight as you grabbed the toes of your shoes."

"Most of us did an exercise like that in school. How was that a punishment?"

"We had to stay like that for a long time, fifteen minutes or more. Once our group had to stay like that for a whole hour."

"Your group must have been angry at any boy who caused everyone to pull toes."

"He'd get a beating from the other boys when the guards were gone, that's for sure."

"What other punishments did you see?"

"There was the box. It was a small shed like an icehouse. No light, no breeze. A boy would be put in there for hours. Maybe a day. If it was in the summer, he would come out of there like he had been in the oven. Wet with sweat and red all over."

"You were never put in there."

"No."

"What else?"

"They would hit boys with the bat."

"A baseball bat?"

"It was a thick leather shaving strop, like barbers use. They might hit you with it once or twice to keep everyone in order. A formal punishment would be thirty-nine lashes."

"Thirty-nine lashes. Like Jesus got."

Bobby stared at him, unsure of what he wanted him to answer.

Flewellen put his hands behind his back and paced toward Bobby. "Just how would they administer these thirty-nine lashes?"

"The boy would be laid out on the dirt on his stomach, his shirt stripped off, his britches and underwear down to his ankles. One boy would hold his hands and another would hold his feet, and—"

The defense attorney interrupted. "*Boys* would hold him down?"

"We had boy captains who carried out the orders of the guards."

"And so, the boy captains would hold down this naked child."

"Yes, and a guard would bring the bat down on his back and rear end over and over."

"A boy died from that in 1917. Probably all of us in here read about that. You were at Gatesville when it happened."

"I was nine. The boy had not even been there a week. He would not do the drills. The guards told him he would not eat until he got with the program. He was so weak after a couple of days that I do not believe he could have drilled if he wanted to. They took him behind a shed—"

"They?"

"Some of the boy captains and a guard. He . . . he did not live."

"The guard is serving time for that."

"That is what I was told."

"You never got the bat."

"I never got the thirty-nine. Everyone got a few strikes with the bat every now and then."

"Most of the boys were there for committing crimes."

"Yes, sir."

"But you were there just because you were an orphan. Just because no one wanted you."

"I guess that about sums it up."

"And yet, after a year or two, these boys who had committed crimes would be released. Their sentences would be finished. But not you. You were there until the state said you were old enough to take care of yourself."

"I was there until I was sixteen. Yes, sir."

"The school made sure you got your lessons in. You know how to read and write. You know your arithmetic."

"Yes."

"But you learned some other lessons at Gatesville, too, did you not? From the boys who were sent there?"

Bobby repeated the wording his lawyer had told him to use. "Well, I suppose they taught me how things worked in the real world. They taught me that no one gives you anything and you got to take care of things yourself. And people in authority won't never have you in mind. You got to find someone who'll look out for you and stay loyal to him. Even if he tells you to do something wrong."

The wording was true enough to his mind, though it would not have occurred to Bobby to summarize such lessons in exactly this way without the lawyer's guidance.

"What did you do when you were released at sixteen? Did you go home?"

"I had no home to go to. I boarded a westbound messenger train."

"Where were you heading?"

"Nowhere. Just away."

"In fact, that train stopped here in Eastland County, ten miles west of this courthouse, over in Cisco. That was three years before the robbery of the First National Bank. Do I have that right?"

"Yes. It was not the end of the line. I just got out to stand a while where things weren't swaying."

"You were sixteen, finally free from Gatesville, no family to meet you when you were released. You were heading west trying to decide what to do next. And you were hungry."

"Yes, and I had no money. It was in the middle of the night, and no one was on the streets. All the shop windows were dark. So, I broke into a tailor shop. There was a little cash in the register. I pulled five suits from the rack that I thought I could sell down the line. A couple of train stops later, I tried to sell the suits to a shop owner. I guess he saw the Cisco store tags and reported me to the police. I was arrested and returned to Eastland County, and I pled guilty to the theft. I was sent to Huntsville for a two-year term. That's where I fell in with Marshall Ratliff. When he heard I was sent up from his hometown, he sort of looked out for me there in Huntsville. Everyone seemed to like him, so when I hung around him, no one bothered me much."

"And when you got out of Huntsville, you followed him."

"Yes. He had been released about a month before me. He was living up there in Wichita Falls."

"And it was Marshall who led you back to Cisco to join him in robbing his hometown bank."

"Yes."

"Yesterday we heard all the witnesses describe the robbery. Tell us about it in your own words."

Bobby recounted the events, emphasizing that he did not shoot anyone but only fired overhead to keep people back. He described how he carried the old woman from the Harris car, and how his arm was struck by a bullet as it shielded her head. He told of the firefight at the pump jack near South Bend, how he and Henry wandered the Brazos River bottoms for a week, and how they were captured in Graham.

When Bobby was done, his attorney nodded at him, gave him a reassuring smile, and sat down.

Sparks rose to his feet. "This state of Texas gave you a place to stay and food to eat when no one else would take you. This state of Texas taught you to read and write and do your figures. Our tax dollars funded an institution where you were given everything you needed to get along in life. And yet you seem to blame the Gatesville School for all your choices. Stealing from a tailor shop the moment you got out of Gatesville, and now armed robbery of a bank. According to you, it was all due to your sad childhood. Is that your claim?"

"Well, sir. I pleaded guilty for the tailor shop and now for the Cisco bank. I didn't kill no one, I didn't even shoot at no one. But I went into that bank with Marshall to take the money—"

"With guns drawn."

Bobby hesitated and then said, "With guns drawn, yes, sir."

"Thank you. That is all."

The crowd had been quiet throughout the afternoon testimony. But as Bobby left the witness stand, it seemed the gallery in unison exhaled a breath held for too long, and low chatter hummed in the courtroom.

The judge banged his gavel for order and the prosecutor stood. "Your Honor, we return C. E. King to the stand."

The administrator of the Gatesville School returned to the witness box. Joe Frank Sparks folded his arms. "Mr. King, the point of the Gatesville School for Boys is to reform them—to set them on the right track?"

"Yes."

"And you feel you accomplished that with the boys in your care?"

"I feel that the things we did gave them their best chance to turn their lives around."

"And did they? Did the boys in your care turn their lives around?"

"Very few of the boys were returned to the school on further convictions. So, yes, based on that, I can say we were successful in most cases."

"And yet Robert Hill would have us believe that it was his years in your school that trained him for crime."

The defense attorney stood. "Objection, Your Honor. Does the prosecutor have a question to ask?"

Before the judge could respond, Sparks corrected himself. "Here is my question. Mr. King, do you believe the program you provided at Gatesville set Robert Hill on his path of crime?"

"If . . . if he claimed it did, I would not agree with that conclusion."

"Thank you, Mr. King. Nothing further, Your Honor."

The defense rested, and the court adjourned. The next day, in his closing argument, Sparks recapped the crime, highlighting the violence and terror. He insisted that Bobby deserved the death penalty as a willing participant.

For his closing argument, Bobby's attorney stood and remained behind the table. "Gentlemen of the jury, let me summarize what you heard in this trial." He put his hand on Bobby's shoulder. "This man pled guilty to participating in the robbery. That means he knows he should have made other choices. Keep in mind, though, that he made those choices still a teenager, really. After having spent his entire childhood in hardship, with no mother's guidance. He was placed in the Gatesville School for no crime. Motherless, abandoned, raised with young criminals. You have before you the boy who never stood a chance. You hold in your hands the fate of our own Jean Valjean, as it were."

Flewellen walked to the railing in front of the jury. "You remember the French novel, I'm sure. Someone showed Jean Valjean mercy, and it changed his life." He pointed to Bobby. "You can do the same for that boy sitting there." The lawyer returned his gaze to the jury and leaned both hands on the railing. "Robert did not kill anyone. He did not expect anyone would be killed. You even heard witnesses testify that he only shot overhead in warning. He does not deserve a sentence of death. You must not give him a sentence of death."

After the judge's instructions to the jury, they filed out, and Bobby was taken to an adjoining room to wait with his lawyer for the verdict.

Flewellen lit a cigarette and handed his pack of ready-rolls to Bobby. "That went well. I was watching the faces of the jury as you spoke. They were sympathetic to your story."

Bobby pulled out a cigarette, tapped the end on the table, and lit it. "You called me John Val . . . somebody. Who is that?"

"Jean Valjean. He's the main character in a novel from France. *Les Misérables.*" When Bobby shrugged, Flewellen said, "It's been a very popular novel, even here in Texas. You haven't heard about it?"

Bobby shook his head as he flicked ash into a tray on the table.

"Well, at any rate, the jury would have known the tale. Jean Valjean had a childhood much like yours. Orphaned young, then imprisoned young. When he was shown mercy by a priest, he did something with his life."

Bobby pulled on his cigarette and exhaled a stream of smoke.

It ONLY TOOK forty minutes for the jury to report that they were returning with a decision. Once the court was assembled, the foreman read off the verdict. "Your Honor, we find the defendant, Robert M. Hill, guilty as charged, and assess his punishment as ninety-nine years in the penitentiary."

The judge thanked the jury and turned his attention to Bobby. "Mr. Hill, I believe this jury has passed the right sentence on to you, and I want to tell you that while there is still life, there is still hope. If you will make a good prisoner and not try to get away, you will make friends who may be able to do something for you sometime. This jury has been lenient with you, and I hope you appreciate that fact. Do you have anything to say?"

Bobby stood and pulled at his too-short coat sleeves. "I, uh, I have nothing to say except that I wish to thank everyone who has done anything on my behalf. I am going to make a good prisoner."

Deputies escorted Bobby back to the jail, where Uncle Tom sat at the rolltop desk in the office. But it was another person who had Bobby's attention.

A small, barred window served as the pass-through for meal trays between the office and a kitchen. Through the window, a young woman passed in and out of sight as she bustled about. She was the daughter of Pack Kilborn, and she lived with the family in the private residence that was part of the jail building. Bobby didn't know her name. Her singing would often amble up from the kitchen to the second floor, where he lay in boredom on his bunk. She was singing now. It was nearly suppertime, and the rattle of pans came through the pass-through.

Uncle Tom stood from the rolltop desk. "Well, Bobby?"

"I got my two nines."

"That's a relief, I expect," Tom said in his gentle, grandfatherly voice.

Bobby gave a noncommittal nod and returned his eyes to the girl. On his side of the barred pass-through window, a small table was stacked with cakes and pies and a bottle of cologne. Bobby's name was inscribed on envelopes that sat next to each item.

"What's all this?"

"These came for you today. Gifts from women admirers."

"They must of not heard the verdict."

"No, they did." Tom adjusted an envelope next to one of the gifts. "There are always some women who would rather have a long-distance correspondence with a prisoner than have to come to terms with a man they might have to live with." He waved at the table. "You want Pack's girl to cut you a slice of one of these cakes or pies for supper tonight?"

"That'd be real nice." Bobby smiled at the young woman in the barred window. "Maybe the buttermilk pie?"

She returned his smile and pulled a lock of hair back to hang it behind an ear. When she passed out of view, the sound of clattering pans resumed.

9

THE HOT BUTTON

When Marshall walked into the small private room, his mother greeted him with a bright "Happy Birthday!" Her voice had a forced cheeriness that belied the circumstances. He stood in chains between two deputies, and she was sitting with his attorney.

When the deputies removed his handcuffs, he played along with her merriment for her sake. He held out his arms to model the new outfit his mother had bought him, complete with bow tie and fedora. He grinned. "Here I am in nothing but my birthday suit!"

Jarilla let out a short cackle despite herself and waved her hand dismissively. "Oh, Marshall, don't be bawdy."

He took off his new hat and bent down to kiss her on the cheek. Sweeping his hair back in place, he nodded at his attorney.

It was March 1928. They were in a private chamber adjoining the courtroom in Abilene, about sixty miles west of Eastland. Joe Frank Sparks had not been satisfied with the ninety-nine-year sentence the jury had given Marshall in the first trial. He ordered him returned from Huntsville to appear in court again. The first trial was for armed robbery, but this time, Sparks would prosecute Marshall for the murder of the two police officers. Cearley had requested a change of venue, and it was granted. In fact, the two counts of murder had been split and sent to two different courts. The trial for Chief Bedford's murder was sent to the Taylor County court in Abilene. The trial for Officer Carmichael's murder would take place after that, in the town of Anson in Jones County.

Cearley gestured to a chair, and Marshall sat. "I want you to know a few tacks I'm taking. For one, I am claiming former jeopardy. All the facts of this case were already laid out in your Eastland trial, and they gave you ninety-nine years. The prosecution wants to separate their charge of armed robbery from their charge of murder. But I want to show the jury that all of this was one continuous event you have already been tried for. It will be up to them to determine that."

Marshall was inspecting the unfamiliar lining of his new hat and didn't look up. "Well, it is. They ought to see that."

"The other approach I want to take is what's called imperfect defense. If the chief shot at you first and you were returning fire, you were instinctively defending yourself."

Marshall set the hat on his head, trying out different tilts. "I was only returning fire. And my shots didn't put him on the ground. That was someone else from behind."

"There's another thing I've been going over with your momma." Cearley tapped his pen on the notepad in front of him as if he was still settling his mind on this tactic. "In Robert Hill's trial, it was a good decision for the jury to hear him tell his childhood story. I don't want to put you on the stand and expose you to the prosecution's questions. But it would serve us well to put your mother on the stand. I think the jury needs to see you as a son. As *her* son."

Marshall stopped playing with his fedora and faced his mother. "Do you want to do this?"

"I want to do whatever will help you."

He nodded at Cearley. "It's okay with me, then."

Cearley stood and collected his materials, stuffing them into his brief-case. "As a witness, of course, she cannot sit next to you during the trial like she did the last time. You say your goodbyes here, and I will meet you in the courtroom."

The attorney left, and Jarilla put a hand on her son's cheek. "My baby's twenty-five today. I can't take that in."

He took her hand and kissed it, giving her a confident smile. "Prime of life, Momma. And just getting started."

THE TRIAL BEGAN with the opening statement from Sparks. He walked toward the jury box as he spoke. "Gentlemen of the jury, Marshall Ratliff has already been tried for the armed robbery of Alex Spears, the cashier of the First National Bank in Cisco. Over in my county, they found Mr. Ratliff guilty for that. His defense attorney at that table over there would have you believe that is the end of the story. But after Mr. Ratliff and his gang had sacked the money and prepared to leave through the back alley, they committed a second crime. They found two officers of the law in their way, and they gunned down G. E. Bedford and George Carmichael. We will show that Mr. Bedford is dead specifically because of that man there, the bandit chieftain himself, Marshall Ratliff. This is my assistant, Deputy District Attorney Sterling Holloway. And that man sitting next to him is W. W. Hair. He's the special prosecutor appointed by Governor Dan Moody himself to see that justice for two lawmen is done."

He rested his hands on the railing in front of the jury and contin-ued. "We have come into your county to ask you to help my county. You know that only a thin line exists between order and anarchy. That thin line is guarded every day by a man with a badge. Over in Eastland County, two of those men are no longer standing on that line. They're dead." He pointed to Marshall. "And they're dead because of that man sitting there in his natty new suit and his fine new haircut."

Sparks continued to stare at Marshall until members of the jury turned toward Marshall, too. "You must protect the thin line, gentlemen. You must sentence Marshall Ratliff to die for the murder of Cisco's chief of police, G. E. Bedford."

Cearley stood. "The death of Mr. Bedford is tragic. It is heartbreaking." He put his hand on Marshall's shoulder, and Marshall raised his face confidently to meet the eyes staring at him from the jury box. "But this man did not set out to harm anyone, and we will show he only fired after his life was threatened. His instincts kicked in, same as would happen to any one of us in this room. We've already had a trial over there in Eastland for all of this, and a jury laid out a stiff sentence for him. Ninety-nine years. His whole life behind bars. Young Mr. Sparks over there wants you to decide that each action on that day was a separate crime. That way, he can hand down a separate sentence for each action. But it was all one continuous event. One continuous event for which my client has already been tried."

He walked around the table toward the jury and held up his hands like he was ceding a point. "Now, I'm not fool enough to think you have not already read about this event in the newspapers. But did you read one article about a robbery and then turn a page and read another article about a gunfight? No. You read one continuous article about one continuous event. In that one continuous event, men out in the street heard money was being taken from the bank, and they surrounded it and fired at anyone who came out.

Why? To collect a hefty reward the bank promised for dead bank robbers. *Dead* bank robbers. The bank said 'not a penny' would go to the capture of a live one. It was no use to try and surrender. This man sitting before you found himself having to defend his life, that's all. He's already been tried, and his sentence from that trial is sufficient. This is the conclusion you must draw."

The prosecution called Alex Spears to the stand, and he gave the same testimony he had given in the three trials in Eastland. Jewell Poe testified next, describing how the Santa character came into his teller cage and took the bank's automatic pistol from his station.

Sparks held up his hand. "Just a moment, Mr. Poe." He walked to the exhibit table and picked up a handgun. "Is this the bank's pistol, the one that the man dressed as Santa Claus took from you?"

"Yes, it is. He took it and stowed it in his belt inside his red coat."

The prosecutor walked to the jury and paced the length of the box, holding up the weapon for each juryman to see.

"It was the Santa Claus that took this very pistol?"

"Yes, sir."

Sparks tucked the gun under his belt. "And he put it in his waistband like this."

"Yes, sir."

Sparks continued his line of questioning with the handle of the pistol jutting out prominently above his leather belt and dress trousers. Poe was asked to complete his story of being herded into the alleyway, and he told of his injury and escape. When he left the witness stand, Sparks returned to the table and flipped a page on his notepad, with the pistol still in his leather belt.

Sparks called Marcel Bedford to the stand. The thirteen-year-old son of the chief had not been called to testify in the previous trials.

"Son, you were with your father in the police station on the day of the robbery, weren't you?"

"Yes, sir. We were out of school for Christmas."

"Tell us about that day."

"Well, a woman come in the station with her daughter. She was shouting that the bank was being robbed."

"She had been in the bank, and she and her daughter had escaped."

"Yes, that is what she told my father."

"What did your father do?"

"He asked her how many robbers there were and if they had guns. He then took a shotgun and left with a couple officers. He told me to stay at the station."

"But you heard the gunfire a block away."

"Yes."

"What did you do?"

"I couldn't hear any more shooting, and my daddy wasn't back. So, I ran to the bank." He paused. "There . . . there was a crowd around the alley." He paused again. "My daddy was on the ground."

"Was that the last time you saw him?"

"I saw him at the hospital. He told me to take care of my mother." His voice cracked at the last word, and he put a hand over his eyes and sobbed quietly.

In the gallery, purses snapped as women searched for handkerchiefs to dab their own tears. After a moment, Sparks spoke quietly. "He would have been proud of you today, Marcel." He nodded at the judge. "Nothing further, Your Honor."

Cearley began his cross by walking to the witness stand and offering the boy a handkerchief. "Do you need a moment, son?"

Marcel shook his head. He ignored the offered handkerchief, pulled out his own, and wiped his face.

"I am very sorry about your father." Cearley paused. "Now, you say the gunfight was over when you arrived. You did not see any of the shooting, then?"

"No, sir."

"And you did not see who shot your father."

"People told me about it. Told me it was the bank robbers."

"But you did not see this for yourself."

"No, sir."

"Thank you, Marcel. Mr. Sparks said right. Your father would be real proud of you."

Ellis Oder, the radio repairman, was called to the stand. He testified to running toward the alley when the gunfire began, darting his head around the corner, and seeing the Santa Claus in the alleyway next to the car.

Sparks faced the jury. "Mr. Oder, you say the Santa character was standing in the alleyway just a few feet from Chief Bedford when he pulled out a pistol and fired at him."

"Yes, that is what I saw."

The prosecutor paused, as if thinking about the next question to ask. Then in a quick motion, he reached for the pistol still stowed in his waistband. He yanked it out and pointed it at a member of the jury. He pulled the trigger of the empty weapon, yelling, "Bam!" The juryman jerked in surprise, but Sparks was already pointing it at another member of the jury, yelling again, "Bam!"

Marshall's lawyer was on his feet. His shocked shout of "Your Honor!" and the prosecutor's third "Bam!" and the judge's banging gavel came at the same time.

The judge pointed his gavel at the prosecutor. "Mr. Sparks, I do not know how they do it in Eastland County, but your theatrics are not welcome in this county's court."

"My apologies, Your Honor." But he still faced the jury, and several of the jurymen alternated tense looks between the prosecutor's eyes and the pistol that hung by his side. His grip around the handle remained tight, as if he would raise it again. Then he grinned at the jury and winked. He crossed to the witness bench as he turned the weapon over and back, over and back, in his hands.

"Now, Mr. Oder, we have not established who the Santa character is yet, but we have shown that he is the one who took this pistol that belonged to the bank. You're saying it was the Santa character that fired this pistol at the chief."

"Yes."

"Did the chief remain standing when this happened?"

"No, he fell to his knees. He was in pain, from what I could tell. He was hit."

"Then what happened?"

"Well, Uncle Bit, meaning the chief, he raised his shotgun at the Santa. It must have been empty because it did not fire. The chief tossed it beside him and reached for his pistol."

"Did he get off any shots with it?"

"No, sir."

"Why not?"

"It looked to me that his arm was tore up real bad. He was struggling to get the pistol out of his holster when another bandit at the back door of the bank took aim at the chief."

"In the trial of Henry Helms, you testified that man was, in fact, Henry Helms."

"Yes, sir."

"So, after Marshall Ratliff shot up the chief, tore his firing arm all to pieces, then Henry Helms took aim at the chief."

"Yes."

"And fired at him."

"Yes, sir."

"And the chief collapsed on his back."

"He did. He fell to the ground and did not move."

Sparks turned to the jury. He displayed the pistol again, but this time, he held it out in both open palms in presentation. "So, the Santa Claus fired at him with this weapon right here, and the chief dropped to his knees. His right arm, his firing arm, was hanging by his side. Then Henry Helms finished him off. Was that the sequence of events?"

"That is how I saw it, yes."

Sparks started to bring the weapon to the exhibit table, but he turned around. Fingering the weapon in thought, he said, "Do you think . . ." He paused and began again. "Do you think the chief could have defended himself against Mr. Helms if the Santa character had not already wounded him?"

Cearley objected to the speculation, and the judge sustained the complaint.

"I withdraw the question." Sparks placed the weapon on the exhibit table. "I have no further questions for the witness."

Cearley stood and flipped a page on his notepad. "Mr. Oder, you testified in the Helms trial that it was Mr. Helms who killed the chief."

Oder pointed to Marshall. "Well, him in the Santa suit was shooting, too."

"But now, you arrived late, after the shooting had already begun."

"Yes."

"You could not say whether it was the chief or the Santa character who shot first."

"I cannot see why that should matter."

"Mr. Oder, it is not for you to decide what matters. It is your job to tell us what happened. You cannot tell us that. You cannot tell us who fired first, can you?"

"I suppose I cannot."

"So, the chief could have fired first."

"I cannot say who fired first."

"And you were doing some shooting, were you not? You took the chief's unfired pistol and sprayed bullets into the alley. Your own neighbors huddling there with you flinging bullets all around."

"I—I wanted to do my part."

"And get that reward."

Oder set his jaw, resentful. "I wanted to do my part."

The man was dismissed, and Sparks called Laverne Comer to the stand. The child described the robbery and how she and Emma Mae Robinson were taken as hostages in the escape. When she got to the part where the Santa Claus yanked off his beard, Sparks interrupted her.

"And you got a look at him then, didn't you?"

"Yes, sir."

"Did he have a wound on his face?"

"Yes, along here." She ran a finger down her jawbone.

"The man who took off that Santa beard, do you see him in the courtroom today?"

She pointed at the defense table. "He's sitting right over there."

"You're pointing to Marshall Ratliff?" He swept his finger down his jawbone, as she had done. "The man with the ugly red scar on his face?"

"Yes, sir."

Marshall tried to stare placidly at the girl. He found he wanted to touch his jaw at the smooth, hairless streak of skin that had grown over the bullet wound. He resisted by lacing his fingers together on the table. He could feel the jurymen assessing his face, judging the scar as ugly and red like Sparks had described it.

A lawman testified about Marshall's capture in South Bend. He told of manning the roadblock at the Brazos, how they chased the bandits into the field of abandoned derricks, and how the bandits took a stand behind the pump jack.

The prosecutor interrupted his story. "So, back in Cisco, one lawman was already dead, another was dying, and now you and your men were being fired upon. Your lives on the line, the thin line."

"That was the way of it."

"Now, at the pump jack where Marshall Ratliff and his gang were shooting at you, what happened?"

"Well, they made a break for the woods. We hit all three of them, but two got away."

"Not Marshall Ratliff."

"No, he was passed out when we got to him."

"And you cleared him of weapons."

"Yes."

"What did you find on him?"

"Six pistols and three cartridge belts containing two hundred rounds of ammunition."

"My word. He was ready for a fight, wasn't he?"

"He had all the makings for it."

Sparks walked to the exhibit table and picked up the automatic that belonged to the bank. "Is this one of the pistols you took from him?"

"Yes, it is."

The prosecutor brought it to the witness stand. "Now, I want you to be sure, because we have already heard testimony that a man disguised as Santa Claus took this weapon from the bank. It was this weapon the Santa character used against our chief of police, George Bedford. And we have already heard that the man disguised as Santa Claus was, in fact, Marshall Ratliff." Sparks handed the weapon to the witness. "You are certain that this very pistol was found on Marshall Ratliff when you arrested him?"

The witness turned the pistol over in his hands and returned it to Sparks. "Yes, I am certain."

At the end of two days, the prosecution rested.

The next day, Cearley began his defense by calling Marshall's mother to testify. "State your name and your relation to the defendant."

"My name is Nancy Jarilla Carter. Most people call me Rilla. I am Marshall Ratliff's mother."

"Where do you currently reside?"

"In the Oddfellow's Lodge in Fort Worth. I keep house there in exchange for my room and board."

"But you lived in Cisco for a time. You raised Marshall and your other children there."

"Yes."

"Alone?"

"Yes. My husband divorced me when the children were young. I have never remarried."

"How many children do you have?"

"Five. Three daughters and two sons."

"When your husband abandoned you, he took the boys with him, did he not?"

"Yes, for a time. When they became teenagers, he sent them back."

"What was it like, raising two teenage boys by yourself?"

"It started out as a hardship, it did." She adjusted the pince-nez, snugging it to the bridge of her nose. "The first year they were back, I would tell them to help at the café, and then find the kitchen empty, and the cash register, too. I would make them go to church, and then find later that they had carved their initials on a pew. A few times in the middle of the night, an officer would knock on my door to tell me the boys had found liquor, and there they would be, rocking on their feet beside him. It was humiliating. Boys need to follow a good daddy around to find out how to be men, and my boys didn't have that."

"But then you felt you were making progress with the boys, especially Marshall."

"Yes. Marshall took an interest in church. He liked the singing. He had a real good voice, my Marshall. But at school, well, they had him pegged for a troublemaker right at the start. They just would not see him any other way. Seemed to have it in for him, to my mind. I saw him for what he could be, but they only saw him for what he had been."

"And he started to slide away from you, away from what he could be."

"He did. He never had a chance to do something decent with his life. Even when he came back from prison last year, no one would give him a job. No one would forget his past and let him start fresh."

"I imagine you are hoping the men on the jury will give him that chance."

"Yes, I hope that. I do. Every day, I send my boy poems and scripture verses and little notes, telling him to trust the Lord." She looked at the jurymen. "He's going to be in prison his whole life because of his last trial. I only want you to let him live out his days behind bars and there become the man I know he can become."

Sparks had no questions, and Rilla was dismissed from the stand. Marshall smiled at her, and she moved toward the table as if to join him by his side. Cearley shook his head at her. Rilla clutched her purse and walked past the table, through the staring eyes of the gallery, and out the back door.

The defense rested, and the judge adjourned the court for lunch. A reporter leaned over the gallery railing. "Say, Marshall, you called yourself a high-stepper in your last trial. Do you think you'll be stepping over this hill?"

Marshall grinned at the reporter. "I'd take that bet."

"The prosecutor, Mr. Sparks there, he sure seems to have it out for you. I've never seen him so intense. What do you have to say about that?"

Marshall's grin dissolved into a smirk. He opened his mouth to speak, but Cearley took his arm. "Mr. Ratliff has nothing further to add at this time."

When the court reconvened after lunch, the prosecutor began his closing argument. "In my county, George Bedford is no longer guarding the thin line between order and anarchy. He's dead. He's dead because of that man sitting over there with his high-dollar lawyer and his dandy suit. He wasn't wearing that dandy suit on December 23 last year, though. No, indeed. Marshall Ratliff disguised himself behind a Santa costume that day. A suit that's meant to bring joy to children's faces. Instead, he brought terror and grief to the town of Cisco. He gunned down George Bedford, the chief of police, the man everyone fondly called Uncle Bit. He gunned him down and left him to die in the dust."

He walked to the jury box. "You know, a few of our forefathers came out West with a few saddle horses, and to have one stolen was hard. And then some high-dollar lawyer would get the horse thief freed, and men had to resort to other methods to get justice. They had to bring him to a noose and string him up in the nearest tall tree. You do your job here, and no mob has to do it for you."

Marshall's attorney raised his hands to the judge in a gesture of protest, and when the judge said nothing, Cearley huffed loudly to the jury in frustration.

The prosecutor ignored him and continued. "You're not going to consider a ninety-nine-year verdict, are you? Don't do it. I can see Mr. Ratliff and his fancy lawyer laugh at a ninety-nine-year verdict, and I can hear them say, 'Well, well, didn't we put it by that jury of half-wits?' Gentlemen, Marshall Ratliff's hands are red with the blood of Uncle Bit Bedford. But if you don't give him the death penalty, the blood of Chief Bedford is on *your* hands. Help me protect the men on the thin line."

Cearley shook his head as he stood to begin his closing argument. "A rope over a tall tree." He stood in front of the three prosecuting attorneys and rested his fingers on their table, still addressing the jury. "He says you should kill him to keep a mob from doing it for you." Maybe that is all we can expect from Mr. Sparks after his antics in this trial."

He pointed at Sparks. "Why has he even made it necessary for any of us to be here? Marshall Ratliff has already been tried for this crime. He has already been found guilty. He was already in Huntsville to serve his sentence. But young Mr. Sparks had him taken out of prison and brought him here to waste all your time. Marshall's serving a ninety-nine-year sentence. He will be behind bars for the rest of his life. But the prosecutor wanted another crack at him, and so he made up this claim that what happened inside the bank and what happened outside the bank were two separate crimes. Common sense tells you that can't be so. How many bites at the apple is he going to get? It's up to you here in Abilene to tell Eastland's district attorney that's not the way the law works."

Cearley walked to the jury box. "If you dismiss this whole case for former jeopardy, you're not setting Marshall Ratliff free. Not at all. He's going to be behind bars in Huntsville for the rest of his natural life. If there was enough evidence to give him the death sentence, the jury in the first trial would have done that. But they did not condemn him to die. Why not? Because Marshall never attempted to hurt or injure or kill anyone until he was fired upon. Men were shooting at him, lusting after the rich reward the bank promised for a dead bank robber. Even Chief Bedford himself was using a shotgun the bank had given him to kill bank robbers. Marshall Ratliff feared for his life, and he shot back in self-defense. How would any of us react if we suddenly found a whole town shooting at us? The same way. The same way."

He raised a finger for emphasis. "Even so, it wasn't this man who killed the chief. Witnesses testified in this court that it was Henry Helms who fired the fatal shots. That's why, in the trial for Mr. Helms, the jury gave him the death sentence. He's lined up to face the chair for that. They decided that's the man who killed Mr. Bedford. No, you send Marshall back to Huntsville to live out the rest of his life behind bars."

He pointed to the empty witness stand. "His mother sat right there and pleaded with you to let him live out his days there, to let him become the man she knows he can be. It's in your power to grant that dear mother's request."

It only took the jury two hours to reach their verdict. As they filed in, Rilla was again by her son's side, her hand wrapped through the crook of his arm. The foreman read the prepared statement. "We, the jury, find against the defendant on his plea of former jeopardy, and we find the defendant guilty as charged in the indictment and assess his punishment as death."

Marshall shook his head in contempt, but his mother cried out, "God . . . my boy!" And she collapsed on the table, burying her head in her folded arms and weeping loudly. Marshall put his arm around her shoulders and leaned his head down to hers. "This ain't over, Momma. You wipe those tears, now. I ain't going down this way."

BACK IN THE Abilene jail, Marshall raised his cuffed hands to his bow tie, unknotted it, and gave it to one of the guards. He was escorted into his cell and uncuffed, and he sat down heavily on the bunk.

In a nearby cell, a voice called out: "Did you get a verdict?"

"Yes."

"What was it?"

"The hot button."

"That's hard, Marshall."

"No, boys." He said it as if the inmates on the entire floor were his audience. He set his jaw and he combed his fingers through his hair. "They ain't going to set me down in that chair, I can tell you that."

CEARLEY FILED A motion for a new trial in Abilene, but none of the arguments persuaded the judge. The attorney told reporters he planned to file with the Court of Appeals after the trial for the murder of Officer George Carmichael.

In the small town of Anson in Jones County, Joe Frank Sparks called nearly the same list of fifty witnesses for the fifth time. In fact, the newspapers reported that the child witnesses, Laverne Comer and Emma Mae Robinson, would have to repeat the fourth grade the next year because the five trials had kept them out of school so many days in the winter and spring.

When the case was given to the Anson jury, it took them twenty-four hours and twenty-one ballots before they returned a verdict and a sentence. They did not grant the prosecution's demand for the death penalty, but they did sentence Marshall to another ninety-nine years. His attorney did not ask for a retrial or file an appeal in the Anson case. On April 28, 1928, Marshall was transported to Huntsville.

He had walked through the prison entrance twice before. Three years ago, after being convicted of the Valera robbery, and then three months ago after his first trial in Eastland. Still, he couldn't help but be impressed as they drove up to the prison. The entry building was three stories tall, with elaborate Victorian-style details and topped with a clock tower that chimed the hour. To the right and the left of this elegant building ran a whitewashed brick barrier over twenty feet tall. It was easy to see why inmates referred to the Huntsville prison as "the Walls."

In the admissions room, he stripped off the suit and shirt his mother had given him for his twenty-fifth birthday. In its place, he put on the prison-issue coarse duck-cloth shirt and trousers in solid white. He was escorted into the massive East Building, three towering floors of cells that housed the prison's general population.

But he wasn't going to be assigned with the general population this time. His guards reached the opposite door of the hall and escorted him through it. They were bringing him to a special section of the South Building.

Inmates called it death row.

10

DEATH ROW

The first thing Marshall noticed was a windowless metal green door at the opposite end of the hall. He suspected the death chamber was behind it and he stopped. A guard nudged him, and he began walking again, passing cells in a line to his right.

Concrete blocks separated the compartments from each other, but he could see into each cell through bars set in the front. Two Mexicans occupied the first two stalls, and two black men occupied the next two cells. As he passed the fifth cell, a middle-aged white man sat at a desk piled with thick books. He was rolling a sheet of paper into a typewriter. The man stared briefly at Marshall before he began typing, the clatter ringing off the solid surfaces of the death row.

Marshall was taken to the sixth compartment. Inside was a single bed, a desk with a chair, a toilet, and a sink. Above his head near the ceiling was a horizontal window. It was too small to crawl out of it, but it let in a slit of sunlight. The death row was mostly belowground, and blades of grass waved mildly against the pane. If there was a way to crawl up to it, he knew it looked out on the exercise yard for the general population. In his previous stay in Huntsville, he would sit in that yard and stare at the death row windows, wondering about the men on the inside.

He heard the cell door close behind him, and he turned to survey the corridor from the perspective of his cell. To his left, his escorts walked out the door they had brought him through. Keys jangled on the other side of the door as the death house was locked from the outside. A guard, unarmed, sat at a desk that held a telephone and an AM radio. The guard chewed an unlit cigar and read a newspaper, his feet propped on the desk.

"Marshall Ratliff. In the flesh."

The statement came from the cell to his right. Black hands hung over the crossbars into the corridor, fingers woven together.

"That's me."

"Yeah, we get newspapers in here. Dressed as Santy Claus to rob a bank." The man chuckled. "I'da loved to of seen that."

"What about you?"

"They got the wrong man, but my side of the story don't count."

Marshall expected a wisecrack from the other cells at this claim of innocence. When he was in the general prison population, someone always had a joke about what he was doing, or whose wife he was sleeping with, during the crime he was accused of. In this hallway, no one responded to the complaint of innocence.

"Name's Lawrence Davenport." A thumb gestured to Marshall's left. "The one on your other side is Harry Leahy. You're almost as famous as him."

The clacking typewriter echoed from the cell to his other side. Marshall had read about Harry Leahy. He got forty-five years for the torture and premeditated murder of a doctor over a land dispute near San Antonio. When Leahy appealed for a new trial in another county, the new jury gave him the death sentence. It made Marshall think of his own poor luck in moving his second trial to Abilene.

Lawrence's voice rose. "Leahy. Leahy!"

The typewriting stopped.

"Ain't you about done with that racket?"

The clacking resumed without a comment from Leahy.

"Looking for an exit in his own way," Lawrence said to Marshall. "He's a lawyer. Or was. He's a good one for advice."

"Has he helped you?"

"Me?" He paused. "Naw. That stream's done dried up."

Marshall wanted to ask how long Lawrence had left, but he didn't.

Through the month of May, Marshall got used to the routine. In the morning, newspapers were shared from cell to cell, and every afternoon, mail was distributed if any had been delivered. Every Saturday night, the radio on the guard's desk would be tuned to the Grand Ole Opry, and every Sunday morning, they would get the broadcast of a local worship service. The lights in the corridor stayed on throughout the day and night, and Marshall got used to falling asleep with his forearm over his eyes.

Everything was done within a man's six-by-ten compartment. Meal trays were slid on the floor through a slot in the bars. If a man chose to exercise, it was done within his cell's available floor space. If he had any visits from lawyers, ministers, or relatives, the guard would pull chairs up to the cell for the visitors, and he was required to sit in on the conversation.

The only time an inmate left his cell was for the weekly shave and bath. A barber chair sat in the middle of the corridor next to a large tub. To fill the tub, guards dragged a hose through the door that led to the exercise yard. Then each cell would be opened, one at a time, beginning with the whites. The inmate was escorted to the barber chair and his arms restrained. After a shave and, if needed, a haircut, the man stripped down and stepped into the tub. As the newest member of death row, Marshall was the last white man to be released into the corridor. The bathwater was gray by then, but he welcomed the opportunity to wash and get fresh clothing and bedsheets. It was also a chance to see into the cells and make eye contact with men whom he only knew by voice throughout the week.

On the thirty-first of the month, Marshall woke to a new routine. It wasn't the day for the weekly washings, but the barber was waiting, and the tub was filled. Guards released Lawrence into the corridor. The barber lathered up his face and shaved it, and then lathered and shaved the top of his scalp as well. Lawrence looked like a medieval friar Marshall remembered from a book illustration. The barber also shaved the hair off the calf of the left leg. After Lawrence was released from the chair, he undressed and stepped into the tub.

After his bath, Lawrence toweled off and reached for the clothes laid out for him. Today, it wasn't the prison-issue white trousers and shirt. A dark dress suit of cheap material lay over the chair next to the tub.

Lawrence zipped up the pants, shrugged into his suit coat, and struck a pose for the men in the cells. "How do I look?"

Voices called out from the other cells: "Be the man tonight, Lawrence" . . . "Show them you can take it" . . . "Hold your head up."

As he was escorted back into his cell, the left trouser leg flapped from where the seam was open from the cuff to the knee. When the cell door clanged shut, Lawrence hung his arms out the bars, his fingers laced, like the first day he and Marshall talked. Marshall tried to think of something to say to him like the other men, but nothing came to mind. He stood at the door with his arms out the bars, his fingers laced together, in the same position as Lawrence.

Later, a guard asked Lawrence if he had any special request for his last meal.

"Stewed cabbage, a pork chop . . . Too early for fresh tomatoes and peas, I guess."

The guard said, "I'll see if we got anything canned from last year."

As he left to fulfill the order, Lawrence called out to the cells, "Otis, I'm sending you my shoes and socks. I got a couple of dime store novels in here if anybody wants them."

A voice called out: "I'll take them."

"What about these cigs. I've got three packs here. And a couple oranges that ain't gone bad."

Men jutted their hands from the bars and passed the condemned man's belongings to the different cells.

A chaplain visited with Lawrence after supper and left. Hours passed, but none of the men fell asleep. Marshall lay on his bunk, hands folded over his stomach.

After the clock tower finished ringing midnight, keys rattled at the outside door. The death row guard stood from his desk and nodded at the man who entered. Marshall assumed he was the warden, because he walked up to Lawrence's cell and made the pronouncement.

"Lawrence Davenport. You have been found guilty of murder by a jury of your peers. You have been sentenced to die by the state of Texas. May God have mercy on your soul."

Lawrence was told to leave his cell, and he walked down the corridor between two guards on either side, and two guards in front and behind. His house slippers made an odd fashion contrast to the suit he wore, and the soles slapped on the concrete with each step. The fabric at the open seam of his pants fluttered behind his left leg like a flag of surrender.

The procession stopped at the metal door at the end of the hallway.

The death row guard placed his hand on the latch, and he raised his voice in a clear, formal pronouncement. "The little green door opens." He swung the door out into the corridor toward the cells.

Marshall figured the green metal had to be at least four inches of solid iron. He strained to see what was beyond it, but the angles blocked his view. The men in the hallway passed into the next room, and the death row guard shut the door and stood by it, avoiding eye contact with any of the men in the cells.

There were muffled voices behind the green door, but Marshall could not make out what was being said. A faint crunching sound came from the room, followed by a steady hum that rose in intensity until it became a loud whine and finally an unnatural snarl. The volume fell and rose again, fell and rose again once more, and dropped into silence. After a few moments, more muffled voices came from behind the door, then nothing. The men who had entered the death chamber must have left another way, because they did not return through the row.

For the next two months, the routine fell back into place. An oppressive summer heat settled over the prison, and the house was rank with the sour smell of bodies and bedding and clothing that weren't washed often enough. The men became lethargic, lying in their bunks with sweat matting their shirts to their skin.

In August, the routine that was followed with Lawrence was repeated with a black inmate named Garrett Thomas. Garrett had attempted to rape a fourteen-year-old and then killed the girl's father when the man walked in on the assault. Like Lawrence, the crown of his head was shaved, and his left calf. Again, the cheap suit he was given had the seam of the left leg open to the knee. Again, that call: *The little green door opens.* Again, Marshall strained to see into the chamber behind the door, with no luck. The same muffled voices, the same crunching that rose to a hum and then to a snarl, more muffled voices followed by silence.

The next day, Harry Leahy invited Marshall to play chess with him, and they set the board on the floor in the corridor between their cells. Reaching through the bars, Marshall slid his pawn two squares. Leahy's hand moved a knight, and Marshall countered with a knight to guard his pawn.

"Tell me something, Leahy."

"Yeah?"

"Davenport and Thomas. They both had rips up the seam of their trousers. What for?"

A voice called out from another cell, "Electrodes." The voice was high-pitched and nasally. The man spoke like he took a dark pleasure in initiating Marshall into the routine.

Leahy slid a pawn forward and said, "They send the current through the body between a connection on the scalp and one on the leg. That's why they shave those spots. Once they get a man in the chair, they'll soak a sponge with briny water and snug it between the electrode and the skin. They want a clean connection for that current."

"Is it painful? You know . . . when they send it through you?"

The nasal voice from the other cell called out again: "Ain't nobody come back through that little green door to tell us." Then he sniggered.

Leahy cleared his throat and made another move. "Tell me about your trial."

Of course, Leahy was trying to change the subject, but it was a subject Marshall wanted to talk about. He laid out the details of his three court cases in Eastland, Abilene, and Anson.

Leahy's arm stretched through the bars to move a rook. "So, your momma wasn't sitting next to you during the Abilene trial like she was in Eastland."

Marshall shook his head, then remembered Leahy couldn't see him. "No. My lawyer wanted her to testify."

"I would not have had your momma testify in the Abilene trial. In Eastland, every time the jury looked over at you, they also saw her, and I think that made them more sympathetic to you. In Abilene, as a witness for the defense, she couldn't be in the courtroom until her time on the stand. To win the jury over, those few minutes on the stand weren't near as effective as them seeing her by your side whenever they looked your way."

Leahy moved his bishop diagonally four squares. "It's hard to know whether that decision made any difference, though. Two lawmen were killed. The surprise isn't that you got death in the Abilene trial but that you dodged it in the Eastland trial." His queen made a slight *clack* as he relocated it on the board. "Checkmate."

Leahy reset the pieces. "Has your lawyer filed an appeal?"

"He said he would."

"The state of Texas has a Court of Criminal Appeals. You don't show up. All the paperwork gets sent to Austin. Three judges vote. It will take several months."

IN EARLY SEPTEMBER, on a single night, two Hispanic men in their early twenties were scheduled to be executed. They had been sentenced for the gang rape of a San Antonio high school girl.

Marshall had once touched a frayed wire in the kitchen of his mother's café. He remembered how his muscles throbbed until he released it, and how a gritty sensation at the touch site slowly gave way to normal feeling again. What would he feel when the current was sent through those electrodes? Would his limbs thrash involuntarily as the electricity coursed through? Would his body smolder and catch fire, like the singed wallpaper he once saw near an overloaded outlet? How long would it take before he slipped into oblivion? Texas had replaced hanging with electrocution five years ago, following the lead of New York. East Coast experts claimed it was a more scientific and humane way to put someone to death, but the newspapers never reported on the grim details. At least not any of the newspapers that made it into the death house.

Marshall had not heard a scream or a cry of pain during the executions of Davenport and Thomas, but he listened for it again. As the first condemned man was taken behind the little green door and the hum rose in intensity, he heard nothing. Maybe death was instant. The second man came into Marshall's view and passed by, his scalp shaved like a monk and the left trouser leg flapping at the open seam. Marshall became conscious of his own hand rubbing his left calf. He shuddered and then shook his hand as if to flick away something unpleasant.

MARSHALL PASSED THE empty breakfast tray through the slot in the bars. A lanky trustee took it and placed it on a cart. He continued his methodical lope past the other cells, stacking trays as he went. The trays clattered as the trustee rolled the cart to the outside door that led to the exercise yard of the general population.

Marshall stood at the bars in front of his cell and waited. He never missed the moment the outside door opened. Since the door was on the same wall as the cells, he could never see the door or the outside beyond it. But when it opened, bright beams of sunlight streamed into the corridor, along with the fresh air of a mild September front. It was only for a moment. Then the door closed, sending a metallic *clack-clack-clack* down the concrete walls of the death house.

A voice called from one of the cells to his left: "Hey, Marshall."

"Yeah."

"Your boy, Bobby Hill, he's in the papers."

"Let me see."

He waited for the newspaper to be passed from one cell to the next until it reached him.

Someone called out, "What's it say? Read it to us."

Sitting on the edge of his desk, he unfolded the newspaper and found the article. He read it aloud. Bobby had escaped with five other men from a prison farm in Brazoria, south of Huntsville. The six were part of a work unit sent to clear timber off a prison-owned field. It only took five hours for bloodhounds to track Bobby to a clapboard church building a few miles away. The dogs cornered him inside the building. When the handlers followed the dogs' pitched bays, Bobby was found cowering in the corner, scratched and bitten. As of the date and time of the newspaper report, the other five convicts were still at large.

Marshall shook his head. "Well, he had the right idea, anyway, didn't he, boys?"

A FEW WEEKS later, two more executions were scheduled on the same night. Both were black men. Forty-year-old O. T. Alexander was sentenced to die for killing his wife. He had claimed she was trying to poison his food, but Marshall suspected he had a paranoid streak. Whenever a trustee brought in the meal trays, Alexander would insist the trustee taste it in front of him before he accepted the tray. On the night of his execution, the man fainted when the warden entered the hallway, and he had to be carried into the death chamber.

Marshall pressed his face to the bars and whispered, "Leahy."

White hands came to Leahy's cell door. "Yeah?"

"Did you notice that? Fainted dead away and they carried him in anyway. Do you think they'll revive him before throwing the switch?"

"They'll have to. Texas law says they can't execute a man if he's not in a condition to know what's going on." A pause. "That's right . . ."

Leahy's hands disappeared. At the sound of riffling pages, Marshall assumed he was flipping through one of his law books.

"Leahy?"

"Later. I've got to look something up."

The unearthly snarl on the other side of the green metal door rose and fell, rose and fell, and then rose and faded away.

A thin, timid voice came from the cell to Marshall's right. "I know I have to go, but I am going to take it like a man."

Voices came from the other cells: "That's it, Tom" . . . "Show them, brother."

Six minutes later, Tom Ross was taken away to die for the killing of a logging camp paymaster in East Texas.

RILLA SAT IN a chair in front of Marshall's cell. He was mindful of the scent surrounding her. Bathed skin and talcum powder and fresh air. She smelled of the outside world.

Her brow wrinkled. "You're so pale. And your eyes . . . such dark circles." She reached out to his face in a mother's impulse. The guard who sat a few feet to her side shifted in his chair and shook the pages of the newspaper he was pretending to read. She withdrew her hand. "Are you bearing up?"

He broke down weeping, trying to keep the sobs quiet from the other men on the row. He hadn't planned to. His mother made the long trip on the Greyhound to Huntsville as often as she could, and he did his best to appear cheery for her sake. The act had gotten harder to pull off as the months passed.

He wiped his nose on his shirtsleeve and sniffed, then leaned forward and spoke in an urgent whisper. "Momma, I've seen six men walk this corridor into that room over there." He pointed to the green door at the end of the hall on his right. Her eyes trailed reluctantly in the direction he was pointing. When she turned back to him, her lower lip was quivering.

He continued in his low hiss. "They keep taking people in there, but this death house don't never empty out. They just keep filling these cells back up with more men for the chair. One day, they'll walk me through that door. And for what? For *what*?"

By the time he got to the question, his voice had risen in an urgent mix of frustration and desperation. But then he dropped it again so low he hoped even the guard would have trouble hearing. "I don't belong in here. These men, they've raped and killed in cold blood. One white man they brought in, a couple of cells that way"—he gestured to his left—"he tortured a whole family before killing each one of them, one by one, right in front of the others. I don't belong in here with the likes of them. I only defended myself. I was *defending* myself, Momma!"

Tears welled up in her eyes, and she reached a hand toward him again, glanced at the guard, and put the hand to her mouth instead. She drew in a long breath to compose herself, straightened her back, gripped her hands together in her lap. "You stay strong, Marshall. I pray for you every day. You know that, don't you?"

He nodded, wiping his cheeks with the heels of his hands.

She continued. "Mr. Cearley, he's working on getting you moved out of here while your appeal is being heard. He says others who have been sentenced to—" Her eyes went sidelong to the little green door and back to Marshall. "He says they wait in the county that tried them while the Appeals Court decides whether they get a new trial. This isn't right, having you in here for so long . . . what it's doing to your health . . ." She trailed off as she worriedly scanned his face.

At the news of a possible move from the death house, his mood changed. He hoped none of the other inmates had heard how he had broken down in front of his mother.

TWO WEEKS LATER, a guard walked in with a stack of envelopes and pack-
ages, already opened by the front office. He called out, "Leahy, Ratliff,
Blake, Sanders. Mail's come for you."

The guard stood in front of Leahy's cell with a small stack of books.
"The books you requested from your lawyer." He read off the titles from
the spines before passing each one between the bars. "*Ten Days in a Mad-
House . . . The Experiences of an Asylum Doctor . . . A Text-Book of Psychiatry for Students and Practitioners.* That's some nice bedtime reading for
you, Leahy."

"Mm-hmm" was all that Leahy replied. Marshall heard pages flipping.
The ex-lawyer was already at work on the new volumes.

The guard read Marshall's name off an envelope as he stepped in
front of his cell. He thrust the envelope through the bars. "A letter from
your lawyer."

Marshall pulled out the pages. The cover page explained that the complaint about premature confinement to the death house had been rejected
in Taylor County, but Cearley had already protested this decision to the
Appeals Court in Austin.

His mother's own testimony was included in the appeal. She wrote
that the prison authorities had confined her son in a little six-by-ten cell
without proper ventilation or exercise and near where people were being
electrocuted frequently. It was her opinion that it was affecting both his
physical and mental health. He couldn't argue with her claim that the
death house was taking a toll on him. The little green door was never out
of his mind.

LATER THAT WEEK, the death row got a new resident. His name was Bob
Silver. Marshall was as interested as the other men in getting a look at him.
The press called him "the Kansas City crooner," and they had covered his

trial and sentencing on the front page for months. He and another man were convicted of killing a Fort Worth theater manager who resisted their attempt to rob him. The other man got a life sentence, while Silver was condemned to die.

Silver entered the death house like he was leading the guards instead of being escorted by them. As they removed his shackles, he took in the stark surroundings, returning the gaze of each inmate who stood at the bars to watch him. He seemed to be about Marshall's age, show-business handsome, with a full head of dark hair. The guards escorted him into the vacant cell that had briefly housed Tom Ross, and when they left the death house, Silver began to hum. Then, in a good imitation of Vernon Dalhart's mild country twang, the Kansas City crooner sang a popular tune.

I'll be carried to the new jail tomorrow
Leaving my poor darling alone
With the cold prison bars all around me
And my head on a pillow of stone
Now if I had wings like an angel
Over these prison walls I would fly
And I'd fly to the arms of my poor darling
And there I'd be willing to die

As the plaintive tenor voice trailed off, Harry Leahy spoke up. "Well, now, Bob Silver there sings as good as what we hear on your radio, Boss Cole." He was addressing the guard at the desk with the title all convicts were required to use of any prison authority.

Across the next two months, Silver entertained the men with his singing. Usually it took only a snippet of conversation to send him off into a rendition of some song with a similar theme.

The governor granted him a stay of execution, and then a second one, but on October 24, Bob Silver's time was up. He was to be electrocuted after midnight.

As they strapped him in the barber chair for his shave, his cocky confidence melted. His voice quavered as he spoke to the row. "Boys, I'm all out of songs, I'm afraid. Looks like I'm really going down this time."

Replies came from the cages: "Bear up there, Bob" . . . "Make us proud tonight."

The barber trimmed his thick locks and shaved a bald tonsure on his scalp. He knelt and rolled up the cuff of Silver's left pants leg, but before he could scrape the hair off the calf, keys clattered at the outer door. The assistant warden walked in with a slip of paper in his hand.

"Hold up there, Wayne," he said to the barber, who stood and stepped aside.

The assistant warden placed himself in front of the chair. "Bob, we can all be grateful for mommas like yours."

Fear and hope mingled in Silver's expression as he fixed his eyes on the slip of paper the assistant warden held.

"Your momma's pleas must have worked. The governor called us just five minutes ago." The official paused, knowing the attention of the entire room was on his next words. "Bob, he's commuted your sentence to life behind bars."

Cheers broke out from the cells, but Silver fainted and slumped in the chair, his body held in place by the constraints still around his arms. He wasn't out for long, and when he came to, he peered around, dazed. The men in the cells laughed and congratulated him.

He gaped up at the assistant warden. "Did I dream it, boss, or is it true?"

"It's true, Bob. I'm glad to report it's true."

Now he laughed, too, and fidgeted impatiently as a guard unbuckled the constraints that held him to the barber chair. He jumped up and struck his best Al Jolson stance. He sang out as if the corridor was a stage.

I'm sit-sittin' on top, top of the world

I'm rolling along, Yes, rolling along

The men in the cells laughed and hooted as Silver paced back and forth in front of their cell doors in a rhythmic skip.

And I'm quit-quittin' the blues, blues of the world

Just singing a song, just singing a song

He laughed and went along the row, shaking the offered hands through the bars, and then entered his cell to collect his few belongings. He held them in his arms and said, "I'm ready, boss. Even a work farm's better than this here death row."

"You'll stay here at the Walls for now, Bob. We're going to take you to general population now. Tomorrow you'll start in the laundry, where we have an opening."

Silver laughed and turned back to the cells again. "You hear that, boys? You be thinking of me every time you put on a clean uniform, now."

The men in the death house shouted out more congratulations to Silver as he disappeared through the entry door with the assistant warden and two guards. They laughed as someone recounted again how Silver fainted into a slump at the news of his good luck. Then the cells grew quiet, and Marshall was sure that each man was thinking the same thing he was. Maybe the cards would come their way, too. Maybe the governor would listen to a relative's appeals. And maybe each of them would finally walk out the same door like Bob Silver, singing a song, just singing a song.

OCTOBER GAVE WAY to November and November to December. In January 1929, Floyd Byrnes passed Marshall's cell and was escorted into the death chamber. Byrnes had always seemed distant, and Marshall had never liked him. The man had been convicted of a triple homicide, including the gruesome mutilation of a twelve-year-old girl. Byrnes seemed indifferent to both the accusation and the approaching execution. Still, he was about Marshall's age and the first white man that Marshall had seen taken behind the little green door.

For weeks after the execution, he had a recurring dream about Byrnes being marched to the death chamber. In the dream, just when Byrnes reached the thick iron door, he stopped and turned to Marshall. But it wasn't Byrnes's face. It was like gazing in a mirror because Marshall's own face stared back at him. He woke up at that moment in the dream every night.

The next month, he received a letter informing him that the Court of Criminal Appeals had denied his lawyer's request that he be moved off death row while his murder trial was being appealed. He would have to stay in the death house indefinitely.

11

THE MIDNIGHT SPECIAL

Bobby Hill swayed in unison with the other prisoners as the buckboard wagon made its way over the gravel road. Seven of them sat facing each other on two long benches, their knees nearly touching. Guards used a motorized truck for longer trips, but they were only going a few miles today. Two donkeys were harnessed ahead of the wagon, and two donkeys carried guards behind it. The men who followed had shotguns draped over the crook of their arms, and their bodies rocked to the loping clop-clop of their mounts. The prisoners all wore handcuffs and leg irons, but Bobby stood out from the rest. Unlike them, he wore a baggy outfit with wide horizontal black-and-white stripes. The stripes marked him as a runner.

Bobby tried to calculate the day. Sometime in February 1929. Back in September, he had fled with five other men from a work farm, but they had all been caught and returned to the Walls Unit in Huntsville. There they were "dark celled" together in an unlit room only eight feet long, six feet wide, and six feet tall. The men bumped into each other any time they moved, and they had no room to lie down. The guards left them there for three days and nights, feeding them only cornbread and water once a day. The men had only a single bucket for a toilet. It was never emptied, and it stank. When the exhausted prisoners were marched out again, squinting in the sunlight, they were all wearing the stripes.

For five months, he had been back on the "dummy." That was the name convicts gave to the bottom-rung work crew. They broke rocks into gravel for road repair or they chopped wood for the prison's cookstoves and furnaces. At the end of January, his fever spiked enough for the guards to admit him to the hospital ward. The prison doctor didn't like his wet, rheumy cough.

That was why he was on the buckboard wagon. He was among men suspected of having tuberculosis. He and the others were being brought to the Wynne Unit a few miles from the Walls. There a persistent respiratory illness could be monitored safely away from the crowded prison population in Huntsville.

The driver reined in and pulled the brake lever. A guard opened the front gate, and the driver called out to him, "New lungers for you."

The guards who had escorted the wagon dismounted from their donkeys. They stood gripping their shotguns, fingers on the triggers, and one of them commanded the prisoners to climb down. One by one, the men shuffled to the back of the buckboard, and the chains of their leg irons scraped loudly on the wooden planks beneath their feet. They dropped to the ground and ambled forward awkwardly in their constraints and, as they entered the prison yard, the bloodhounds bayed and paced in their cages. The guards removed their chains and escorted them into the bunkhouse. There the building tender inspected his new charges. He was a trustee who was responsible for keeping everyone within the schedule and the rules. These he now introduced to the newcomers in a rapid monotone.

It was the same orientation Bobby had heard in other labor camps, and he began to look around at his new surroundings. Where he was standing must be the dining section. It consisted of two long rows of tables with benches on either side. An open corridor ran down the center of the building, with the tables on one side and two rows of bunks, three deep, on the other. He imagined the building could house about fifty. There were doors to the outside on either end of the long building. Near the entrance, a guard stood in a picket office behind bars that extended from the floor to the ceiling. At the opposite end from which they entered was a large room for showers and toilets.

"Is he boring you, Stripes?"

It was a new voice, and he was speaking to Bobby in his striped uniform. The way the building tender stepped back to let the man have the floor, Bobby guessed he was being addressed by the unit's captain.

"No, boss."

The captain kept his eyes on Bobby as he asked a guard, "Who's this man?"

The guard read off a sheet of paper. "Robert M. Hill."

He assessed Bobby for a moment. "I'm not going to have any trouble with you, am I, Robert M. Hill." It was more like a statement than a question.

"No, boss."

"Good." He addressed the entire group. "Because this ain't no East Coast sanatorium where consumptives sit on a porch in the sunshine and *re-hab-ill-a-tate*." He emphasized each syllable with sarcasm. "If you can work, you're going to work. And I'm the one who decides if you can work." He squinted at Bobby again, assessing him. "Stripes, I decide you can work in the kitchen. You'll start now."

"Yes, boss."

"The rest of you will be assigned to field squads tomorrow. Today, you're going to clean up this bunkhouse."

The building tender barked out orders to the men while a guard escorted Bobby into a smaller building that housed the kitchen. A crew of convicts moved between the stoves and the ovens. Pans of cornbread cooled on a wooden table, and steam rose from a pot on the stove.

All the kitchen workers were white except one. An old black trustee carried a stack of tin plates toward the back door. He was muscular and trim for his age. He had a full white beard, and he was bald at the top with white hair at the sides in tight kinks.

The guard called out to him: "Another one for you, Willie."

Willie considered Bobby doubtfully. "You seen him spitting any blood, boss?" The voice was gravelly but sonorous, like the low notes on a church organ.

"Not this one."

Willie gestured at Bobby with his head toward a stack of plates. "Well, then. You get those plates over there and follow me." Willie kicked open the screen door at the back of the kitchen and disappeared.

Bobby wasn't accustomed to a black man giving orders in a room full of whites, and he turned to the guard for confirmation. The guard broke off a corner of the cornbread without looking at him. "Get to it now."

"Yes, boss."

As the guard ambled out the front door wiping crumbs off his shirt, Bobby took the stack of tin plates out the back door. Willie was adjusting the bridle on a donkey hitched to a wagon. He nodded to the back. "Put them in the John Henry."

In the other prison farms Bobby had worked, that was the name the convicts gave the wagon that brought noontime dinner to the fields. Two white men were at the back of the John Henry securing the covered pots and pans. One was an old man with thin, wiry arms, and the other looked to be about thirty. The younger one pointed to a box in the wagon, and Bobby lowered the plates in.

Willie climbed onto the raised bench and took the reins. "Hoppy," he said to the younger man, "you bring this new one—what's your name?"

"Bobby. Bobby Hill."

"Hoppy, you bring Bobby Hill and go feed the new arrivals and the sick. Pops here will go with me to the fields."

Pops climbed up on the bench next to Willie, and the wagon pulled away.

Hoppy stood next to Bobby and glared at the departing wagon. "It ain't right for him to give orders to white men like that." He hocked and spat and turned to Bobby as he wiped spittle off the corner of his mouth. "What did you do for the captain to put you on this crew so soon?"

"I don't know. I just got here."

"Well, Bobby Hill, he already has it out for you. Probably those stripes."

The man started for the back door of the kitchen. His arms and shoulders hitched up in a little leap each time his left foot came down, as though he wanted to put as little weight on it as possible.

Hoppy said, "When the captain was transferred here, he brought Willie because he liked his cooking. Then the captain found the best way to humiliate a white man was to put him in the kitchen taking orders from Willie. He won't let no one touch his house boy. It just ain't right."

Hoppy pointed to a tall, covered pot. "It's time to feed the new crew that came in with you, and then the lungers. You take that—watch it, it's hot."

Bobby touched the handle lightly, testing the heat. "Ain't everyone consumptive here?"

"Not everyone. Some just got too old for the fields—"

"And some just got too stupid for the fields." It was another convict in the kitchen who had interrupted Hoppy. His mop of white hair jutted out like wads of cotton from a boll. "Hoppy here, he cut off two toes to get off the Retrieve Farm."

"Worst in the whole system, Boll. I would have given up all ten toes to get out of that place. But this ain't no resort itself, Bobby Hill. They sent you here with us knockouts on suspicion you're a lunger. But they'll work you till you cain't work, and work you again if you get better."

"*If* you get better," the man called Boll repeated. He picked up a box of plates and spoons and walked out the front door of the kitchen.

Hoppy lifted a large basket filled with cornbread that had been cut into squares. "Bring those peas and follow me."

On the work farms where Bobby had served time, men lined up to enter a dining hall that was in the same building as the kitchen. Wynne had a smaller population, and the cookhouse stood alone. The meals had to be carried to the bunkhouses.

It took both hands for Bobby to lift the pot by the swinging handle. He followed Hoppy from the kitchen and into the main building to a serving table. The men who had been on the transport wagon with him were occupied with brooms or wet mops or dusting rags. They moved with the bored motions of men who knew they had been given pointless make-work. They had only been cleaning the bunkhouse for twenty minutes or so, but the dust and exertion had fired up hacking fits among most of them.

Hoppy leaned toward Bobby and spoke in a low voice. "Not all of them come in with you are lungers, I'll reckon. Looks like two of them got too old for the other farms. Some of them with coughs will find their lungs clear in a few weeks."

Boll leaned in. "You better hope that's you."

A jaundiced man's hacking fit turned into wheezing gasps, and he wiped his running eyes.

Hoppy pointed to him. "I'll wager that one's got it bad, though."

The building tender tucked his lip under his teeth and gave a loud whistle. "Dinner. Leave the brooms and mops where you can come back to them and line up."

The men shuffled in lethargic steps to the serving table. Bobby and the two kitchen workers ladled up peas and cornbread and thick molasses.

When the short line was served, Hoppy picked up his basket of cornbread. "Now for the lungers. Bring that pot."

Bobby followed him across the open corridor toward the bunks that were closest to the toilets. When he first scanned the building, he had assumed all the bunks were empty. Now that he drew nearer, what he had thought were lumps of unmade blankets were men. Maybe seven of them, all in lower bunks. Thin arms with skeletal hands emerged from the blankets and pushed emaciated bodies into a sitting position.

The man in the bunk closest to Bobby coughed into a rag and wiped blood off his chin. His face turned weakly up to Bobby with an expression of weary resignation.

Her eyes had been the same color, with the same dark rings.

It had been a February day like this one, and Bobby was eight years old. His mother's eyes had followed him as he dragged a chair across the floor to sit at her bedside. The sound of the scraping brought her husband into the room. As the man shooed Bobby out, his mother gave him a weak smile. She said in a gentle whisper, "Be a good boy."

It was his last time seeing her alive. Later that day, while the grown-ups were in the kitchen talking in low tones about where to bury her, he snuck into the room and stood over her body. Her skin was like candle wax. Her concave chest was at rest, no longer struggling for wet and wheezing breaths.

He reached out to move a strand of auburn hair off her face. Behind him, a form darkened the doorway, and her husband's voice was annoyed. "Bobby."

A voice called him again. "Bobby."

It was Hoppy. He held out a tin plate that had a piece of cornbread on it. "Dish out those peas."

Hoppy, Bobby, and Boll had their own lunch and a little rest until the John Henry returned from the fields. The afternoon was spent cleaning up from the noon meal and getting supper ready.

Toward sundown, prison bosses brought in their squads. The whites were led into the bunkhouse Bobby was in earlier, and the black prisoners were escorted to a bunkhouse on the other side of the kitchen.

When a small crew of black men entered the kitchen, Willie pointed to pots and baskets they were to take back to their bunkhouse. Willie and the kitchen crew gathered up their pots and serving spoons and entered the white lodging.

It was the same menu they had served at noon, but the scene was different. Nearly fifty men filled the space. It was obvious why Hoppy had called them knockouts. Some were old and nearly toothless or had thick cataracts that nearly blinded them. Some were young but hobbled with foot injuries like Hoppy. Some would start into consumptive coughing fits, trying to clear the disintegrated lung tissue that rumbled deep in their chests.

After the line had passed the serving table and all the men were settled onto benches, Willie picked up the pot of field peas. He pointed to the basket of cornbread and waved at Bobby to follow him. "Bring those squares."

They walked the length of the tables, adding cornbread or peas when men asked for more.

It was then that it came.

"Hey. Boy."

Henry Helms had always used that taunt with Bobby, and in that same snide tone. But it couldn't be Henry. Last Bobby had heard, Henry was idling away in a Dallas prison, waiting for his death sentence appeal to be decided in Austin.

Bobby turned around. The man who had spoken was a surly thick-necked man who had come in on the transport wagon with him that morning. His gaze wasn't on Bobby but beyond him to Willie.

"Boy, you come and take a look at this."

Willie remained where he stood, holding the ladle in the pot.

"I told you to come here now." The man held his plate toward Willie and pulled up the shriveled body of a lizard by the tail. Three of the legs were folded in on the body, but one leg splayed out stiffly from its side. "You tell me why this here's in these field peas you give me."

The rows of men grew silent. Even the clacking of spoons on tin plates stopped. Their eyes alternated between the new convict and Willie, the only black man in the room.

Willie showed no expression when he said, "How long you been in?"

The man squinted at Willie. "What?"

"How long you served so far?"

"One year on a five-year sentence."

"Well, then. I made a mistake."

The convict nodded, pleased. Willie waved the ladle toward the lower end of the table. "You ain't been here long enough for a whole lizard. You give half of it to someone else."

The room erupted in hoots and laughter. The thick-necked man stood, humiliation and wrath in his face.

But before he could step over his bench, a prison guard shouted: "Quiet!"

The man stopped and the room went silent again. The guard pointed at the man. "Sit down."

"Sitting down, boss."

The guard waved his hand toward the back door. "Move it along, Willie."

"Moving it here, boss."

Spoons scraped on plates again, and a low, cautious hum of conversation rose. Bobby followed Willie to the serving table, where the old man put down his pot. "You men bring everything back and start the washing. I'm going to check on my bunkhouse."

He left, and Hoppy scowled after him. "He better enjoy playing boss while he can. The captain's going to leave him high and dry one day."

It took another two hours to clean up from dinner. When Bobby returned to the white bunkhouse, he found a spare bunk to drop into. He shifted to settle his body into the mattress, hearing the muffled crunching of the shriveled corn husks it was stuffed with. His pillow had no slipcover, and it smelled stale with the dried sweat of a dozen previous owners. It didn't matter. He was so tired that even the always-on lights in the corridor couldn't keep him from falling fast asleep.

It seemed like he had just dozed off when someone shook his shoulder. "Get up, Bobby."

It was Hoppy's voice. Bobby peeked open his eyes. "What time is it?"

"Biscuit time."

Bobby sat up, squirmed his feet into his brogans, and followed Hoppy to the cookhouse. Willie and the crew were already at work on scrambled eggs and biscuits. Dawn still had not arrived when they returned to the bunkhouse an hour later with breakfast. The men shuffled past the serving table with the look of sleep still in their eyes, and with pillow creases still on their faces. There was little conversation. By the time the men assembled in separate squads in the yard, horses were taking shape in the first faint streaks of dawn, blowing and champing. Prison guards sat in the saddles with shotguns bridged across their forearms. Bloodhounds bayed from their pens at the commotion, and the prisoners silently filed out. Each one waddled in leg irons, their white outfits glowing dimly in the twilight. If it were like the other farms Bobby had been on, they would march on foot like that for several miles, arriving in the field by the time it was light enough to begin the work.

After the kitchen crew had their own breakfast and washed up, Bobby shook out a cigarette from his pack and put it to his lips. A burner emitted blue flames under a large pot of field peas for lunch, and Bobby lowered his head and puckered his lips to get the cigarette tip into the fire. He stretched as he walked out the back door of the kitchen. After the heat of the stoves and the wash water, he welcomed the crisp February air of the southeast Texas morning.

Willie sat on the stair landing of his bunkhouse. Bobby nodded at him and lowered himself onto the landing of the cookhouse. He turned his head to the right and left to stretch the weariness out of his neck.

Willie squinted at him. "How old are you?"

"Ninet—well, twenty now."

Willie chuckled. "I got socks older than you." He picked a tobacco flake off his tongue and flicked it away. "They bringing young fellas like you in here and it's changing this place. It used to be a bunch of white-hairs with stiff joints and ropey arms, their life about spent. Mostly harmless. Now the hospital at the Walls Unit sends us someone if the guards think they got the TB. Or if they run out of beds for all the men injuring themselves to get off the work farms. This little unit can't keep up with that. Ain't no good going to come of it."

Willie tipped ash off his cigarette and studied Bobby like he was coming to some decision about him. Finally, he asked, "Who are your people?"

"My people?"

"Yeah. Who you belong to?"

"Most people want to know what I did."

"Okay. What did you do?"

"I robbed a bank." Bobby's hands hung over his knees, and he tapped the cigarette, sending the ash floating to the ground. "Don't got none, I guess. People."

"Everyone got people."

Bobby thought of his dead parents and the man whose name he carried.

"Not me," he said.

Willie pursed his lips a moment, and he peered off into the distance as if trying to recall something. "'Of what people art thou?' That's from the book of Jonah. If you don't know who your people are, how you goin' to know who *you* are?"

Bobby pulled on the cigarette and exhaled a stream of smoke like a sigh. "Who are *your* people?"

The old man grinned. "Well, now. Most people want to know what I did."

Bobby smiled back at him. "Okay. What did you do?"

Willie scratched his bearded chin with his thumb, and the cigarette between his fingers sent up a meandering vine of smoke in front of his face. He stared off like he was watching a film unspool in his head, and he spoke in his deep church-organ voice, low and sad. "When I was a young man, I killed my brother. I found him on a bed with the girl I was sweet on. They had their clothes on, but I knew. I walked away, and I should of kept walking. But I turned around. I went back in the bedroom and beat him till he wasn't moving no more. He died the next day. I ran and hid myself in a barn. Then the Lord come to me in a dream and said, 'Where is your brother, his blood crieth to me from the ground.' I woke up when I heard the dogs baying for me. I been in a prison uniform ever since."

Willie's untended cigarette had a long line of ash, and he tapped the stub.

Bobby flicked his own spent cigarette into the yard. "You a preacher? You sound like one."

"I ain't had no church ordain me." Willie jutted a thumb to the building behind him. "But they seem to like how I preach on Sundays. That's my church. They's my people now."

BOBBY GOT USED to the daily routine, and he found himself awake at three each morning without Hoppy shaking his shoulder. By the end of March, the captain let him exchange his striped outfit for the coarse white shirt and trousers that the other prisoners wore. The rheumy cough that had gotten Bobby sent to the Wynne Unit had long since cleared up. He wasn't sure whether that meant he didn't have TB or that the symptoms had merely receded for a time. Either way, he remained with the knock-outs, and he was fine with that.

The only change to the routine was on Sundays. After breakfast, Willie held church inside his bunkhouse, and Bobby sat on the kitchen stairs by himself. He liked to listen to the singing that came from the open windows. Some of the songs were hymns faintly familiar to Bobby from Sundays at the boys home. In other songs, a lone voice rose, and the men responded in unison, accompanied by rhythmic clapping and defiant shouts in response to the lyrics. After the music, Willie preached. The volume of his voice rose and fell, helped along by affirmations from the men. The sermons Bobby remembered at Gatesville were lectures from well-meaning pastors with a visitor's pass, but with Willie, it was different. When he preached on hope, or patience, or courage, it was like he was offering to share a drink of clear water from his own cup.

The last Sunday in March was Easter, and Bobby listened as the men in the bunkhouse sang of suffering and new life. Willie continued the theme in his preaching. "He was *abandoned* on that cross." He raised his voice at the word "abandoned," straining it out in a gravelly voice, highlighting the misery. "His father walked *away*. Jesus cried out, 'My God, my God, why hast thou *forsaken* me?' But there was no answer. No answer! All the sins of the world were on him, and his father turned his *face* away from him."

A slap of a hand on wood accompanied the word "face," and Bobby imagined Willie smacking a table where the men sat for their meals during the week.

"But that ain't the *end* of the story—you know it, don't you?" The men responded to the question with triumphant laughter and clapping, and someone said, "That's right, that's right!"

"His father told the angels to roll *back* the stone, to *open* that tomb." Someone shouted, "Hallelujah!" Willie continued. "His father said, 'Get up, son. Get up!'" Willie laughed. "Can't you see it? Here come Jesus out of that tomb, and then he turn around and he *mock* that dark shadow inside. 'O death, where is thy sting? O grave, where is thy victory?'"

The men clapped and shouted. Someone started singing and the rest joined in.

THE NEXT MORNING after the breakfast chores, Bobby sat at his familiar spot on the landing and lit up. He drew the smoke into his lungs and released it with a long sigh as he stared off in the distance.

"Fine day," Willie said.

Bobby glanced at Willie and returned his gaze vaguely to the landscape beyond the fence. He put the cigarette to his lips, blinking at the smoke streaming off the tip.

"Gonna get hot soon enough," Willie added.

Bobby nodded without looking at Willie. He wasn't in the mood for conversation, but he knew Willie was waiting him out.

"Yep . . . hot and sticky," Willie said, and when Bobby finally faced him, Willie had his head up to the sky but his eyes were on Bobby, sidelong, with a faint hint of amusement.

Bobby smiled back. "I just got things on my mind."

"Like what?"

Bobby hesitated, and then spoke. "You said Jesus was abandoned. In your sermon yesterday. I never heard that before."

"That's what he cried out on the cross: 'My God, my God, why hast thou forsaken me?'"

Bobby rubbed the soreness at the back of his neck and propped his wrists on his knees, fidgeting with the cigarette. His mind went back to the day he was abandoned to the Gatesville School. Bobby remembered pressing his little hands on the window of the administrator's office while he stared out at the man whose name he carried. The man never looked back as he climbed into his car and drove away.

"It ain't like that, Bobby."

Bobby gaped at Willie in surprise, wondering how he knew what Bobby had been thinking.

The old man continued. "'When my father and my mother forsake me, then the Lord will take me up.' That's in the Psalms. You know the Psalms?"

Bobby returned his gaze to the stairs. Willie hadn't read his thoughts after all. "That ain't the way of it. My father and mother didn't abandon me. They died, is all."

"You telling me you never blamed them for leaving you alone in this world?"

Bobby didn't answer. Of course he blamed them, foolish as it was. And it sat as a hot stone in the pit of his gut.

He stubbed out his cigarette and stood. "I'll go harness up the John Henry."

THAT AFTERNOON, BOBBY brought a bucket of drinking water to the guards at the front gate. Outside the fence line and beyond the bend in the road, a faraway voice was singing.

Gonna pack up all my care and woe
Here I go, singing low

Bye, bye, blackbird.

The tenor voice was fit for a stage, like it was some live a cappella performance on the radio. Bobby heard the squeak of a wagon and the arrhythmic clop of two donkeys in harness. Soon, the same clapboard wagon that transferred Bobby to the Wynne farm came into view. Two men were in chains on the back benches. One of them raised his hands toward the fields, rattling the chains that bound his wrists, flushing crows up from the plowed earth in a snapping flutter of wings. He laughed and sang out to the fleeing birds.

Make my bed and light the light,
I'll arrive late tonight.
Blackbird, bye, bye.

The singer appeared to be in his mid-twenties, a full head of dark hair, and Bobby thought of Marshall. The singer even carried himself with that cocky confidence Marshall had. His companion in the buckboard looked older by a decade, jaundiced, with dark circles under his eyes.

The driver reined in at the gate, and at the guard's command, the two prisoners jumped off the back of the wagon. They were marched through the gate and to the captain.

"Who'd they send me today?"

A guard pointed to the jaundiced man, who wheezed out a long, rolling cough. The guard stepped back from him with a look of disgust. "This one's Marvin Azbell. He was sent up for marrying too many women."

"Marrying too many women?"

"And none of them knew about the others."

"Son, how many women you have for wives out there?"

"Four," Azbell said, his voice only a hoarse whisper after his coughing fit.

"You a glutton for punishment or something?"

The guards around the yard chuckled.

"And now you've come down with the consumption."

"That's what they tell me, boss."

"From the look of you, they telling the truth."

"I hope not, boss."

The captain made a nod of his head toward the other prisoner. "And what about our Al Jolson here?"

"This one's Bob Silver."

"The one who was on death row?"

"Yes, sir."

"He don't look consumptive."

"No, sir."

"You belong with the TBs, Bob Silver?"

Silver smiled at the captain. "I don't know, boss. They ran a test, but I feel fine."

"What did you do?"

"Armed robbery, boss."

"No, what did you do at the Walls, after the governor took you off the death row?"

"I was with the laundry, boss."

"Well, you'll boil laundry here, too. And our marrying man…" The captain assessed Azbell doubtfully. "We'll just have to see."

The captain stepped aside and waved the guard on. Silver and Azbell were marched into the bunkhouse to be presented to the tender.

Inside the yard, Bobby still held the water bucket. A guard lifted the dipper to his mouth, took a drink, and dropped the dipper back into the bucket. "You go on now and get back to the kitchen."

"Going to the kitchen, boss."

THE NEXT AFTERNOON, Bobby was alone in the cookhouse when Bob Silver entered with a neat stack of laundered towels.

"Where do these go?"

Bobby had both hands in the dishwater at the sink, so he gestured with his head. "Put them in that cabinet right there."

Silver slid the towels onto a bare shelf and took in the room. "Those stoves and ovens make it hot in here, and it's only April. This cookhouse ain't the place to be come summer."

"I've only been here since January, but I guess you're right."

Silver strolled around, exploring the kitchen, pulling out drawers and opening cabinets.

Bobby reached for a steel-wool pad and scoured a pan. "I heard you was in the death house."

Silver seemed satisfied with his quick investigation of the place, and he fished in his shirt pocket for his cigarettes. "I was. For three months. The governor commuted my sentence to life on the very day I was to go down."

"You ever talk to a guy named Marshall Ratliff in there?"

Silver was shaking up a cigarette and he stopped, surprised. "All the time. How do you know Marshall?"

"We robbed that bank together, him and me and two others. My name's Bobby Hill."

"For sure? Small world, as they say." He pulled out a cigarette and offered his pack to Bobby, but Bobby presented his soapy hands in answer. Silver took a match from a box above the stove, lit up, waved out the stick, and dropped it into an empty tin can. He leaned his backside against the countertop next to where Bobby stood at the sink. "I would have guessed you was his little brother the way Marshall went on about you." He squinted at Bobby and pursed his lips, thinking. "Said you could handle cars."

The Gatesville School sometimes leased boys to nearby farmers for work, and Bobby learned how to drive and repair their machines. He found he liked working alone under the hood of a truck or riding by himself in the fields on the coiled-spring seat of a tractor. It put him far from the school guards and their boy captains, at least for a while.

"I do alright."

"Yeah, he said you were fine with cars and guns, but you wouldn't know what to do with a woman." Silver chortled at that.

Bobby figured it was true enough, but he ignored the jibe. "How is he?"

Silver blew a stream of smoke to the side, away from Bobby. "No one's doing too well on that row. I was there for three months and nearly lost my mind. He's been in that cell now, what, a year?"

Bobby returned to his scouring. "Just about."

"They send you here to Wynne because you got the TB?"

"They suspected it, but I feel fine now."

"Me too, me too." He tipped ash into the can. "It seems like a terrible way to go, though. You've seen the lungers, I guess."

Bobby nodded as he rinsed out the pot.

"I had to change their bedding this morning," Silver said. "Skin and bones was all they was. I'm turning them this way and that way to get the sheets out from under them, and all the while, they're looking at me like they're asking me to help them breathe—or maybe help them not need to breathe no longer."

"They're in a sorry state."

Silver shook his head. "I tell you, we may not have come in as lungers, but we got a good chance of catching what they got if we're here long."

He pulled on the cigarette one more time and then stubbed the butt and dropped it in the tin can. "Cars and guns," he said, musing. "Marshall sure liked the way you handled cars and guns."

Outside the back door came the sound of stomping as someone kicked mud off his boots on the landing. Willie entered, and when he saw Silver, he said, "The Laundry finally send you over with my towels? I expected them yesterday."

Astonishment flickered on Silver's face.

Bobby said, "This here's Bob Silver, Willie. He's done put the towels in the cabinet."

"Good." Willie gestured to a stack of soiled towels and dishrags. "Then Bob Silver can bring back that pile there to be washed."

"Now, listen, boy," Silver said. "They tell me the captain's got you high and mighty over this cookhouse, but I ain't on your crew."

Willie stared steadily at Silver. "You standin' in my kitchen, though. So, you go on with that pile of laundry."

Silver scowled at this cheek and took a step toward the old man, but he stopped when the front door of the cookhouse opened and a guard entered.

"Willie," the guard said, "you got any coffee left from this morning?"

"On the stove, boss. Bobby, light that burner under the coffeepot for Boss Fowler there."

Bobby struck a match and put it to the burner, and when he turned on the gas, it lit with a faint *whump*.

Silver watched all this, then returned his attention back to Willie. His lips curved up in a cool grin. He gathered the laundry in his arms and sang out to Willie like a minstrel in a vaudeville show.

Mammy, mammy
The sun shines east, the sun shines west
But I know where the sunshine's best

He gestured with his head at the back door. "Get that door for me, boy." When Willie opened the door, Silver stepped out as he continued his song.

Mammy, oh, my mammy
My heartstrings are tangled around
Alabammy.

Willie shut the door, unfazed by Silver's provocation. He went to the icebox and pulled out a glass bottle. "You want some milk in that coffee, boss?"

DON'T GET NOTICED. That's what Bobby learned from surviving his boyhood in Gatesville, and he was good at it. At Wynne, his kitchen duties helped with that. He was in bed earlier than the rest because he was up earlier than the rest. While everyone else was sitting at the meal tables, Bobby served provisions or cleaned up. Even as the camp enjoyed Sunday idleness, Bobby and the kitchen crew were sequestered away in the cookhouse to prepare the meals that still had to be set out.

But once Bob Silver took an interest in him, Bobby suddenly became visible to everyone. They called him by name. They chatted him up at the serving table. When he ventured to tell a funny story from his time at the other work farms, they laughed. He hadn't sought it out, and no telling long it would last, but it did feel good to belong.

It was the same thing that happened when Marshall had drawn Bobby into his orbit that first stay in Huntsville. The only difference was, when Marshall had taken a liking to him, Bobby had liked him back. He still wasn't sure about Silver.

The next Sunday morning was a fine one. A mild breeze sighed through the screens of the open doors and windows of the cookhouse. Hoppy was setting a pot of field peas on the stove for lunch while Bobby mopped the cookhouse floor. Voices from Willie's bunkhouse were starting in on a song.

Outside the cookhouse, someone called in a loud whisper, "Bobby. Hey, Bobby."

Through the screen, Bobby saw a convict under the window. He had his back to the cookhouse, and his hands were in his pockets, trying to look like he was lounging in the shade of the building.

"What?"

"Silver wants to know how long you got till your break."

Bobby raised his eyes to look farther out into the yard, where Silver stood with two other men under a tree. Silver was saying something that Bobby couldn't hear, and the men were laughing.

"About five minutes, I guess. Why?"

The man kept his back to the window. "He wants to see you when you're done in there."

Hoppy stood next to Bobby. "The boy's got church to go to," he said in a voice raspy with needling sarcasm.

The man under the window turned around, confused. "Church?"

Bobby ignored Hoppy. "Tell him I'll be there."

He returned to mopping, but Hoppy continued to stare out the window at the cluster of men around Silver. "So what do you think he wants?"

"Beats me."

"He's hatching something."

Bobby went through the back door to rinse out the mop at a spigot near the base of the stairs. He hung the mop to dry and stretched his back as he listened to voices from inside the segregated bunkhouse. They were lifting up a song to rhythmic clapping. He turned the corner of the kitchen, and as he walked toward the tree where Silver was holding court, the sound from the bunkhouse faded.

When Silver saw him, he broke into a wide smile. "There he is!" The others turned to Bobby and opened the circle for him. One offered him a cigarette, which he accepted and lit up. "Bobby, Azbell here, he's been telling us about all his adventures. Did you know he's broken out five times?"

Bobby flicked his cigarette. "Which wife did you run to?"

Silver guffawed. "That's a hoot! I never thought to ask that."

Azbell grinned weakly. "Different ones different times."

Silver beamed confidently at the little group. "Boys, I think Azbell here's got another run in him, and I think we could join him. He knows the train routes. He knows the boardinghouses where the clerks won't turn you in. We stick with him, we could get safe all the way up to Chicago."

The two men who were standing with Bobby and Azbell glanced at each other doubtfully. One of them spoke. "I hope you make it. With everything in me, I hope you make it. But I've only got another year left on my dime. I'm going to ride it out."

The other one nodded. "Yeah, I'm out, too."

"That's okay, boys. That's okay." Silver grinned, adjusting to this change in his vision. "It'll be Azbell and me—and Bobby makes three." He laughed at that.

Bobby hadn't signed on for any plans for a breakout, and he was about to say so when Hoppy approached them with the little hitch in his gait.

Silver said, "This is a private meeting."

"I'm guessing you're talking about a break, and I want in."

"If we were making a plan, why would we include you? You'd just slow us down."

"You'll want a way out of that fence line, is my guess. I can get us some bolt cutters."

"How you going to do that?"

"I've got my connections. Bolt cutters and maybe even a pistol. You think you might could use any of that?"

A wide grin spread across Silver's face. "Hoppy, I think you're my new best friend."

THE NEXT DAY, Bobby sat on the back steps of the cookhouse for his morning smoke break, and he stared at the fields beyond the fence. Tiny buds of cotton plants had pushed up from the raised rows. Silver and Azbell and Hoppy would soon be cutting across those rows on their way to a railyard and an empty freight car.

"You been staring at them fields for three days now."

It was Willie's voice, and Bobby turned to him. The old man sat leaning back against the frame of the screen door, and he assessed Bobby through lids half closed over his yellowed eyes.

"Men get to staring out there for as many days as you been staring out that fence—I know what that means. You've got running in your eyes, Bobby."

Bobby stubbed out his cigarette and stood. "I don't have anyone to run to."

"It don't matter you got no one out there to run *to*. You looking for someone to run *with*."

Bobby didn't reply, and he returned his gaze to the fields.

TWO NIGHTS LATER, Bobby was awakened by the flicker of lightning through the windows. At the crack of thunder, the power to the building went out. Rain began pattering on the tin roof in a comforting drizzle. Bobby was falling back into sleep when Hoppy was at his ear, speaking just loud enough to be heard over the rain.

"It's now or never. Let's go."

Bobby had not told any of them he would go along, but he couldn't argue with the timing. He climbed down from his bunk and slipped on his clothes and brogans. Silver and Azbell and Hoppy were at the rear door farthest from the picket room. As Bobby watched the men slip out, he had an impulse to return to his bunk. Then a hand grabbed his wrist, and a long strobe of lightning revealed one of the tuberculars. The man's pale skin stretched taut over the jawline and cheekbones, and his shallow pants for breath shaped his mouth into a slight grimace. He looked like a carved cemetery death skull except for the eyes, which stared mournfully at Bobby in a silent plea to be taken along. Bobby shook off the grasping fingers and scurried out the door.

At once, the rain increased into a roaring chorus around him, and hail began to fall in a loud rattle on the tin roofs of the buildings. Most nights, the fence line would be illuminated with little islands of light every twenty yards, but the storm had knocked everything out. Through the rain, Bobby could barely see the faint forms at the chain-link fence. He ran to them as icy pellets thudded against his bent back.

Silver cut through the galvanized wire with tin snips that must have come from Hoppy. Minutes later, the four were through a gap in the fence and Silver led them across an open field. The hail stopped, but a steady drizzle continued to fall.

"We'll find us a car near the college in town." Silver pressed the grip of a pistol into Bobby's hands. "Take this."

Hoppy grabbed Silver's elbow. "Hey, why does he get the pistol?"

"You ever fired at a man? You ever even drawn down on one?"

Hoppy didn't respond.

"Of course not. All you ever done on the outside was hang paper on suckers." Silver put his hand on the man's shoulder. "I'm glad you got us the gun, Hoppy, but it goes to Bobby. Count yourself lucky you ain't never had to pull the trigger on anyone. Bobby here, he's shot it out with lawmen. We may need that experience. Now let's get us a car before they find out we're gone."

The rain had let up by the time they reached the college campus, but gray clouds hung low and heavy. The men were soaked to the skin, and strands of hair lay matted to their heads. They crept along the side of the road and peered inside the parked cars, but no keys hung from the ignition.

A mechanical chug in the distance made them scramble for cover. A long hiss of tires on wet pavement grew louder, and light from headlamps reflected off the shiny asphalt. A roadster passed them and slowed to a stop thirty feet away, in front of a dormitory entrance. Two silhouettes moved in the window, and a girl's brief giggle lifted over the putter of the idling engine.

Silver whispered. "A boy's dropping his girl off. Hurry now, before he drives away."

The four of them came up to the roadster in a running crouch. Silver opened the driver's side and grinned. "Evening, lovebirds." On the passenger side, Bobby opened the door and leveled the gun at them.

Silver shoved his hip against the driver, making him shift sideways until Silver had replaced him behind the wheel.

Bobby waved his free hand at the girl. "Get in his lap."

Even as she crawled onto her boyfriend's legs, Bobby sat on the bench and shifted his hips against her so he could close the door. With all four of them in a seat made for two, and with Hoppy and Azbel in the rumble seat at the rear, the car swam slightly on the overloaded suspension when Silver pulled away from the curb.

As they passed the city limits sign, the college boy spoke for the first time. "Say, now—" His voice cracked, and he cleared his throat and tried again. "You can have the car, but you best drop us off and let us walk back to town."

Silver grinned. "We're on an adventure, all of us together."

On her boyfriend's lap, the girl's head was bent down against the ragtop, her chin nearly to her chest. "Where are you taking us?"

"What's your name?" Silver asked.

"Loree. Loree Harrison."

"Well, Loree-Loree Harrison, I have a mind to go to Houston."

"My guy's got to be at a baseball game tomorrow. He's captain, if you don't know."

"Oh, is he now?" Silver chuckled at her annoyed tone. He nudged the college boy's shoulder. "What's your name, Cap'n?"

"Hayden Malone."

"Well, Cap'n Malone, you'll be missing that game tomorrow."

They stopped at a gas station in Conroe, but the lights were out, and the pumps were locked. Since Malone was the only man not in prison clothes, Silver ordered him to knock at the house adjoining the shop and wake the owner. Malone was to explain that his mother had been taken to a hospital in Houston and he was on his way to her. The story worked, and while the four convicts hid with the girl in the shadows at the side of the station, the owner took the lock off one of the pumps and sold Malone five gallons.

When the shop owner was back in his house, the six crawled into their places and Silver drove away. Twenty minutes later, raindrops began spattering the car. Hoppy and Azbell drew their legs into the rumble seat and tucked down to get as much of the turtleback over them as they could. In the cabin, Silver and Bobby rolled up the windows.

Despite the cramped space, the gentle thump of rain on the ragtop gave the cabin a cozy feel, and the light from the headlamps turned the drizzle into a glittery curtain in front of them. Loree started to cry in little muffled sobs.

"Hey, now," Silver said in a soothing tone. "Don't neither of you have nothing to worry about."

She sniffed. "We saw you in our side mirrors sneaking up to the car. We thought you were friends of ours out to scare us."

"Well, now. Why can't we be your friends?"

Silver's question went unanswered, and he mumbled, "We only want to get to Houston, is all." It was pouty and resentful, and the car fell into silence again.

The rain drummed on the roof in an increasing roar. The wipers couldn't keep up, and Silver and Bobby lowered the side windows a few inches to watch for the ditches.

The roadster shuddered, slowed to a crawl, and finally stalled out in the middle of the highway. Silver tried to crank it a couple of times before dropping his hands to his knees. "What's wrong with your machine, Cap'n Malone?"

"I don't know," Malone said. "I think water must have got in the engine."

The rain diminished after a few minutes. When it let up, they got out and stretched muscles that had gone numb on their cramped ride. It was impossible to see each other, and when they talked, their voices came disembodied out of the black. Bobby opened a wing of the hood, felt carefully over the hot engine until he found the carburetor, and opened the cover. In the dark, he couldn't see if it held any moisture, but he ran a rag over it just in case. Screwing the cover back down, he told Silver to try to start it, but the engine didn't turn over. He felt for the spark plugs. He polished each connection and snugged the caps back in place.

"Try it again."

Silver cranked the key and pumped furiously on the gas pedal. Hoppy shouted from somewhere in the dark, "Stop that. You probably flooded the engine now."

Headlights peeked over a rise in the distance, and the rhythmic beating of a motor grew louder. Azbell said, "Hey, we got someone coming."

"Well, flag it down," Silver said. "Bobby 'll flash his pistol and we'll switch out."

Bobby asked, "What if it's the Law?"

"Shoot it out with them. We'd just as well be dead as be back in the pen."

Bobby fidgeted with the gun Silver had given him. The vehicle slowed, but when the headlamps luridly illuminated the prison whites of the convicts who stood around Malone's car, the gears shifted, and the car accelerated. The headlights passed by them, enveloping them in darkness once again.

The girl spoke. "Why didn't you take that car and let us go?"

Silver said, "I'd like to know the same thing, Miss Loree-Loree."

Bobby didn't reply. He thought about the man Silver had recruited for the crooner's Fort Worth robbery. Bobby wasn't going to be the second verse of that song.

Silver turned the key again, and the engine chug-chugged, and then sputtered to life. "Hey, now. She's back from the dead."

By the time they reached the outskirts of Houston, the clouds had cleared away and the first streaks of morning light stretched toward them from the east.

Silver yawned and pushed his arms against the steering wheel in a stretch. "Cap'n, we're going to need your daddy's machine a bit longer, but we'll drop you two off. What's your pleasure?"

Loree answered for them both. "How about the Rice Hotel?"

"La-tee-da," he said, with mock elegance.

"Well, you asked me."

Silver chuckled. "No, ma'am. I'll find us a quieter spot."

The city wasn't awake yet. He pulled into a wide alleyway and parked with the engine idling. "Cap'n, you and me are going to switch outfits."

Silver climbed out and Malone shifted toward his open door. The girl had to twist toward Bobby and prop herself up to let Malone out. As she hovered over Bobby in a near embrace, the softness of her sweater and the smell of her neck was his for a moment, and then she settled back down on the bench next to him.

Hoppy crawled out of the rumble seat. "Why do you get the street clothes while the rest of us sit here in our prison whites?"

"You wouldn't fit in them, anyway."

Hoppy alternated his scowl between Azbell in the rumble seat and Bobby in the cabin next to the girl. "You okay with this? I say we draw straws."

Silver unbuttoned his shirt. "We'll all have street clothes soon enough. It'll be the first thing we look for."

Hoppy wagged his head and his finger. "No. No. I'm on my own from here on out." He gave a slight salute to Azbell and Bobby and started toward the street. His arms and shoulders hitched up in his little leap each time his left foot came down.

Silver reached into the car across the girl and took the gun he had given Bobby. "I can't let you around that corner." He cocked the pistol, the metallic click audible in the confined alley.

Hoppy stopped and turned back to Silver, who stood with his shirt unbuttoned and untucked, pointing the gun at him.

Silver said, "You walk out of this alley in your prison whites, Hoppy, and in two blocks, you'll be caught. Which means we'll be caught. Now, here's how it's going to be. I'm going to wear Cap'n Malone's shirt and trousers, and Bobby's going to put on his cap and jacket. You and the marrying man there will tuck down under the turtleback. That's how we're going to get out of town. We'll find clothes for everyone then."

Hoppy stared at the gun a moment longer, then limped back to the rumble seat with a scowl. Silver handed the gun back to Bobby, and he exchanged shirts and trousers with Malone. The girl was told to slide out, and she joined her boyfriend, who was now dressed in Silver's prison whites. Azbell and Hoppy lowered the turtleback over them, and Silver drove the coupe back onto the streets of Houston.

Bobby put on Malone's flat cap and worked his arms into the jacket. "They're just going to go to the cops."

"And in those white duds the cops'll think he's an escapee and his girl is an accomplice." Silver chuckled. "We'll be long gone before they figure it out."

THEY FOUND STREET clothes and evaded capture for two days, but they didn't think they could push their luck in Haydon Malone's stolen roadster any longer. By nightfall on Sunday, they left the motorcar in a stand of live oak northwest of Houston and hoped to find an outbound train in Hempstead.

In a railyard, they knelt inside the shadows of the tree line and inspected five parallel rail tracks in front of them. A high, metallic screech groaned as an engine passed on the line closest to them. A long row of boxcars sat on the second line, connected to an engine fifty yards up, which hissed and *thump-thumped* as it idled. The doors were open on both sides of one of the freight cars. A faint beam of waxing moonlight lay on the empty floorboards.

Hoppy stood. "That engine's gone past. Let's make our play."

Azbell took his elbow. "Not a one of you has done this before. I have. Lots of times. We got to wait till it starts moving. If it's standing still, the bull might come along looking for hoppers to roust."

Hoppy shrugged off Azbell's grip. "I won't be able to catch anything on that freight line once it starts moving."

Silver scanned the rail yard. "It looks clear to make a run. Let's go."

The four left the tree line, with Silver leading the way and Hoppy limping at the rear. They climbed through the open doorway of the boxcar and crawled into the shadows. The exertion fired up a wheezing fit in Azbell. He released a long, rattling cough, burying his mouth in the crook of his arm to muffle the sound.

Footsteps crunched rhythmically on the track ballast, and a beam of light swung back and forth on the ground on one side of the freight car.

Silver whispered to Bobby, "Now's the time to put that shooter to use."

The footsteps grew louder and the beams grew brighter.

Bobby felt a draft by his side and found a floorboard crack. He pushed the pistol through the opening so he wouldn't be arrested with it.

A voice called out: "I thought you said it was this one."

Another voice responded, "No, I saw them crawl in the next car."

A burly man wearing a striped railroad cap appeared in the doorway. The propane lantern he held emitted the sound of a steady huff as it cast a harsh beam of light on the four fugitives.

The man with the lantern said, "Think these are your runners?"

"I think so, Bull."

The four shielded their eyes against the light and saw the gleam of a badge on the man in the Stetson. He was pointing a shotgun at them.

ON MONDAY, THREE days after the breakout, the four shuffled from the Waller County jailhouse chained together in a coffle. Bobby turned up his collar to reduce the chafing from the iron band around his neck, a ring linked by chains to hoops around the necks of all the other prisoners. Together they lurched awkwardly toward a truck with a two-door cabin and a cargo area. They lowered their heads to duck into the covered truck bed, and sat on two long benches facing each other.

When a big man crawled behind the steering wheel in the cabin, Bob Silver said, "Boys, I do believe we're being chauffeured today by Bud Russell himself."

Bobby had heard of Bud Russell, the transfer agent of so many prison songs. His twenty-eight-seat truck had various names, the three most popular being Black Annie, the One-Way Wagon, and the Midnight Special.

It was this last nickname that got Silver to humming as the transfer truck idled at a railroad crossing. A train passed in front of them, and the rail cars raced across a seam in the tracks with a *clack-clack, clack-clack, clack-clack.* Silver hummed to the rhythm, then sang the words.

If you evah go to Houston, you better walk right;

You better not drink, boys, and you better not fight.

The train passed, and the transfer wagon lurched forward. Silver continued singing.

For the sheriff will arrest you; he'll surely take you down;

And Bud Russell gonna get you, then you're chain-gang bound.

He laughed at Azbell and Hoppy, who joined in as he got to the chorus.

O let the Midnight Special shine a light on me,

Let the Midnight Special, shine her evah lovin' light on me.

Bobby didn't sing along. He stared at Bob Silver, wondering why he had run with him. He sighed and looked at the passing fields through the slats of the transfer wagon taking him back to Wynne.

12

WHEN THE ROLL IS CALLED UP YONDER

A guard and a trustee approached Marshall's cell with a large box that had already been opened.

Marshall stood from his bunk. "What's this?"

The trustee grinned. "Your momma sent you a present."

The guard rattled a key in the cell door lock until it clicked open, and the trustee carried the box to Marshall's desk.

A voice called out from one of the cells: "What'd she send you, Marshall?"

He spread the flaps and peered inside. "It's a Silvertone." He lifted the windup phonograph from the box.

Another voice echoed down the hall: "Play us something."

Marshall pulled from the box a handful of disc records in thin cardstock slipcovers. He sifted through them, shaking his head at her selections. All gospel music. Still, any kind of music would be a welcome distraction. As the trustee took away the empty box and the guard locked the cell door, Marshall placed a disc on the Silvertone. He cranked the handle and released the brake to let the turntable spin. The speaker popped slightly as he lowered the needle onto the record. Then a warbling organ began, followed by a solemn singer.

Rock of Ages, cleft for me,
Let me hide myself in thee.

When the song ended, he braked the turntable and replaced the record with another one. A baritone voice came through the hiss and crackle.

What a friend we have in Jesus
All our sins and griefs to bear.

Another voice joined in from the cell next to him. It was Wade Wilborn, a middle-aged black man. Marshall rolled the knob to turn up the volume, and Wade sang along with the record.

Do thy friends despise, forsake thee?
Take it to the Lord in prayer.
In his arms he'll take and shield thee,
Thou wilt find a solace there.

The song faded, and Marshall raised the arm and returned it to the cradle.

Wade spoke quietly. "That's a nice one, Marshall. Brings back memories. My momma, she had us in church every Sunday. My uncle was the preacher. He'd tell the stories like he been there hisself. Made me wish I was out there on the lake catching fish with Peter, or watching Lazarus walk out of that tomb a-wondering why he was all wrapped up."

Wade chuckled at the memories.

The corridor was silent, and he continued. "It was all so real to me, and then other things got more real. Or they seemed that way at the time. Do you—" He paused. "Do you think a man could ever get back there? After I done what I done, is it too late to go back to when all that felt so real?"

Marshall heard quiet sobs from Wade's cell. He knew the man's story. After an argument with his wife over family property, Wade had been sitting in the yard with a bottle. Brooding in his sodden rage, he saw her pass an open window and he shot at her. Just to scare her, he always added when he got to this point in his often repeated account. The terrified shriek of their child had sobered him up immediately.

Wade sniffed, and then released another spasm of muffled sobs. The row had gone quiet, quiet enough for Marshall to hear the strike of a match and the hiss of a flaring flame as someone lit a cigarette.

A man called out from the end of the row: "Play us something with a little life in it. Your momma send you any show tunes?"

"Just hymns."

"Where's Bob Silver when we could use him?"

THE NEXT DAY, Wade was released into the corridor, where guards strapped him to the barber chair and his head and left calf were shaved. He bathed and dressed in his new suit with the rip up the leg.

After midnight, the warden came to Wade's cell and made the pronouncement. When commanded, Wade stepped into the corridor and turned toward the death chamber with his escorts.

Calls came out from the other cells: "Go down gamely, Wade" . . . "Show them, brother."

Then came a sound never heard on the death march before. Through the tinny speaker of the phonograph in Marshall's cell came the recording of a warbling organ and a baritone voice.

When the trumpet of the Lord shall sound, and time shall be no more,
And the morning breaks, eternal, bright and fair;
When the saved of earth shall gather over on the other shore,
And the roll is called up yonder, I'll be there.

Wade nodded at Marshall and smiled. Tremulous, he sang along with the refrain as he walked down the hallway. He got to the end of the chorus as the death row guard announced, "The little green door opens." The second line of the song began as Wade stepped through the door.

On that bright and cloudless morning when the dead in Christ shall rise,
And the glory of his resurrection share—

The door closed, and Marshall turned up the volume in case Wade could still hear it.

When his chosen ones shall gather to their home beyond the skies,
And the roll is called up yonder, I'll be there.

The song continued playing over the unearthly snarl coming from the other room. The needle tracked toward the label, making a *ka-thunk, ka-thunk, ka-thunk* through the speaker. Marshall returned the arm to its cradle and shut off the turntable.

"WHEN THE ROLL Is Called Up Yonder" became a new addition to the execution routine. Robert Blake heard it next. He was a twenty-five-year-old white man convicted of murdering a traveling salesman who had picked up Blake as he was hitchhiking. As the song played, he walked through the little green door with a look of grim resignation.

Mathis Sanders heard it next. He appeared to be about Marshall's age, a black man sentenced to death for rape. Marshall had marked off eleven months on the row, but Mathis had been arrested and tried only last month, and two weeks after entering the death house, he was marched to the chair.

The next to hear Marshall's improvised death march was Silas Jarman, a black teen convicted of severely injuring the wife of his white boss while trying to steal her car. His last words to newspapermen visiting the death house were, "Tell my mother, don't worry about me. I'm going on to rest. My heart is right, and I am sorry that I committed the crime." As Silas was escorted down the corridor, he hummed along to the hymn from the Silvertone.

O. C. Wells heard it, too. He was a white man in his early thirties who had been convicted of killing a grocer in Coleman County. His brother had presented affidavits quoting another inmate admitting he had done the killing, but the governor allowed the execution to proceed. While Marshall played his hymn, Wells walked the corridor with resentful defiance.

MARSHALL DRAGGED THE desk chair to the back of his cell and climbed up. Stretching on the balls of his feet, his eyes could just clear the sill of the window on the back wall. It looked out on the exercise yard. He had peeked outside like this many times, though he couldn't last long before his legs started to cramp from the tension of balancing on his toes.

Outside, men from the general population had the run of the entire yard, but they seemed to stay away from the narrow slits of windows that lined the death house at ground level. The men walked aimlessly in the late-spring weather, or exercised, or gathered in groups like he once did when he held court out there with Henry and Bobby and a few others. When he was in the general population, he used to stand in that yard and think about freedom outside the walls. Now it would be fine just to get outside this cell and walk the yard.

One year. He had been one year in the death house. How many people had he seen go into the chamber? Nine?

He counted. No, twelve.

At eye level, grass waved gently against the pane. A ladybug ambled from a green blade onto the window. *Twelve dead and buried*, he thought, *and the rest of us here waiting, already half buried in the ground.*

His calf muscles quivered. The cramp was coming. He stepped down to the floor and sat on his bunk.

"Boss Owen—"

The corridor guard interrupted before he could finish his question. "It's only fifteen minutes since you last asked me what time it was, Marshall."

So that would put it about one thirty in the afternoon. His lawyer had written him saying he and Rilla had planned a visit for today. When his mother and Cearley finally arrived, Marshall couldn't guess their news simply by their expressions. But he figured if they had happy news, they'd be smiling, and they weren't.

The guard in the corridor lined up two chairs for them to sit in front of Marshall's cell. He joined them in a chair of his own and worked a crossword puzzle in the newspaper.

Cearley began. "Well, Marshall, we've heard from the Appeals Court, and they've turned down our argument for a new trial. I expect we'll get paperwork within a couple of months ordering you back to Abilene."

His mother's lips were pursed like she was making a grim effort to keep her emotions in check.

"To Abilene?" Marshall shrugged. "So, what happens there?"

"They bring a man to the county where his trial took place to announce the date set for the"—he looked at Rilla—"for the execution." He cleared his throat. "But I came here in person so I could tell you not to lose heart. There are still some things I'm working on."

Marshall let out a cynical grunt. "Like what? What's left?"

"Well, for one, I'm filing a motion for a second hearing at the Appeals Court. It's near the end of the term, but that may be in our favor. No date for an execution can be set while our motion's pending. So, if they don't act by summer break, well, there's three more months for us, and—"

Marshall interrupted. "Three months? You say that like it's a good thing. Three more months with my nose above the quicksand before I'm sucked down." He waved his hand toward them. "Don't bother. Neither of you."

His mother wrung her hands in her lap. "Don't say that, Marshall. I'm not giving up."

He kept his eyes on the floor between his feet and he spoke in a voice of quiet resignation. "It don't matter no more, Momma."

"You matter." She said it with such fierce resolve that it made him look up at her. She leaned close to the bars. "You matter. To me, you do."

His scowl melted away into hot tears, and she repeated the words in the same tone she had used to soothe him as a small child. "You do . . . you do . . ."

THE NEXT DAY, Cearley filed the motion for a second hearing at the Appeals Court. As he predicted, they took their summer break before acting on it. But it was their decision on another case that didn't bode well to Marshall's mind. He saw in the newspapers that the Appeals Court had turned down Henry Helms's motion for a second hearing before the court closed for three months. After more than a year in a Dallas prison cell, Henry was scheduled to be electrocuted behind that little green door a few minutes after midnight on September 6.

A day after Marshall read the newspaper report, a guard escorted Henry Helms into the death house. As Henry stood in the corridor and the guards unclasped his restraints, Marshall and Henry regarded each other.

"You've gone skinny."

"You've gone pale."

WHEN HENRY HELMS woke his first morning on the death row, sunlight streamed through the bars and lay across him in bright, warm bands. He tried to remember what his mother called the streaks of light when he was a boy.

God's fingers. That was it.

He would have been about nine years old in the memory, and it was morning. His mother entered the bedroom, and he pretended to be asleep as he watched her. She was at it with her usual bustle of energy, gathering clothes from the floor like a gleaner in the harvest. Then she stopped, her typical businesslike demeanor melted, and she admired him with a sentimental smile. The Venetian blinds made streaks of sunlight across his bed, and she murmured to herself, "God's fingers, Henry Helms. God has got his hand on you."

The memory came to him in his cell as the beams of morning light lay over him.

God's fingers.

He groaned and covered his eyes with a pillow.

An execution was scheduled for that evening. Willie Grady was a black teen condemned to death for the rape of a white woman. The boy passed Henry's cell, telling the guards, "I'll pray to the Lord to have mercy on whoever did this. I hope you will catch him someday." The guards nodded and kept marching him toward the green door at the end of the hallway. Marshall's Silvertone death march began, and Grady sang along as the guards escorted the nineteen-year-old into the death chamber.

When the roll is called up yonder
When the roll is called up yonder I'll be there.

Henry pressed his face to the bars of his cell to get a look at what was beyond the door. He couldn't see anything, and the thick green door closed.

THE NEXT MORNING, Marshall was absently humming the tune to his death march.

Henry said, "The newspapers say you play that song for every man who takes the hike."

Marshall stopped humming. "The last five, I guess. No, six."

"You promising them heaven after all they done?"

"Just bringing them a little comfort."

"Ain't none of it true."

A voice came from another cell: "You don't believe in a beyond?"

"I don't believe in fairy tales of no kind."

Marshall said, "Why does something have to be true as long as it brings some comfort?"

ON THE DAY two lawyers visited Harry Leahy, Marshall came to the bars at the front of his cell and watched the corridor boss set out chairs for them. The attorneys smelled of high-dollar cologne and pomade, their trousers bore sharp creases, and cuff links peeked from the sleeves of their suit coats.

When the chairs were in place, Leahy's lawyers sat, with the corridor guard arranged to the side.

Leahy spoke. "Books coming through, boss."

"Yeah, Leahy. Put 'em through."

As the prisoner threaded each book between the bars, Marshall read the printing on the spines from the titles that had been delivered to Leahy months ago: *Mad-house . . . Asylum . . . Psychiatry . . .*

The corridor guard took each book, thumbed through the pages to check for contraband, and handed the books to the lawyers.

Leahy spoke, his words deliberate, like he was reading off a script. "Boys, I thank you for the books. They confirm the symptoms that I feel have been coming on me in the last few months. It feels like I'm heading downhill in a wagon with no handbrake."

Marshall heard something sliding across Leahy's desk, and the big man said, "Another book coming through, boss."

"Send it through." The guard took a thick law volume from Leahy's hand and fanned the pages. He paused at a dog-eared page, but seeing no forbidden material inserted at that spot, he snapped the book shut and handed it to the lawyers.

The two men opened to the dog-eared page and read for a moment, and then one of the attorneys nodded in staged sympathy. "Mr. Leahy, I'm sorry to hear of your symptoms. We'll get someone down here soon to give you a checkup." The lawyers departed with the books.

From that day, Leahy's behavior changed. He left his food untouched, and he wouldn't come out of his cell for his weekly shave and bath. Sometimes he lifted a loud, wailing moan that sent goose bumps up Marshall's arms, but when a guard or another inmate asked Leahy what was bothering him, he wouldn't respond. Sometimes he mumbled a string of words that made no complete or coherent sentence. An alienist sent by his lawyers sat in front of his cell for an hour, asking him questions about his mental state and taking notes.

A sanity trial was scheduled for Leahy. Guards entered Leahy's cell with restraints for the transport. It had been three weeks since Marshall had seen him, and when Leahy emerged from the shadows of his stall, Marshall gaped at the man's transformation. For the year Marshall had known him, Leahy had been fastidious about his appearance. But the man he now saw waddling in leg irons between four guards wore a wrinkled dress shirt and a brown suit that had lost its shape. His hair was disheveled, and his face bore three weeks of salt-and-pepper stubble. He had a trapped, desperate expression, and he swept his eyes past the other men in their cells with no sign that he recognized any of them.

Four days later, the death house door opened, and they escorted Leahy back in. He was still in his rumpled suit and he was still unshaven. But his desperate and wild-eyed expression was gone, replaced by an exhausted resignation. As Leahy waited for his cell door to be unlocked, he shrugged at Marshall as if he was about to apologize. The guards brought him into his cell, and chains rattled as the restraints were removed.

Every man came to their cell bars, and Marshall spoke the question they all wanted answered. "You ain't crazy no more?"

Leahy's voice was tired and stoic. "I never was, boys."

"You sure looked that way to me."

"There's a law I found that says a condemned man can't be put to death if his mind can't grasp why they're killing him. If he turns insane, they have to put him in an asylum instead." The big man sighed. "Boys, I hated to take that route, but it was the last thing for me to do."

"What happened? At the trial?"

"I just couldn't put it over, is all."

Henry Helms let out a raspy laugh. "Well, watch me take a run at it."

A couple of others joked they might have a good shot at convincing a jury they were insane, too, since they were half the way there already.

Across his remaining weeks, Leahy had visits from several friends and family members. He told them he wanted his body buried close to where he hoped they would visit his grave. He didn't want to be in the prison graveyard the convicts derisively called Peckerwood Hill. Only unclaimed bodies were tucked away there, down in holes dug by trustee convicts.

On the morning of Leahy's last day, Marshall talked him into a game of chess, and their arms reached out through the bars to move the pieces on the board set between their cells. Marshall could tell the mind of the legal strategist wasn't engaged with the game. When Marshall beat him in short order, Leahy said he didn't want to play a second time. The day passed tediously, and the prison officials followed the execution routine Marshall had seen thirteen times before.

At midnight, the warden called Leahy into the corridor, and Marshall lowered the needle onto the now familiar song about the roll call up yonder.

When Leahy disappeared behind the little green door and Marshall's recorded song was over, another song started up. It was Henry Helms. In a high, thin voice, he sang a parody of "It Ain't Gonna Rain No Mo'," a song favored by Boy Scouts and barflies because of its ever-expanding number of stanzas and its repetitive nonsense chorus. Henry sang his own version.

Oh, I ain't gonna sing no mo', no mo'
I ain't gonna sing no mo'
I'll stay right here in this jailhouse cell
I ain't a-gonna sing no mo'.

No one laughed or said anything. Marshall felt it was disrespectful for Henry to break the silence so soon after Leahy's execution. Especially with such a flippant ditty. He began to say something to Henry when he heard the man shout.

"Hey, Captain!"

The corridor guard stood in front of Henry's cell. "What do you need there, Henry?"

There was no response. The guard returned to his desk and opened his newspaper.

"Hey, Captain!"

The pages rustled as the guard lowered the newspaper. "What do you want?"

Silence.

Then Henry started the song again, slurring the words in a high whine and repeating the first two lines like a flawed record that sent the needle back a groove.

Oh, I ain't gonna sing no mo', no mo'
I ain't gonna sing no mo'

Oh, I ain't gonna sing no mo', no mo'
I ain't gonna sing no mo'
Oh, I ain't gonna sing no mo', no mo'
I ain't gonna sing no mo'
The guard raised his voice. "That's enough tonight, Henry."
It seemed Henry had gone to sleep, but then he shouted, "Hey, Captain!"
The guard sighed heavily.

13

PECKERWOOD HILL

Henry Helms squatted naked in the back corner of his cell, hugging himself and rocking back and forth. He stared blankly between strands of hair raked down over his forehead. His father stood in front of his jail cell with the prison chaplain, but Henry didn't acknowledge the presence of either man. He gazed vaguely at the bare wall on the other side of the corridor, talking to himself in a hoarse mumble. *"I ain't gonna sing no mo', no mo'. I ain't a-gonna sing no mo . . . Hey, Captain!"*

John Helms squatted down at eye level with his son, leaned sideways to get into Henry's line of sight. "Henry, it's your father. Don't you recognize me?"

Henry's eyes didn't lock on anything, and the chant went on: ". . . no mo', no mo'. Ain't gonna . . ."

John stood. "Why did they take his clothes?"

"They didn't. He rips them off as soon as they get any clothes on him."

"Can I—" His voice croaked with grief, and he paused to gather himself. "Can I get in there with him?"

The chaplain shook his head.

"What do we do now?"

The chaplain shrugged. "Well, Reverend Helms, a sanity hearing will have to be held in the same county where the death sentence was handed down. So, that means he goes back to Eastland County. A jury will decide whether to proceed with the sentence or transfer him to an insane asylum."

AT THE END of August, John sat behind his son in the Eastland courthouse. On the same bench, Henry's mother stared ahead grim-faced, her gloved hands gripping the purse in her lap. Next to her sat Henry's wife, Nettie, who held their baby daughter. The other children had been left with a relative in Wichita Falls. A year and a half ago, a jury in this room had sentenced Henry to die. Now another twelve men filed in to determine if he was sane enough for that sentence to be carried out. Henry's scheduled electrocution was a week away.

At the defendant's table, Henry wore the pressed slacks and dress shirt that his father had brought for him. Before entering the courtroom, the guards had forced the clothing on him and then cuffed his hands to a leather strap around his waist to keep him from ripping at the garments. He had resisted a shave in the last month, and whiskers coiled out from his face in the meager beginnings of a thin, patchy beard. His mop of hair was in disarray and the bangs were raked down over his eyes. He sat between two guards, rocking forward and back in his chair, mumbling the incomplete lines of his nonsense song.

John took the stand and explained to the jury how Henry had always been peculiar, even as a boy, often suffering with headaches and spells of melancholy. Nettie also took the stand to describe her visits to the Dallas jail. She reported how much her husband had wasted away in body and mind across the past year. A pastor from a church near the jail and two women from the Dallas Women's Christian Temperance Union had often visited prisoners during Henry's stay there. They testified that Henry didn't recognize them on their later visits before his move to the death house. One of them recalled he had developed a "queer expression" in his eyes.

At the prosecution table, Joe Frank Sparks listened placidly to each witness, raising no objections during their testimony, and dismissing them from the stand without cross-examination. The court took a brief recess, and the noise from the gallery rose as spectators stood to share with each other their opinions of the trial so far.

John walked through the low swinging gate that separated the gallery from the lawyers. He squatted at the table in front of his son.

"Henry . . . Henry."

The rocking continued, as well as the song, now in a hum without the lyrics.

John opened his Bible. "Henry, do you remember the Babylonian king in Daniel's day who went mad? You remember how it ends? 'And at the end of the days I Nebuchadnezzar lifted up mine eyes unto heaven, and mine understanding returned unto me.'" John leaned toward Henry. "That's my one request to the Lord, Henry. That's the only thing I talk to God about. Just to see you lift your eyes to heaven and come out of this."

John laid the Bible on the table in front of Henry, open to the story. Henry stopped rocking. He pulled the Bible toward himself with his shackled hands and stared at it for a moment. Henry then mechanically wadded up a handful of pages and tore them free from the binding. The guards got the Bible away from him, but they were unable to free the ripped pages he held tightly in his fist. When the trial resumed and witnesses testified for the county, Henry shredded the onion-thin Bible pages, releasing tiny pieces to flutter to the floor.

For the county, Joe Frank Sparks called six experts in the field of mental hygiene, including the director of the Abilene State Hospital. The doctor testified that Henry's behavior was not what he regarded as "true to type" for an insane man. There had never been, as he put it, "the foul odor about the mouth which comes with swift and acute mania." A lawman then told the jury how he had visited in the Dallas jail and negotiated with Henry for the purchase of two of the six pistols that had been taken from Henry at his capture. The convict had conducted the deal in what the lawman called an "intelligent manner." Two jailers who had served at the Dallas jail throughout Henry's confinement reported that not once had he displayed any indication of mental instability. A guard on the death row in Huntsville attested to a conversation he said he overheard days before Harry Leahy's execution. According to the jailer, Leahy had said, "I couldn't play the part, but Henry's schooling himself and he will get by with it." Henry's lawyer objected to this, and the judge ordered the jury to disregard the claim.

The jury recessed to deliberate, but they returned in ten minutes. Henry Helms was sane, they said. The execution would proceed.

HENRY SAT IN the death row barber chair. His face was clean of the scraggly beard. His thick and unruly hair had been trimmed down to a burr. The barber had tonsured his scalp and shaved his left leg below the knee for the electrodes that would be fixed to his skin in a few hours.

The barber stood back and assessed his work. "I expect it feels better to be trimmed and shaved again, don't it?"

Henry didn't answer.

The barber gathered his razor and scissors into a box and left.

When Henry's restraints were removed, he stood from the chair, took off his clothes, and stepped into the tub. He ran a bar of soap under his arms and across his chest. He lathered up his hands and ran them over his head, feeling the new experience of baldness. Holding on to each side of the tub, he plunged backward under the water to rinse off the soap.

As a boy, his father had lowered him like this into a creek, intoning the words, "Buried with Christ in baptism . . ."

He wondered what it was going to be like to be buried, and he held himself down as long as he could. He opened his eyes under water. The refracted light from a bulb in the ceiling above him expanded and contracted like a glaring white blob. When his body convulsed with involuntary gulps for air, he pulled himself up and drew deep, welcome breaths once again.

He didn't want to be buried. He didn't want none of this.

Henry toweled off and reached for the clothing laid out for him. He put on the underwear and white shirt and slipped on the trousers with the seam on the left leg open to the knee. He shrugged into the jacket and sighed. Several of the men stood at their cell doors and called out to him: "Bear up there, Henry" . . . "Hold fast, brother." Marshall stared at him from his cell door, too, but said nothing.

For his last meal, Henry asked for sausage, creamed potatoes, rolls, and milk. But an hour after delivering it, a trustee came to his cell to take away his untouched plate.

The phone rang at the desk and the guard picked up the handset.

A voice came from one of the cells. "It's the governor, Henry. I just know it. He's calling to commute your sentence to life."

The guard listened, mumbled a response, and returned the handset to the cradle. He walked to the front of Henry's cell. "Your daddy's here. He's asking to see you."

Henry shook his head.

Another hour passed, and the prison chaplain came in and stood at the bars in front of Henry's cell.

"Henry, your daddy's in my office. He wants to visit you."

"No."

"You know, other men on the row don't get visits from relatives this late in the process. The warden, he's made an exception for your daddy being a preacher. Might be a comfort."

Henry released a short, contemptuous grunt.

"You want me to help you settle anything with the Lord before you meet him?"

Henry said nothing, and the chaplain left. He felt flush, and he laid himself out on the floor and pressed his face against the concrete to cool it.

HENRY WAS STILL lying on the floor when gongs rang out from the clock tower. He counted them. Twelve. September 6 had arrived. The chaplain returned to the death house behind the warden and two guards.

As the warden read the formal pronouncement, the condemned man didn't lift his face from the cool concrete floor. But when the cell door opened, Henry crawled to the corner and sat up with his back against the wall. The two guards reached for his arms, but he kicked at them.

"Henry, it's no use," one of them said, and reached for him again.

He crossed his arms and bowed down to his knees. "No!"

The warden puffed out his cheeks and blew out a sighing breath. He waved the two guards from the cell.

"Go get a couple more."

When two more guards entered the hallway, a call came from one of the other inmates. "Go down gamely, Henry."

The four guards reached for him, but Henry flailed and twisted. "No," he demanded, and when they had him on his feet, he said it again in a whimper.

They pushed and pulled until they had him at the door of his cell. He reached out to grip the bars and missed, and he was in the corridor. The inmates frowned at him in dismay, and he abruptly regained his composure.

He walked past each cell, and the inmates called out to him: "That's the man, Henry" . . . "Carry that to the end, brother." But Marshall sat on his bunk with his back to the corridor. The phonograph was not turning, and what had become Marshall's traditional death march was not playing.

The corridor guard called out, "The little green door opens."

Henry stared at Marshall's back as they shuffled him through the doorway. The man who had talked him into the Cisco robbery never turned a glance his way, and the door closed.

In the death chamber, the air vibrated with a mechanical hum. Henry stood before a thick oaken chair with a tall back. Whoever had built the macabre throne had applied a rich stain to the wood. Wide leather straps dangled from it at the legs, feet, and back. A leather cap hung over the top. Light shimmered off brass fittings attached to cables that ran behind a wall where some sort of engine emitted an unearthly thrum.

The medical gurney in the corner caught his attention. He imagined his charred body being wheeled away on it, and he thrashed against the grip of the guards. But they wrestled him into the chair, and two held him while another secured the straps. He fastened Henry's arms to the supports and wrapped a wide belt around his torso, pulling it until his spine pressed against the straight wooden back. A leather belt bound his right leg, and another strap pinched a wet sponge and an electrode to his left leg.

They started to wad cotton into his nostrils, and he shook his head away from their hands, shouting in a panicked, high-pitched voice, "What's that for? What's that for?"

The guards didn't answer him as they locked his head in a vise of hands and forearms and finished plugging his nose. They pulled a hood over his face, and everything went dark.

The death cap was lowered to the place where the hood opened at the top of his head. Fingers worked a strap under his chin, which snugged the cap down on his shaved scalp. The pressure on the briny sponge at the top of the cap released a trickle of water down his back, and he shivered.

The hands that had been working over his body withdrew, and his eyes darted uselessly to the right and left in the darkness of the bag. It was coming. He felt the hood enter his mouth as he drew in a breath, and it billowed away as he exhaled.

It happened a second time, but not a third.

WHEN THE EXECUTIONER rolled the dial to twelve hundred volts, the body in the chair surged against the leather straps and the limbs thrashed in violent spasms. The current dropped, and it was spun up to run through the body again at eight hundred volts, and once again at five hundred volts. Finally, the snarl of the generator dropped to a purr and faded to silence.

No one moved in the room. Faint streams of smoke twirled from the electrode attached to the limp left leg.

The prison doctor held a handkerchief to his nose to stanch the smell of charred flesh. He asked if the current was off, and the executioner nodded. The doctor placed a stethoscope on the steaming chest, stepped back, and pronounced the prisoner dead.

TWO TRUSTEES SLICED their shovels into the dirt again and again until they were satisfied the hole was long enough and deep enough. After laying two lengths of lumber at the head and foot of the hole, they crawled up and sat on the edge to rest, letting their legs dangle in the grave. They lit cigarettes, absently gazing across the lichen-covered headstones marking the bodies of abandoned prisoners on the gentle pine-shaded slope of Peckerwood Hill.

At the squeaks from an approaching wagon, they took a last puff on their cigarettes, flicked the stubs into the hole, and stood. They nodded at the driver and the prison chaplain on the front bench of the buckboard and passed them to retrieve the cheap pine casket from the back. They carried it to the hole and used ropes to lower it to the lumber at the base. They retrieved their ropes and looped them and removed their caps for the chaplain to read scripture and intone a prayer.

As the chaplain and driver departed, the trustees returned the caps to their heads and reached for the shovels.

One said to the other, "I hope my family comes for my body if I die in this place." He kicked his shovel into the pile of dirt beside the hole. "It's a sorrow when a family's got no money to claim the body theirselves."

The other one slung a shovelful on top of the casket, which landed with a hollow *thump* on the wood. "Naw, son. I don't think this family run out of money. I imagine they just run out of hope."

14

MY SONS AND DAUGHTERS

A door banged, and Marshall woke with a start. The trustee with the meal trays pushed his cart into the death row. Marshall sat up and yawned. After Henry's execution, he had not been able to eat breakfast that morning and he slept right through lunch. Still, as the trustee offered him a supper tray, Marshall shook his head. The trustee shrugged and pushed his way down the rest of the row.

Marshall stood stiffly and went to the basin. He splashed cold water on his face, then cupped a hand under the flow and took a sip, smacking at the taste of pennies it always left in his mouth. He turned the handle off and watched a bead of water well up at the end of the faucet. It grew until it was too heavy to stay there, and then dropped to the metal basin with a thin *ting*.

Another bead welled up.

Ting.

Then another, and, after a moment, another, each one plopping on the brown streak that ran down the sink to the drain. For seventeen months, he had tried to twist down the handle tight enough to stop it. In his first few weeks on the row, he had complained to the guards that it kept him up at night. They never did anything about it.

Marshall reached for the handle and paused. Who was that man in the mythology stories condemned to push a rock up a hill only to see it roll back down again and again and again? His high school teacher had told the class about him—what was his name? He snugged the handle once again, as firm as he could make it, and waited to see if it would work this time.

Ting.

He sighed and lay on his bunk, pulling the sheet over his shoulders.

BOBBY WAS BACK at the Wynne Unit and back in the stripes. So were Azbell and Hoppy. Bob Silver had been returned to the Walls. Bobby was also back on the kitchen crew, and on Saturday morning, he took his break in his familiar spot on the stoop behind the kitchen. He finished the newspaper article about Henry's execution and he put the paper down. The man was no prize, but that was a terrible way to go. The report said Marshall was the next one up if the Appeals Court turned down his motion for a rehearing in a month. Would two executions satisfy Eastland County, or was Joe Frank Sparks going to take another crack at Bobby, too? The man had told reporters he was considering it.

Bobby took a sip from his coffee cup as Willie sat on the opposite stoop and lit a cigarette. The first few weeks after Bobby's return, the other convicts had been cold to him, but not Willie.

The reaction from the others didn't really surprise him. During his earlier two-year sentence for breaking into the tailor shop, a man escaped and got caught two days later. When the guards led him back inside the gate, the man's stride was reduced to a pigeon-toed shuffle from the leg irons, his clothes were muddy and ripped from running through the brush along some waterway, and his face was gaunt and drawn from lack of sleep. But to Bobby's mind, the man's incapacity highlighted his own, and he took offense at the failed prisoner. So, Bobby had expected a cold reception when he returned inside, and he got it. It took a couple of months for them to quit being offended by his presence. And, since he was no longer in his unchosen role as Bob Silver's sidekick, he simply became invisible to them once again.

Willie was different. On the first day Bobby returned to the stoop for his morning break, Willie nodded at him with equanimity, and they fell back into whatever kind of relationship this was.

Now the old man flicked ash off his cigarette and said, "I hear your friend went down this morning, Bobby. I was sorry to hear that."

Bobby never considered Henry a friend, but he let that go. He stared absently into his tin cup at the oily ribbon curling on the surface of the coffee. "You ever think it could have been you walking to that chair instead of making soup in here for the rest of your life?"

"Sometimes I do. Sometimes I wonder if it'd be easier to just get it over with."

"The jury tucks away in their little room and come out to tell one man he'll die and tell another he'll spend his life in prison." Bobby shook his head in bafflement. "It feels like a crapshoot."

"'The lot is cast into the lap, but the whole disposing thereof is of the Lord.'"

"That one of your Bible verses."

"It is."

Bobby changed the subject. "You got your sermon ready for Sunday?"

"Just about."

"What are you preaching on?"

"Sin."

"What are you going to say about it?"

"I think I'll say I'm against it."

It was an old joke between them. Bobby stood. "I'll go hitch up the John Henry for you."

"You got to get up, Marshall," said a guard at his cell door. "The barber can't stay here all day, and we got to empty the tub. Come on now."

Marshall remained on his side, his face to the concrete wall, the sheet up over his shoulders.

"Your momma will visit you this afternoon. You want to be cleaned up for her, don't you? Let's get you a shave and a haircut. And you need a bath and a fresh uniform before she sees you."

He didn't move.

He was still in the same position when his mother arrived, and he didn't respond to her first greeting. She called him again, and he rolled over and sat up. He stared at the wall opposite his bunk for a moment, as though he had been roused from a deep sleep.

"Marshall, honey. Come sit with me."

He stood with a faint groan as his dormant muscles rebelled against the activity. He dragged his desk chair to the bars, and his body collapsed into it like deadweight.

His mother spoke softly. "They tell me you haven't eaten in nearly two days."

Marshall scratched his head, and half-heartedly raked his fingers through his matted and tangled hair.

"I brought you an apple pie." She held up a box to the corridor guard who sat to her side. The guard nodded.

Rilla inserted the tin dish through the pass.

"Marshall, you take this now."

Marshall took the dish and held it in his lap. His mother showed the guard a spoon, and when he nodded, she passed it between the bars.

"I want to see you eat some while we visit."

Marshall sighed and took the spoon. He dug through the flaky topping to the baked apples inside and brought a spoonful to his mouth.

"That's better," she said, and the tension in her shoulders loosened. "Take another bite."

Marshall mechanically obeyed, but after swallowing the second spoonful, he stopped.

She said, "Get some more," but Marshall put the dish and spoon on the desk.

His mother leaned toward the bars. "You got to take care of yourself, Marshall."

"I'm fading."

"You're fading? What does that mean, you're fading?"

He put his hands on his chest, fingers splayed. "I'm shrinking inside. I'm . . . fading."

"You're not making any sense, Marshall."

"It don't matter." He stood and returned to his bed.

"Son, I traveled a long way to see you today."

He lay down with his face to the wall and drew the sheet back over his shoulders. Rilla tried to coax him back into conversation again, but when her efforts proved fruitless, the guard suggested she try again the next visitors' day. His mother left in tears, and when the door closed behind her, the *clack-clack-clack* echoed down the hallway to the little green door.

BOBBY'S HANDS WERE deep in suds when the screen door slapped against the frame, and Hoppy entered with a stack of plates. Like himself, Hoppy wore a baggy shirt and pants with wide black and white horizontal stripes.

Hoppy set the plates beside the dishes Bobby was washing. "The guards at the front gate said we left the biscuits in the oven too long this morning. Told me they planned to shoe the horses with them."

Hoppy crossed behind Bobby, and he tripped over the edge of a floorboard that jutted up half an inch. He righted himself in time, swearing at the offending board.

"A nail's come free at the end of this plank." He pressed the edge of the board down with his foot and then squinted out the open window to the fence line. Dropping to his knees, he pried at the edge of the raised plank with his fingertips. Hoppy stood and hobbled to a drawer and pulled out a serving spoon with a straight handle. He fell to his knees again and worked the handle into the seam until he found the leverage to pry the board up.

"Step aside, Bobby."

Hoppy lifted the plank that ran parallel to the sink. It let out a slight creak as the nails gave way along the seam, releasing the board from the joist underneath. Most of the wide planks that made up the kitchen floor were long, but two in front of the sink were shorter.

"These been cut before," Hoppy said. "Probably to give access to the plumbing under the floor here at the sink." He pried up the second one and dropped through the narrow hole to the dirt three feet below. He peered around. A skirt encircled the outside base of the building and hid him from the eyes of anyone in the yard.

He gave Bobby the spoon and lay down in the dirt. "Put those planks back in place. I want to see something."

Bobby lowered the boards in place and pressed his brogans over the nailheads until the nails slipped back into their holes. A few minutes passed of muted shuffling under the floor. Hearing a quiet knock on the plank, Bobby pried it up.

Hoppy grinned at him. To the left of the opening in the floor, he had dug out a hole about three feet in diameter and maybe six inches deep. "And that was just with my fingers." He pointed to the serving spoon he had given Bobby. "Give me that spoon and put the boards in place. This time, though, don't wait for my knock. Leave me down here until morning break's over. When the coast is clear, you open the boards and let me out."

Bobby replaced the boards, pressed the nail heads down, and returned to his washing.

In a few minutes, Willie came through the back door and walked over to the oven. He wrapped a cloth rag around the handle and lowered the oven door to squint at the pans of cornbread. "Ten more minutes." He closed the door. "Hoppy ain't back from the front gate with the plates?"

Bobby shrugged.

"Still yakking with them, I bet. That man can talk the hind leg off a donkey." He pointed to the oven. "Ten minutes on that cornbread, now, and when you put the other pans in, you can take your smoke break."

"You got it." Bobby lowered another pot into the suds. The coiled spring on the screen door twanged as Willie walked out, and the door slapped back into the frame.

After his break, Bobby pried up the boards. Hoppy climbed up through the opening, the serving spoon in hand. He had widened the hole to a diameter of about four feet, with two feet of depth.

Hoppy stood at the sink and washed the spoon, ran his forearms under the water, and splashed water on his face and neck to remove the sweat-streaked grime.

Bobby pointed to his uniform. "You ain't got a spot of dirt on your clothes or brogans."

Hoppy grinned. "Took everything off and worked in the altogether. I got grit in crevices I didn't know I had, but at least my skivvies and clothes are clean."

Bobby squinted toward the fence line. "That's a long way."

Hoppy dried off with a towel and joined Bobby at the window, calculating the distance in his head. "On a straight line, it would come out between the perimeter lamps just right. But, yeah, it would still need to come up far enough out there to get away from the light. I'd say about eighty feet from here."

"Seems like that would take a while."

"Well, I guess we got the time for it."

"'We,' you say? No, Hoppy, that ain't for me. I can't abide caves and tunnels."

"Well, Bobby, you just keep a watch up here on the surface and cover for me while I dig. If you change your mind when the time comes, you can go with me. It won't take nothing to crawl that length of tunnel."

That evening, Hoppy scrambled under the kitchen with instructions to let him out before Willie and others got to the kitchen to start on breakfast. The next morning, Bobby arrived early, switched on the kitchen lights, and pulled up the boards so Hoppy could crawl out. Bobby looked down at what he had accomplished in five hours. The hole was about five feet deep now.

"What'd you do with the dirt?"

"Scattered it evenly all under the joists."

Bobby put the boards in place, and as Hoppy washed at the sink, he continued to talk about his night. "It's hard to get much leverage lying down flat and working with just a spoon. And then whatever I dig up has to be spread out thin so it don't build up. It makes for slow going. And there's a lot more dirt to come."

A sneeze roared in the yard, and boots clomped up the steps. Hoppy put down the dish towel and started filling a pot as Willie entered the back door.

Willie took down a can of ground coffee. "I saw the lights on. Seeing as how you two are up before the chickens, go see what they've laid." He waved Hoppy away from the pot he was filling. "I'll finish making the coffee."

That evening, Hoppy dropped into bed early, and immediately deep snores came from his exhausted body. He returned to the project the next night. When Bobby entered the kitchen in the morning, he didn't turn on the lights. He pried up the boards and Hoppy crawled out. In the dark, Bobby couldn't see what kind of progress had been made on the hole. As he replaced the boards, Bobby spoke in a low voice.

"How far you get this time?"

Hoppy helped Bobby press the nails back in place and whispered in reply, "Maybe just a couple feet more." He scrubbed at the sink. "I bent the spoon, so I'll need something else to dig with."

Two nights went by before Hoppy was ready to dig again. When it was down to the two of them in the kitchen, Hoppy showed Bobby the heavy metal blade he had pulled off the wooden handle of a garden hoe.

Bobby nodded. "Looks like that'll do you better than a serving spoon." He bent down to the boards at the sink, but Hoppy stopped him.

"Hold up, there, Bobby."

Hoppy switched off the kitchen lights and opened the door. A figure entered in the shadows.

"Oscar's going to help me tonight."

Bobby opened the boards the next morning without switching on the kitchen lights, and Oscar and Hoppy crawled out. Their arms and faces were streaked with grimy sweat, but both had clean prison uniforms.

Hoppy lay the boards back in place. "Me and Oscar here switched off all night, one of us digging and one of us scattering the dirt. I expect we made it straight down to eight feet tonight. Next time we can make the turn toward the fence."

Word about the tunnel spread, and more wanted in on it. The scheme expanded to twelve diggers on four teams, including one team of three men from Willie's bunkhouse. Each evening, a team slipped into the cookhouse and dropped into the floor opening, and Bobby closed the boards over them for the night.

The teams were reporting four and five feet of progress each night. But they were running out of room under the kitchen for all the excavated dirt. They decided to shorten the tunnel by ten feet. They also agreed to tighten the tunnel, cutting the height by half for the remaining excavation. To compensate for the fact that they would surface closer to the fence line, their escape was scheduled for the last Sunday of the month. The moon would be waned out by then, and the day off would give them enough rest for a good run once they were on the other side of the fence.

ON THE SUNDAY morning of the planned escape, Bobby had the long, dark tunnel on his mind. He had told Hoppy he would go, despite his misgivings about having to crawl underground. The capital sentences for Henry and Marshall were never off his mind. He feared Sparks was plotting some bench warrant even now, especially after Bobby's escape with Silver back in April. Any day, an Eastland County sheriff's cruiser might show up to cart him off to a new trial.

He sat on the kitchen stoop and listened to the men from Willie's bunkhouse sing and shout. At the sermon time, Willie's voice broke out clearly through the screens of the open windows and doors.

"'But Zion said, The Lord hath forsaken me, and my Lord hath forgotten me.'" There was a pause, and Willie continued. "You gonna feel like that sometimes."

From the bunkhouse came a "That's right," and a "Mm-hmm."

Willie said, "I know I do." And someone replied, "Have mercy, Lord."

"But the Lord, he say—" There was a pause, and Bobby imagined Willie was looking down in the pages of his Bible, finding his place. "He say, 'Can a woman forget her sucking child, that she should not have compassion on the son of her womb?'" And his voice rose to a shout. "'Yea, they may forget, yet will I not forget thee.'"

Men clapped in response.

"You know why?"

"Tell us, tell us."

"The Lord, he say, 'Behold, I have graven thee upon the palms of my hands.'"

"That's right," someone said again.

"You see this? I got this scar on my hand here, right under my thumb. I remember the man who gave it to me. A big Mexican. He come at me with a shiv. I remember how I knocked him cold, too!"

The men laughed.

"I may forget a lot of faces, a lot of names. Old people do—ain't that right, Jefferson?" It must have been Jefferson who replied with a gravelly chuckle. "But that man I ain't never going to forget. Ever time I see this scar here on my hand, I remember. I remember!"

Bobby rubbed the hairless scar on his left arm and remembered the pain of the bullet that pierced him there, and the whimper of the old woman he had protected and carried to safety.

Willie wasn't finished. "The Lord, he looks down at his hands and he sees the scars. The only manmade thing in heaven, you know. The scars! And when he sees them, he remembers when he died for you. He don't never forget you!"

And the most beat-down men in the most beat-down place clapped and shouted.

After the last song, Willie walked out the door, mopping off the sweat his preaching had worked up. He sat and began to build a cigarette.

The expression on his face reminded Bobby of a man he knew once. The reform school had leased Bobby to a farmer for the summer. After working all morning in the cornfields with the man, they broke for lunch under the spreading shade of a post oak where the farmer's old father sat. As they ate their sandwiches, the farmer updated his father on the farm. The old man nodded and gave his son an affectionate pat on the leg, and the farmer straightened his back and grinned.

Willie had that same smile.

"Good sermon today," Bobby said.

"You say that ever Sunday." Willie lit the rollup and shook out the match. "You think you might decide to go from liking it to believing it?"

"I think I'll just stick to liking it." Bobby inspected how much was left on the smoldering nub in his fingers. "I'm glad you found something that gets you through, but taking to religion ain't the way I'm whetted."

"Whetted?" Willie grunted. "You sure that's the way you want to put it? No one ever whetted you."

Bobby frowned and stared out at the fields beyond the fence.

Willie rubbed a hand over his face and his voice softened. "Aw, now. You ain't the only one. In my bunkhouse, I seen a lot of fatherless boys. They all men, but really they just still fatherless boys. I try to tell them it don't have to be that way. 'I will receive you and will be a Father unto you, and ye shall be my sons and daughters, saith the Lord Almighty.'"

Bobby groped for something to say and settled on, "How much of your Bible you got memorized?"

"A lot. And you're interrupting an old man." He let out a weary breath and continued. "My daddy, he wouldn't never speak to me after I killed my brother. Half brother, really. The boy was born in Daddy's old age, the child of his second wife, and she died giving birth to him. He doted on that boy." Willie paused, and a sadness came over his face as if it had all happened only yesterday. "I never heard from my daddy once I was sent up. At first, I thought, alright, Willie, alright. There ain't no one you got to please now. That felt free for a while, me making my own way. But that led to nowhere happy."

Willie was quiet as his eyes scanned memories Bobby couldn't see. Then he continued. "I remember as a little boy, I'd say, 'Daddy, look at me!'" Willie grinned. "I'd be balancing up on a fence or sailing way up on a tire swing. And I'd say, 'Daddy, you watching, you watching?' A man don't never outgrow that need for a daddy to *see* him . . . to be *pleased* with him."

Bobby gave a grunt of frustration. "Must be nice you at least had it for a while."

Willie gestured at Bobby with the hand that held his cigarette, the vine of smoke swaying with the movement. "See? Just because you didn't never have that don't mean you never needed it. Back when you was a foster boy, I bet you wished someone would come along and adopt you. All those other boys, they'd spend only a few years with you, then one by one they got to go home to families. Didn't you ever dream back then some Daddy Warbucks would come for you?"

"There's no denying I did. When I was little, I thought about it a lot. But it was best to give up on that fairy tale. It wasn't no good always living with the ache it caused."

"Maybe you had that ache for a reason. When your stomach grumbles, that must mean there's food somewhere."

Bobby shrugged. "People starve to death. Just because they got a gnawing for something don't mean nothing."

"Aw, Bobby, think now. That don't mean there's no such thing as food. It only means no one's brought them any, or they too sick or too sad to want what's brought them. That's the only reason someone dies of hunger."

Willie pulled on his cigarette, let out the smoke, and continued. "'A father to the fatherless,' Bobby. That's what King David called God in the

Psalms. I was in the stir for years before I saw the Lord like that. But when I finally did, it was like I got adopted from your old foster home. I had somebody I wanted to make proud, and somebody I could come back to in sorrow when I didn't make him proud." Willie paused. "I needed God to give me what I used to have, and you need God to give you what you never had."

Bobby stubbed out the stump and flicked it to the side of the stoop as he stood.

Willie looked disappointed. "Now, where you running off to? You always running."

That surprised Bobby, and he stammered, "I ain't running." His tone was more defensive than he intended, but Willie gave no hint that he knew of the plans for that evening. Bobby relaxed and shrugged. "I just got cornbread to make for dinner, is all."

Willie chuckled and waved him off. "You go get things started, Bobby. I'll be in to join you in a while."

THAT EVENING, EVERYONE in the bunkhouse had a role in the choreographed plan. Bobby and nine other men arranged their bunks to make it look like they were settled in for the night, and then they slipped out the back door in groups of two or three.

Each exit was covered by a distraction arranged to occupy the attention of the building tender and the cage boss. Three slipped out while men ginned up an argument over a poker game. Two more exited during a convict's complaint about a bunk frame coming too loose to sleep in. Two got out while an inmate showed the guards his photo of Clara Bow swimming nude in a lagoon. Bobby and two more disappeared when the earlier argument over the poker game escalated into a fight.

When Bobby entered the crowded kitchen, he thought he saw Willie among the black men, and he brightened. But the old man wasn't in the crowd, and there was no reason to expect otherwise. Bobby had never told Willie about the tunnel under his kitchen. Now it felt like a betrayal. He had an impulse to leave a note and say goodbye, but the crowd behind him pressed toward the opening at the sink until Bobby stood at the edge of it himself.

He shimmied through the floor gap and dropped into the hole in the dirt. With no light to guide him, he felt for the tunnel he had been hearing Hoppy talk about for a month. Finding it, he entered on his hands and knees. He shuffled forward in the inky blackness and bumped into the legs of the man in front of him. He raised his head in a vain attempt to see forward, and his cap scraped on the tunnel ceiling. Loose dirt cascaded down his neck and into his shirt collar. The whole thing made him uneasy, and he changed his mind about joining the escape. But Hoppy was behind him now, and he saw the shadowy form of another man dropping through the faint light from the hole under the kitchen floor. All he could do was crawl forward in the line, keeping his head below his shoulders to avoid dislodging the dirt right above him.

When Bobby got to the place where they had changed the size of the crawl space, he had to lay on his belly to continue. He figured it couldn't be higher than eighteen inches. He rotated his knees out, right and then left, so he could push with the insides of his feet and pull with his elbows to propel himself forward. He was kicked in the face a couple of times when the feet in front of him slipped trying to find purchase.

Abruptly, the whole line stopped. No one dared make a sound, so no news came down the line as to why things weren't moving. With nine men in front of him and three behind, he could do nothing but wait.

In the inactivity and blackness, the sensations of his surroundings began to occupy his mind. The tunnel air was humid and stifling and smelled of organic decay from the dirt. It was inches around him on every side, and he imagined the whole thing sagging down and burying them all. Bobby rested his face on the crook of his arm and tamped down the rising panic by concentrating on his breaths.

The line started moving again, and soon a faint stir of fresh air passed his face. The silhouette of the man in front of him took shape, then the man stood, clambered up, and disappeared. Bobby found himself at the end of the tunnel, and the opening was above him. When he stood, the top of the hole was still over his head, and he found toeholds and handholds until he cleared the lip.

Men convicted of assault and rape and murder were running out into the free world ahead of him, shredding the ribbons of fog that threaded across the low areas of the field. Their white uniforms faintly reflected the lights on the prison fence line, giving them a spectral appearance of phantoms disappearing into the low brush under the trees. Bobby ran toward them, expecting at any moment to hear a shout from the corner pickets and the crack of a firearm. But no cry of alarm was raised from inside the prison fence, and all thirteen escaped successfully.

Once in the woods, Bobby separated from the men and struck out on his own. Sticking together on Bob Silver's escape had done him no good, he figured, so he wasn't going to repeat it.

When the sun was above the trees the next morning, he approached a lone farmhouse and peeked in the windows. He suspected the farmer was in his fields, and from the look of male neglect, the man had no one living with him.

The door was unlocked. Inside, Bobby exchanged his prison duds for clothing he found in the closet. He ate his fill of cold pork chops from the icebox and a square of cornbread from a plate on the counter, and he stood at the sink and drank cupfuls of tap water as if he could store it up for the uncertain days ahead. On the windowsill, the corner of some folding money stuck out from under a jar, and he put the bills in his pocket. He went through the larder shelves and stuffed a pillowcase with as much as it would hold. A single-barrel shotgun leaned in the corner, which he took. It wasn't for defense. If someone saw him in the woods, a shotgun would give the impression that he was hunting.

He stretched out the farmer's food for as many days as he could, but the pillowcase was empty only a week after his escape. Raiding the trash behind a diner for table scraps, he found half a can of baked beans and a peanut butter and jelly sandwich with only a bite out of it. Bobby sniffed the sandwich, shrugged, and ate it. Seeing a recent newspaper in the refuse, he pulled it out and brushed off the coffee grounds. The front page had information about the escape. Though food stains marred some of the report, he could make out that most of the men had been caught and returned to prison. It was hard to know from the readable portion of the report, but he seemed to be the only escapee still free.

He didn't know what to do next. He had no one to trust and no place to go. He was out of food, and he wasn't sure how to safely ask anyone for a job. That evening, he walked deep into the woods and bedded down in a pile of decaying leaves. He'd begun to fade into an exhausted doze when somewhere up in the trees he heard the hollow call of a great horned owl. It sounded like someone blowing across the mouth of a bottle, and at the same time it sounded like a question.

"Who? Who-o-o?"

15

LONG ENOUGH

In front of Marshall's cell, a guard said, "I'm telling you he's been in that position for two straight days."

Another one said, "He ain't gone and died on us, has he?"

Keys jangled, an ungreased hinge groaned, and a hand was laid on his shoulder.

"Marshall . . . Marshall, you look at me now."

They pulled Marshall over on his back, but he stared vaguely toward the ceiling.

One guard put his hand to Marshall's forehead and said to his partner, "He don't feel like he's got fever, but guess let's get the doctor in here."

When the doctor came later in the afternoon, he wrinkled his nose. "It's rank in here. When was the last time this man had a bath and a change of clothes and bedsheets?"

"Almost a month. He's refused to come out for wash day the last three Saturdays."

The physician sat in a chair next to Marshall and checked his temperature. He felt for any swollen glands in his neck, pressed his gut, and listened to his heart and lungs through a stethoscope.

"You say he hasn't been eating regularly?"

"First part of September, he'd pick at a plate ever now and then. Here on the row, we paid no never mind at first. His friend Henry walked the mile back then, if you remember. Men'll sometimes lose their appetite for a time after that, as you know. When he still turned away most of his food after a couple of weeks, we started reporting his meals and manners to each other at shift change. We got it all in a ledger back at the desk."

"You say he hasn't eaten in two days. What about water? Has he had any water?"

"We ain't seen him go to the sink. We ain't seen him move at all."

"Well, let's see if we can get some water in him."

They pulled Marshall into a sitting position. One guard brought a cup to his mouth, and Marshall drank deeply, letting out a satisfied sigh when it was empty. When they asked him if he wanted more, he didn't reply or look at them, so they lowered him to the mattress again.

One of the guards said, "My cousin, he got to where his arms and legs didn't work like that. They said he had encef—encef—"

"Encephalitis," the doctor explained.

"Is it contagious?"

"No, it's not contagious, but that's not what we have here, anyway. Let's just monitor it. You boys did a good thing starting that ledger. Y'all keep this chair next to his bunk and set his plate on it at mealtime. Maybe he'll eat something if he can reach it. If he doesn't come out of whatever's causing this paralysis, we'll have to feed him. But a body can go a lot longer without food than without water. Don't let a day go by without him getting a drink. If he doesn't rise to get it himself, pour it down his gullet again."

The plates they put by his bunk were never touched, and by the third day of this unfruitful routine, they brought the food to his mouth like they had been doing with the water. They started with a small spoonful of mashed potatoes, shoving it into his slack mouth. Only part of the mash stayed in, while the rest oozed down his chin and onto his chest. After wiping off the mess, they laid him back down and left the cell.

"GOD, THAT SMELL." It was one of the guards, talking to another about the fetid odor of excrement in Marshall's bunk.

The other man said, "His momma's bringing his lawyer today. The warden says we got to get his clothes and bedding changed and give him a bath before they come see him this way."

"I didn't sign on to change diapers."

"You're right about that. Go get the trustees."

Minutes passed, and keys rattled at his cell door again. Hands pulled at his body until he was up in the arms of two trustees.

They shuffled him into the corridor and sat him in the barber's chair. His limbs hung as limp as a rag doll, and he stared, expressionless, into the distance. While one removed Marshall's bedsheets in the cell, the other stripped his pants and boxers. He held the damp and soiled clothing by the tips of his fingers and wrinkled his nose in disgust. "I done lost my appetite for the rest of the day."

A guard said, "Just pile all that laundry over there with the sheets for now and sponge him off."

The trustee dipped a sponge in the bathtub, wrung it out, and worked it over Marshall's naked body. He was unresponsive except for the goose bumps that pimpled on his skin. After the sponge bath, the barber snapped a sheet over him, snugging it around his neck, and shaved his face and trimmed his hair.

After the trustees put fresh clothes on him, they started to return him to the cell, but the corridor guard stopped them.

"No, leave him there. His mother sits at that cell door every week and calls out to him lying in that bunk with no response. She's going to get to sit face-to-face with him today. Empty out the tub."

They drained the tub and mopped the floor and carried out the pile of filthy laundry. Marshall was left alone to maintain his blank stare down the corridor.

When his mother was escorted in with Marshall's lawyer, she cried out in delight to find him sitting up. But as she passed the chair to face him, his glassy eyes didn't register her presence, and her smile faded.

"Marshall, it's me. You still don't recognize me?"

He gave no response.

She turned to the guard next to her.

"Has he been eating?"

"We've been feeding him, and about half of it seems to get down him."

"Thank you for taking care of my Marshall." She reached a hand toward her son's face and withdrew it, remembering the rules. "And thank you for shaving him and cutting his hair. He looks more like himself."

The guard dragged over two chairs for Rilla and Cearley and positioned his own chair a few feet away. The three sat in front of Marshall.

Rilla spoke to the lawyer. "You see what I'm saying now, Mr. Cearley? He's not in his right mind. He's been nearly a year and a half in this death house. He's watched fifteen men go by his cell to the electric chair, including his friend Henry. It's done broke his mind. I don't have my Marshall anymore."

"Yes, well . . ." Cearley's voice trailed off as he gaped at the pale, emaciated figure in front of him. "Marshall, do you recognize me? It's your lawyer, Lee Cearley."

The vacant eyes stared dully ahead, so Cearley turned back to his mother. "Rilla, the Appeals Court is back in session and they have agreed to a second hearing on our motion for a new trial. That's promising news, considering they turned down a second hearing for Henry Helms, if you remember. I say we wait until we hear from them. If they turn us down, we can file a motion for an insanity hearing then."

Rilla shook her head. "Why wait? Anyone can see he belongs in an asylum no matter what the Appeals Court decides on your motion. Besides, it's my understanding that if we wait until a formal death sentence is handed down, the county that condemned him determines whether he's sane enough to be . . . for them to proceed."

"Yes, a jury at the Taylor County courthouse in Abilene would decide that."

"I don't want him back there. I don't want anyone in Abilene or Anson or Eastland to have any more say over his fate. I've talked with Judge Singletary right here in Walker County and he's sympathetic to my cause. If we schedule a hearing with him, Marshall will be in the care of an asylum as soon as possible."

Cearley waved his hand before Marshall's face. "Marshall, if you got anything you want to say about this, anything you *can* say about this, you need to let me know. Are you okay with what your momma's proposing?"

Cearley received no answer, so he made a notation on the paper pad at his knee. "Alright, Rilla, let's go see this judge you've talked to."

THE SCUFFLE OF shoes drew closer, and then the voices of two prison guards came from the front of Marshall's cell.

"Eastland? What do you mean he's going back to Eastland?"

"We got their county sheriff and his deputy out front waiting to take him back."

"Don't he have a sanity hearing with Judge Singletary here in Walker?"

"All I can tell you is the Eastland sheriff is standing out front with a bench warrant. Something about a new trial for attempted armed robbery of a car. Him and his gang ordered some family out of their machine on the streets of Cisco during the getaway."

"He's been on this row for nearly two years for killing a police chief, and now they want to try him for car theft?"

"I don't figure Eastland County wants Judge Singletary down here to decide the man's future."

"Guess it's all above our pay grade."

"Tell me what ain't."

They chained Marshall, and then used the medical gurney from the death chamber to wheel him out to where the Eastland County sheriff and his deputy waited.

WHEN THE CRUISER pulled up to the Eastland jailhouse six hours later, the sun was low in the west, and long shadows stretched out from the buildings and bare trees.

The deputy said to Marshall, "Guess you know this place. You been here plenty."

Marshall made no acknowledgment that he had heard the deputy. They carried him through the jailer's office and mounted the iron staircase that ran up the back wall.

The Eastland jailer, Pack Kilborn, led the men carrying him. "There's an open cell on the east side of the second floor. We're going to turn right at the top of the stairs." Keys jangled at a cell door. "Lay him down in here."

They lowered Marshall to a bunk, and Kilborn stood over him, assessing him. "So, the claim is that he's gone crazy since we sent him down there to Huntsville?"

The sheriff nodded. "They say he's got some sort of paralysis that's got no physical cause. You'll have to feed him and bathe him."

"As if me and old Tom here ain't got enough on our plate already. We got a full house, and some pretty rough company, at that."

The grandfatherly jailer everyone called Uncle Tom leaned into Marshall's line of sight. "Aw, now, we'll be fine, Pack. You and me can handle him." He pulled a wool blanket up to Marshall's shoulders and snugged it around him.

The men left the cell, and once their steps faded down the stairs, a low voice came from the compartment across the corridor. "Hey." A pause. "Hey, you there . . . Marshall Ratliff." A pause. "You really crazy or you trying to beat the chair?"

No answer came from Marshall.

The next morning, Pack propped Marshall up while Tom brought spoons of oatmeal to his mouth. Most of the mushy cereal ran in streaks down his chin by the time the bowl was empty, and Tom cleaned him before helping Pack lower him back down to his bed. The feeding was no different at lunch and supper, though they learned that tying a bedsheet around his neck for a bib made cleanup easier.

As they left his cell that evening, Pack said, "Hang on, Tom." Pack took Marshall's right leg and crossed it over the left leg at the ankles.

"What'd you do that for?" Tom asked.

"Just you wait," Pack said, and turned the key in Marshall's cell door.

The next morning, they found Marshall in the same position, his right leg crossed over his left.

"You convinced now, Pack?"

Pack let out an unsatisfied grunt and unlocked the cell door. He stood over Marshall, who stared at the same spot at the ceiling where his eyes had been fixed when the jailers left him the night before. Pack waved his hand in front of Marshall's face and got no response. Then he pointed his index finger and slowly lowered it toward Marshall's right eye. He got about six inches away and shouted, "Yah!" while darting his finger toward the eye, stopping an inch above.

Not a muscle in Marshall's body flinched, and his gaze never left the ceiling.

"Well, I'll be."

"Pack, cut it out now and prop the poor boy up."

The next morning when Pack and Tom brought breakfast, the sharp tang of ammonia filled the cell, and a rank odor of excrement.

"Oh, Pack, that's just pitiable right there. You still think he's faking it? Who in his right mind could sleep in his own filth like that?"

"You've always been an old soft-touch, Tom."

"Well, we ain't never seen anything like this, have we? He's been two years living next door to a death chamber. That tension's bound to do something with your mind."

"I wouldn't know nothing about that, Tom. Don't you turn your back on him, is all."

They stripped his clothes and bedding, washed the urine and feces off his skin, and got him in dry clothing. After breakfast, Pack took the oatmeal-streaked sheet they used as a bib and bundled it with the soiled clothing and bedding.

"My wife'll be none too pleased at having to wash this nastiness today."

Tom turned the key in the lock. "Want me to do it for her today? Guess I know how to boil clothes."

"That's kind of you, but I was only bellyaching. It's the life of a jailer's family, Tom. You're doing more than enough by staying on two more months. Your wife was all set for your retirement last week, I figure."

"I couldn't have gone and left you by yourself, what with the jailhouse so full. Besides, my wife's willing to wait a couple more months before she has to put up with me full-time." He chuckled.

RILLA CARTER AND Lee Cearley stood in front of Marshall's Eastland cell. She had given up trying to get Marshall's attention on these visits, and she turned to Cearley.

"I haven't heard any date for a trial on their charge of the car theft."

"No, not yet."

"So, no insanity trial in Walker County, no car theft trial in Eastland County, and no word from the Appeals Court about a new trial in Taylor County."

"We're in a sort of legal limbo right now."

"Judge Singletary down in Walker County was ready to set up an insanity trial before the Eastland sheriff kidnapped my boy. Can't we get him back there?"

"I think that route's closed to us. Even Walker County's own attorney didn't agree with the judge's claim to have jurisdiction for an insanity trial. No, our best course is the Appeals Court. I expect we'll hear from them before Thanksgiving. If they rule against us again, we've got a good case for a jury to find him insane then." His eyes returned to Marshall. "A real good case."

TOM AND PACK were finishing up Marshall's supper when angry shouts and a crash rose from the cluster of cells on the other side of the stairway.

Pack shook his head. "I best go see about that, Tom. You okay to clean him up?"

"Sure, Pack. You go ahead."

Pack helped old Tom lower Marshall into the bunk, and he left the cell.

Tom removed the bib and began to wipe off Marshall's chin and mouth. Another crash echoed down the hallway, and more shouting. Pack was ordering two men to stop arguing and clean up the mess they had made. Tom hurriedly collected his washrag and the bib in one hand

and balanced the tin plate and spoon and mug in the other hand. Leaving the cell, he pushed the door shut with his foot, and went to join Pack.

Marshall lifted his head from the pillow.

The lock. He had heard no snick of the lock. He replayed the sequence of sounds: He recalled the creak of the door hinge and the clang of the barred door as it found its place in the metal jamb, but old Tom had not turned the lock.

Marshall sat up and paused, listening. The argument was still going on, and Pack was shouting threats at the fighting inmates. Marshall stood and walked to the cell door, his legs wobbly from two months of disuse. He pushed, and as the door swung out into the corridor, he winced at the faint screech of the hinge.

The prisoner in the cell across the corridor gawked at him in surprise. Marshall paused, waiting to see if he would shout out to Pack and Tom. The prisoner remained silent, though, and Marshall nodded his thanks.

He stuck his head out of the cell and peered down the corridor toward the cluster of cells on the west side of the stairway. He heard Pack's and Tom's voices, but they could not be seen.

Marshall padded in his bare feet to the iron stairway. He descended to the landing and craned his neck to investigate.

No one was in the office.

The door to the jailer's apartment was closed.

The kitchen pass-through was shuttered.

He took the remaining stairs that turned left at the landing, and he ran quietly to the front door.

Locked.

He inspected the surface of the desk for a key, but there were only stacks of paper, an empty coffee cup, and a few framed photos. He crept to the door that would take him to Pack's apartment and paused. He'd walk in on the jailer's family if he went through the door, but he tried the handle anyway.

Locked.

He returned to the desk and quietly slid the lap drawer toward him.

Pens, pencils, a box of .38 caliber bullets.

He pulled open the top drawer on his left.

A can of tobacco, a racy magazine, a blackjack.

He turned to the right and drew the top drawer toward him.

A .38 Colt revolver.

Pack or Tom must have the key to the front door, and he was going to have to take it from them. They didn't carry weapons when they made their rounds through the cells, so he would have the advantage with the pistol.

He checked the cylinder. Empty. He opened the lap drawer again and clawed out six bullets from the box. He crept back up the stairs, loading the chambers as he went. His fingers shook, and he fumbled the last round. It struck a stair and fell to the concrete floor below, bouncing with a faint *tap . . . tap . . . tap-tap-tap* before rolling against the wall. Marshall clicked the cylinder into the frame and continued climbing.

When he reached the top and turned left, he almost collided with Tom Jones.

The assistant jailer froze, his mouth gaping in surprise.

Marshall raised his weapon. "Give me—" After two months of not speaking, Marshall's voice was hoarse and raspy, and he swallowed and said it again. "Give me the keys."

Tom stared at him, assessing him. In a sudden lunge, he clutched the pistol with both hands and tried to wrench it free. Marshall had underestimated this white-haired grandfather who had gently nursed him the last three weeks. Now Tom was all fierce strength and aggression.

Marshall pulled the trigger, and the bullet went through Tom's abdomen. The man's eyes widened in pain. Shouts rose from the cells—encouragement, objections, appeals for Marshall to take them, too. But his mind was on the old man who still had both hands on the gun. Marshall fired again, hitting Tom in the leg above the knee. The old jailer grunted and took one hand off the weapon to claw at Marshall's face. A finger entered Marshall's mouth like a fishhook and yanked his head sharply to the side. The two men lost their balance, and they tumbled and slid down the iron stairway.

When their fall stopped at the landing, Tom was unconscious. The cacophony from the cells above him still rang as Marshall checked Tom's pockets for the key.

He looked up in time to see Pack edging around the corner at the top of the stairs. Marshall fired at him, and Pack arced backward.

He kept the pistol pointed at the opening, waiting to see if Pack would reappear, when he was struck in the groin. He doubled over in pain. Tom was sensate again, and he shoved Marshall down the remaining five stairs off the landing. The old man staggered down the stairs toward him, and Marshall fired. The bullet pierced the jailer in the chest above the heart, and Tom collapsed on Marshall.

He pushed Tom off and straddled him, pointing the gun in his face, but the old man wasn't conscious. His fingers quavered from his ebbing strength as he explored Tom's pockets, now wet with blood.

Marshall heard something behind him and twisted around to see Pack on the landing. He fired at Pack, but too quickly and unsteadily. The bullet lodged in the ceiling with a faint puff of dust. Pack leapt over the railing, his full weight coming down on top of Marshall. The two rolled off Tom's unmoving form, and they wrestled for control of the gun. Pack was on top of him, twisting the gun, sending sharp pains through Marshall's wrists.

Marshall, emaciated and weak, felt his grip give way, and the gun slipped from his hands.

Pack pointed the barrel at Marshall's head, and fierce vengeance was in his eyes. Marshall turned away and winced his eyes shut, waiting for the bullet to rip through his brain.

Click. Snap.

The hammer had fallen on an empty chamber. Marshall peeked open his eyes, and against the wall lay the bullet he had dropped when he was loading the pistol moments ago.

Pack let out a guttural growl of fury and struck Marshall in the head with the pistol grip. He struck him a second time and a third, but he stopped when his daughter came into the room from the apartment door. Her chest heaved, fear and rage on her face, and she pointed a revolver at Marshall. The convict groaned and lolled his head away from her, blood streaming from the blows Pack had landed.

Pack gently pushed his daughter's pistol away and composed himself. "No more." He gasped for breath and turned to Tom lying motionless. "No more bloodshed."

His daughter used her own key to open the front door of the jail and went outside, firing shots into the air to sound the alarm. In moments, men crowded into the room, shouting questions about the status of the other cells upstairs and who else was wounded. They handcuffed Marshall, and when they found Tom still breathing, barely, several volunteered to rush him to the hospital.

As the men left, Pack moaned, "It's my fault, it's my fault. He was to retire a week ago, but I asked him to stay on. He should be sleeping next to his wife in his own bed."

A doctor was called in to stitch up Marshall's wounds from where Pack had struck him. After cleaning up his face and wrapping his head, they returned Marshall to his cell.

MARSHALL AWOKE THE next morning to find Pack staring at him through the bars. The jailer held a tray of oatmeal and coffee, and he set it on the floor in front of the cell.

"Guessing you can get this yourself if you want it."

The prisoner across the corridor asked, "How's old Tom?"

"Touch and go," Pack said to the prisoner without taking his eyes off Marshall. He pulled at the door of Marshall's cell to check the lock, and he left.

Marshall stood, and immediately the floor tilted sharply to the side. Touching the bandage wrapped around his throbbing head, he shuffled over to the cell door and sat on the floor to regain his balance. He had no appetite, but he took the tin cup of coffee and drew it between the bars. Sipping the bitter drink, he leaned his back against the wall and released a long, weary breath.

"You sure convinced me." It was the prisoner across the corridor.

"What's that?"

"Your insanity act. I don't know how you did it for so long."

"A man facing the chair, he'll do about anything to avoid it."

"It may not be the chair what gets you. Old Tom was pretty popular in this town."

Marshall squinted at the other prisoner in concern and turned to the window in the outside wall of his cell. He grunted as he stood and shuffled across the pitching deck. He grabbed the bars in the windowsill for balance and squinted to let his eyes adjust to the sunlight. Below, he saw a small group of men in a cluster across the street. They talked to each other as they stared at the jail.

At this angle, he was above the outside door that led into Pack's apartment. A road ran beside the jailhouse, and across the road was a large lot behind a hotel and theater.

The construction of the Connellee Hotel had been on-again, off-again the whole time he was growing up in the county, but the ambitious project looked finished and open for business now. For the past several nights, as he lay in his false paralysis, faint strains of live music had wafted into his cell, and he figured it must have come through the open windows of the banquet hall he could now see up on the top of the eight-story building.

To the left of the lot was the back of the Connellee Theater. Marshall had been to a show at the theater once as a teenager. Not to see the Broadway tours that oilmen brought in during the boom. Even with the money Marshall got from robbing moonshine stills, he could never afford the grand productions. Instead, he put his money down for the film, *The Covered Wagon*, and sat with several hundred in crushed velvet seats. As someone in the orchestra pit plinked on a piano, up on the screen trail guides on horseback led ambitious families across the Old West.

He smiled at the memory, but his eyes returned to the men talking together in the open lot. They were too far away for Marshall to hear anything distinct, but he knew it had to do with him. A man in the center of the crowd gestured furiously at the jail with the lit end of a cigar as he spoke to the others, and they nodded.

Let them grouse out there all day if they didn't have anything better to do, he thought. They didn't know the whole story. All Tom had to do was hand over the keys and nothing would have happened.

He lay down and managed to doze for a couple of hours. When he woke, he couldn't hear any noise. Satisfied that the men had drifted off to their homes, he shuffled to the window again. The men had not left. The crowd was even larger, gathered in five clusters at different points of the street and the open lot. He saw mostly men, but a few women and children hovered, too.

The crowd continued to swell throughout the afternoon and into the early evening. Marshall lay on his bunk, listening to the low hum of hundreds of voices through the window. Pack was in the corridor, collecting the empty supper trays, when a voice called up the stairwell.

"Daddy, you up there?"

"Here, son."

A young man about Marshall's age appeared in front of his cell. "I ain't never seen nothing like it. I'll bet there's a thousand people out there."

"No one gave you any trouble as you came through the crowd, I don't imagine."

"No, sir. I think most of them are just here for news on Uncle Tom. But there's maybe two hundred men near the building that seems like they want us to give them"—he glanced at Marshall—"more than news."

"I don't think so, son. They're a little worked up, is all. They'll blow off some steam and go home soon enough."

"Well, maybe or maybe not. I don't like the way some of them tried to follow me into the residence before I could close the door."

Pack squinted at his son, a faint look of concern on his face. "Your mother and sister alright down there?"

"They're uneasy."

"Well, you sit with them at the kitchen table while I go out and talk with the men at our door."

"You think that's a good idea, Daddy? With the sheriff off to Huntsville with one prisoner and the deputy off to the state asylum with another? Maybe it's best we keep things locked down and wait out the night."

"Aw, now, you're making too much of this. I expect I know just about everyone out there."

Pack and his son descended the stairs, and Marshall crept to the side of the window and listened. The residence door opened and shut, and Pack's voice came from the stoop.

"Folks, I know you want news on Tom."

A voice near the jail called out, "Your boy come from the hospital just now. Uncle Tom's dead, ain't he?"

Another voice growled, "We want action."

It wasn't loud, and Marshall doubted the outer bands of the crowd had even heard it. They remained silent, probably waiting for Pack to finish telling them about the old jailer.

Pack continued. "Tom's still with us. The news ain't no different than it was this afternoon. Now, everyone go home and we'll all know more tomorrow."

In the silence that followed, Marshall could hear Pack opening the residence door.

Near the jail, another man's voice rose. "Let us have him, Pack."

Marshall peeked out the window, and below him about twenty men surged toward the open door. The wave stopped suddenly, and the men shuffled backward until Marshall could see the top of Pack's head. The jailer had his hands on the chests of two men, and he was gently pushing the crowd back down the stairs of the stoop.

Pack held up his hands to the crowd of men around him. "Now look, boys. This is my own home you're trying to come through, and my family's inside. Just be patient. You know the Appeals Court is going to confirm the conviction and Marshall Ratliff is going to pay for his crimes."

A voice shouted, "He's takin' the scenic route," and there was some harsh laughter at this.

Someone said, "What about old Tom?"

Another voice. "That's right. How many more good men are going to die while things drag on?"

The crowd surged up the stoop again, and this time, hands reached out for Pack and pulled him away from the door. The jailer struggled against them, but he was outnumbered, and they wrestled him to the ground. Pack's son ran out the door to his father's aid, but men pulled his arms behind his back and restrained him. The jailer's pockets were searched, and a voice shouted in triumph, "I got the keys."

Marshall's eyes widened in panic as he saw twenty men flow into the jailer's apartment. From below came the sound of furniture crashing, and a scream of alarm from Pack's wife, and then the heavy thud of multiple boots on the iron stairway. A man appeared in front of Marshall's cell, yelling, "Here he is." Men crowded at the bars and stared at him, grim and determined.

Marshall had his back against the wall under the window, watching a man unsuccessfully try one key after another. Each discarded key meant they were getting closer to the one that would work, and he slid down the wall, moaning in terror.

The lock finally turned, and five men rushed into the cell with arms stretched toward him. Marshall scrambled under the bunk and gripped the frame, but they pulled on the fabric of his pants until his legs were out from under the bed. The pants slipped free of his gaunt waist, and finger-nails scratched and dug into his bare skin as men tried to find a grip on his flailing legs.

They yanked him out from under the bunk, but he kicked free of their hands and scrambled away. The men closed in on him again and grabbed at him, but he twisted until all they had was his shirt in their hands. He ran naked to the back corner of the cell, reaching up the wall as if to find handholds to crawl away from the crowd. They drew him toward them and bound his hands behind him.

When the mob emerged from the jailer's residence with Marshall, most of the crowd gasped at the naked and bound prisoner. But they didn't leave.

Someone growled out the order, "Bring him over to the utility poles there."

The men who held Marshall pushed their way through the crowd until they stood under a support cable strung between two poles. As the crowd parted, a man threw a rope above him with a noose tied at the end. The noose sailed high in the air, arced over the cable, and dropped, coming to a stop with a slight bounce in front of Marshall's face. He whimpered and struggled against the cords that held his hands behind his back. His ankles were tied together, and they draped the noose over his head and snugged the knot to his neck. A dozen men grabbed the other end of the rope, and with a fierce surge, they yanked him violently into the air.

He soared up into the night sky, and then plummeted to the ground in a heap. The powerful yank across the cable had snapped the rope.

Marshall lay in the dust. A sharp pain in both ankles and his left hip provoked a reflexive attempt to gasp, but nothing filled his lungs. He began to wag his head in hopes it would loosen the knot. Someone reached down and released the rope from his neck, and he sucked air in gulps.

"God, oh God," he moaned. "Have mercy on me. Somebody."

A man said, "I've got a new rope in my truck. Three-quarter-inch hemp. It'll do the job. You know where I'm parked."

"Make him decent," another voice said. "There are women and children in the crowd."

They stood him up and tied a gunnysack around his waist, cinching it tight with a length of the rope that had just failed to hang him.

A woman called out from back in the crowd, "That broke rope was a sign from the Lord, boys. This ain't your business."

But the gang under the support cable ignored her. They tied a noose with the new rope and tossed it over the cable. As they snugged it in place, someone said, "Don't try to break his neck this time. Just get him up in the air and let the knot do the work."

Two men got him up on their shoulders and Marshall squinted in the glare of vehicle headlamps that lit up the scene.

A voice called out from the crowd, "Maybe he has something he wants to say."

One of the men who held Marshall on his shoulder said, "You got any last words?"

"Let me down and I'll talk."

They lowered him to the ground again.

As things got quiet for him to speak, he was distracted by music coming from the eighth floor of the Connellee Hotel. Far above, tuxedoed men and their dates leaned out the windows. A live song fell apart as the members of the band joined the crowd to gawk down at the spectacle.

Marshall shuddered at the pain in his hip and ankles, but he straightened his bare torso to address the people surrounding him. Those closest to him maintained angry and resolute expressions, but farther out were looks of horror and bewilderment from people who clearly had not come to the jail for this. Those were the ones he could reach, and they far outnumbered the ones who seemed determined to lynch him.

Marshall flicked his head to get a strand of hair out of his eyes. "Folks, I done wrong. I did. But I just need a chance to—"

Someone interrupted him: "What's he saying?"

"I just need a chance to—"

Another voice called out, "I can't understand him."

Marshall hesitated. Some of the people were leaning in, confused, like he had been speaking a foreign language. Helpfully, he raised his voice and spoke more slowly. "It's cold out here. Have mercy. Let me go back in that prison and—"

A man next to him said, "He's talking gibberish."

Marshall stood open-mouthed, confounded at their inability to understand him.

Another man growled, "Enough nonsense. String him up and make a good job of it this time."

The men hoisted him on their shoulders again, and the slack went from the rope. Slowly he was lifted by the neck until he was free of the men's shoulders and swaying in midair. He continued to rise until he could see even those on the outer edge of the huge crowd. Faces panned across his vision in a swirl as his thrashing spun him in a sluggish clockwise turn.

He could draw no air through his mouth, and he began to spasm. He tried to raise his hands to pull the rope from his neck, but his hands remained securely tied behind his back, and all the twisting to free them made the noose even tighter. His eyeballs bulged and red stars exploded in front of him like bursts of fireworks. Then everything went black.

THE BUCKING STOPPED, and the hangmen tied the rope to the utility pole and stood back to watch the body sway in the garish light of the head-lamps of a dozen cars and trucks. The burlap that hung loosely over the hips flapped mildly in the chill breeze. The body made a quarter-turn clockwise and finally stopped.

A new man pushed his way through the crowd. He gaped at the body, and then glared grimly at the men around him. "What have you gone and done?" He pointed to the end of the rope tied to the pole. "Take the body down."

An unidentified voice rumbled, "Let it hang there."

"No. None of this was legal. Or moral."

"It was necessary."

"Do you know who I am? I'll start calling for arrests if I have to. I'm telling you, bring the body down."

A few men untied the rope, lowered the body, and removed the noose from the neck. As they carried the body away, the crowd fell upon the cord. Men, teenagers, and even some women each cut off a few inches for a souvenir. In minutes, only a few yards were left of the rope that had taken the life of the Santa Claus bank robber.

TOM JONES DIED of his gunshot wounds the next morning. Throughout the day, several thousand people filed by the Barrow Furniture Store, where the body of his killer had been propped up in an open coffin for display. Finally, city authorities ordered the body locked away from view. It would hardly serve to allow the gawking to continue once the county prosecutor ordered an investigation into the illegal hanging.

Joe Frank Sparks called fifty men to testify before a grand jury, but no one said they could identify anyone who had participated in the lynching.

The attorney threw up his hands and growled at the last subpoenaed witness, "Are you telling me that a thousand people could be on hand, and no one can remember a familiar face in the whole mob?"

The witness said, "Well, sir, it's like this. I don't suppose nobody wants nobody to go to jail for this. You cain't deny the man deserved what he got. All these delays, all this coddling of someone who used two of our girls as shields and traded gunfire with our officers." The man pointed a finger at the prosecutor. "It's been two years without justice, Mr. Sparks. I say if the Law cain't do the job, men 'll find a way to do it theirselves."

Sparks didn't respond to the personal attack. "But you tell us you weren't one of those men."

"No, sir."

"And you're claiming you don't remember seeing anyone you recognized."

"No, sir."

"You do understand that most every newspaper editorial in the state—in the nation, even—is calling our town barbaric?"

"Well, Mr. Sparks, I cain't say as I agree or care."

The investigation into the lynching ended a day later, with the prosecutor unable to indict a single person.

RILLA CARTER ARRANGED for her son's body to be transported to Fort Worth for burial. On Saturday, a small group gathered with her in the mortuary chapel. After the service, they filed out behind the coffin to the hearse.

A small parade approached them with drums and brass instruments, led by a man dressed as Santa Claus.

Rilla gasped in dismay. "What is this?" she stammered at the funeral director, her voice quavering with emotion. "Who are these people who've come even here to mock my boy?"

The funeral director stepped out into the street and waved the parade to silence. One by one, the drumming stopped, the trumpets faded, and the entire mob faced Rilla.

The director returned to Rilla's side and pointed out the name of a department store on sandwich boards carried by two women dressed as elves. "It's only a Christmas promotional for a local store, Mrs. Carter. I'm so sorry. I doubt they even know who the funeral is for."

Santa removed his red cap in respect, and the band passed the hearse in silence. When the parade got a block away, the raucous holiday music started up again.

16

THE LAST MAN

Bobby was in Louisiana when he read the newspaper report on the lynching. It was confirmation that he had made a good decision to run. To his mind, Joe Frank Sparks would have taken another swipe at him just like he did Marshall.

He put down the ragged days-old newspaper. The hobo jungle around him was beginning to stir. It was just a small clearing in the woods not far from the railroad, no different than any of the others he had wandered into the last two months. A few men in tattered clothing reignited the campfires that had gone cold in the night. One man, his face shadowed with whiskers, pulled a short stub of cold cigar from his pocket, and lit it with a flaming twig from the campfire. Another walked into camp tittering triumphantly as he unveiled eggs he said he lifted from a nearby henhouse. Someone set water to boil in a scorched tin can, and the man lowered the eggs carefully into the water. Bobby made a quick count of the eggs and the men surrounding the campfire. It looked like enough for everyone. He wouldn't miss out this time.

Local cops raided these sites every so often. Mostly it was to scatter the drifters away to the next town, but sometimes they'd collar one or two and take them in just to see if anyone matched the dispatches on their bulletin boards. For that reason, he avoided the jungles as much as he could. But loneliness would get the best of him, and he would find a camp and stay for a few days. Wherever he went, the talk was of failure. Savings gone after a bank failure, property gone after a crop failure, jobs gone after a factory failure. If someone asked about him, he'd put himself as the main character of a down-and-out sob story he had heard in a previous camp. Men would nod in sympathy and offer him a cup of bitter coffee, or the remaining hunk of a stale loaf flecked with gray-green blooms of mold.

He picked up odd jobs at a farm or a warehouse when he could. He never stayed more than a day before he was off again, finding a spot where trains slowed down enough for him to hop aboard an empty freight car if the bulls weren't watching.

The scenery changed outside the open boxcars as winter gave way to spring. He let the trains take him on a long, meandering arc around the Texas border. Arkansas to Oklahoma to Kansas to New Mexico. At first, he had no plan other than to keep moving. But a vague idea of disappearing into Mexico formed in his mind, and more and more, he chose southbound trains. In May 1930, he found himself in El Paso.

On the first afternoon in the border town, he stood on the sidewalk in the back of a Salvation Army soup line. As he craned his neck to see how many people were in front of him, a cop appeared up ahead. The officer didn't seem to be doing anything but chatting with the tired and ragged men in line, but Bobby got nervous and slipped away. That evening, he lay down on the back porch of an abandoned house and fell asleep.

The next morning before dawn, he snuck behind a diner and lifted the lid of a trash can to see what had been thrown away from the night before.

"I can make you a real plate if you want one."

He jumped at the voice and turned around. A man in his fifties stood behind the screen door that led into the back of the diner.

Bobby put the lid back on the trash can. "I'd like that, yes, sir."

"You can wash your hands at the hose there, and I'll be right back."

Bobby turned on the spigot and rinsed his grimy hands and face and waited by the door with his cap in his hands. The man returned with a plate loaded with scrambled eggs and sausage links and three biscuits. Bobby quickly tucked his cap into the back of his waistband and took the plate with a nod of thanks. He tried to keep composed in front of the man, but at the first bite of the eggs, he whimpered and began to shovel the food into his mouth.

"I'll get us some coffee," the man said, and disappeared into the back of the diner. He returned with two steaming cups. Bobby had the plate scraped clean and the last biscuit in his hand. He tried to offer the plate to the man, who raised the two cups with a shrug. Bobby held the biscuit in his mouth and took one of the cups with his free hand and gave the plate over. The man laughed pleasantly at the awkward juggling exchange, and Bobby took the biscuit from his mouth and smiled, too.

He took a sip of the coffee and inspected the biscuit. "Your oven cooks even. A lot more even than the one I used. We had to tend it, or we'd get the biscuits brown on the bottom and doughy in the middle, or they'd be cooked through in the middle but black on the bottom. I ain't had better biscuits than these here. Thank you again."

"You have experience in a kitchen?"

Bobby regretted letting the food and the kindness make him so free with his talk. He nodded in response to the question while trying to figure out what lie he would have to tell if the man asked anything else about his past.

The man pointed inside with his thumb. "You want some work?"

Bobby stammered. "You mean in your diner? For the day?"

"If that's all you got time for. But my cook's gone, and if you know your way around a kitchen, I can put you to work as long as you want. What's your name?"

"Bobby—" He paused. His last name couldn't be used, no matter how common it was.

The man in the diner didn't seem to notice the hesitation. "Mine's Herb Lashee, Bobby." Herb held out his hand.

Bobby took it and completed the introduction. "Davis—Bobby Davis."

He didn't know why he had used that last name for his alias. He hadn't thought about poor Louis Davis for three years.

"I expect you'll need a room. There's one over the kitchen where the last cook stayed. It ain't much, but it'll keep you out of the rain. I'll give you room and board and five dollars a week for some walking-around money. Can you start now?"

Bobby gave the man an astonished grin, and stammered, "This morning? Yes, sir, I could . . . Thank you."

"Well, you'll have to bathe yourself and wash those clothes another time because the diner opens in fifteen minutes. Just remove your collared shirt and cook in your T-shirt this morning. No one's going to see much of you through the serving window, anyhow."

Bobby had grits on to boil and was cracking eggs into a mixing bowl when a middle-aged woman walked in the kitchen and hung her purse on a peg. She regarded Bobby a moment and said, "Where's Chuck?"

Bobby assumed she was talking to him, and he shrugged. But Herb walked from the pantry with a sack of flour and answered her. "Chuck had his last argument with his last customer. I told him not to come back."

"So, you picked up another stray."

Herb gave her a tolerant smile. "I can always count on you to make someone feel welcome, Claire. This here's Bobby."

She rubbed the corner of her mouth and checked her finger for lipstick. "I'll bother to remember his name if he stays more than three months. For now, he's just Cookie to me, like all the rest."

After the café closed and the cleaning was done, Bobby climbed the stairs to the room that Herb had promised him. Herb's wife had set out a new razor for him, and soap and a fresh towel. He shaved his face and took a long soak in the tub. The narrow bed was made up with laundered sheets, and he slipped between them and settled into a deep, contented sleep.

Herb paid him his five dollars at the end of the workweek, and Bobby got a haircut and bought some new socks and underwear from a small department store. He spent the next few paydays at a secondhand shop, where he found a shirt and a pair of trousers in good condition and shoes his size that weren't too worn, and he replaced his shapeless jacket and sweat-stained cap. After months of wondering if a day would end without any meal, it was good to have three squares every day, and he could tell from his reflection in the mirror that his face was filling back out.

BOBBY STOOD AT the sink scouring a pot, listening to Claire humming as she wiped down the tables. The diner had closed for the day, and Herb was at the bank making a deposit.

"Your pies were popular today, Bobby." Claire spoke it loud enough to be heard in the kitchen.

"What happened to 'Cookie'?

She brought more dishes to the sink for him to wash. "I keep my word. You've stayed long enough, so now you're 'Bobby.'"

"I'm grateful for the work."

"Grateful don't seem to be enough to keep someone in place these days. Herbie's had six men at the grill in the last eight months. And it ain't never been from a proper want ad in the newspaper. It's always strays like you."

She tousled his hair to show him she didn't mean anything by the comment, and she helped him rinse and stack the washed dishes in the strainer. "I think he's rescuing his son by rescuing the likes of you."

"What happened to his son?"

"Herbie's boy had ambitions. Rose up to bank manager at a real young age and was doing good until the stock market crash."

"Stock market crash?"

The line of her rouged lips quirked in surprised confusion. "Back in the fall, end of October."

When he still stared blankly at her, she put her hands on her hips. "My word, you've been riding the rails a long time if you hadn't heard of that. It was in all the papers. New York stockbrokers jumped from ten-story windows. People panicked and withdrew their money from the banks and a lot of banks collapsed. Factories closed. Farms got repossessed. I read unemployment's upward of twenty percent or so these days."

He thought of all the drifters he had shared campfires and boxcars with over the last six months. All their individual stories were part of a much larger drama he had never known about.

"The bank Herbie's son managed was one of them what failed. It broke his son. Just broke him. He up and disappeared one day, left his wife and baby girl behind. I think he was just too ashamed."

She shook her head and sighed. "Last we heard, he was spotted in a soup line in San Antonio. Herbie went there hoping to find him but never did. I'm guessing Herbie figures if he can't help his son, then he wants to help any drifter who reminds him of his son."

The story stopped, and Claire appraised him.

Bobby grinned self-consciously. "What?"

"You really do look like him. In a way."

ON CHRISTMAS EVE, after the diner closed for the holiday and Bobby put away the last clean dish and hung up his apron, Herb entered the kitchen. He fidgeted with a box wrapped in bright-silver paper and then held it out.

"Merry Christmas, Bobby."

Bobby gave Herb an uncertain grin as he accepted the gift. He ripped off the paper and opened the box. Inside he found a new pocketknife enclosed in a smooth wooden handle with a rich stain finish.

"Well, uh . . . ," Herb began, and trailed off.

Bobby realized he had been staring at the gift for so long, the silence had become awkward. He looked up from the box. "Last time I had a Christmas gift, I was maybe seven."

"Never since?"

Never since. At Gatesville one Christmas, he and the boys got some presents from a women's charity group. While they were out working in a field, the women had stacked the boxes in the cafeteria near a big, decorated tree and left. The boys found the presents at dinner. It was a nice surprise, but it wasn't like they had him in mind.

Herb smiled. "Well, I hope you like it, Bobby. You have a merry Christmas, son."

Bobby reached out to shake Herb's hand, and stammered, "You have a merry Christmas, too, Mr. Lashee."

THREE WEEKS LATER, the box sat on the bureau of his room where he had first laid it. The pocketknife was still inside it, and the torn Christmas paper was still beside it. Bobby had not removed the knife from the box even to unfold it and see what the blade looked like. To his mind, it didn't belong to him. It belonged to the son Herb longed for. It was time to go to Mexico, as Bobby had intended when he first landed here.

On Friday afternoon, he went to a pawnshop. A fat man sat at the cash register, and in the glass counter below him was a handgun.

Bobby pointed to it. "What's that .38 cost with a handful of bullets?" He hadn't resolved yet if he wanted it for a stickup in Mexico or just for protection. Either way, he planned on carrying it across.

The man's arms were folded over his chest and resting on his gut. "With the ammo, twenty-five dollars." He said it like he couldn't care less whether he made the sale or not.

Bobby paid the man and pocketed the pistol, but he didn't leave.

"Anything else?" the man asked.

Bobby reached into his pocket, hesitated, then pulled out a box and put it on the counter. "What will you give me for this?"

The fat man opened the box. In it was the knife Herb had given Bobby for Christmas.

The cashier pulled out the blade and snapped it back in place. "Good steel . . . strong tension . . . beautiful handle . . . kinda small." He stared at it, running a calculation in his head. "I can give you three dollars."

"I figure it's worth at least ten."

"Take it or leave it."

After a pause, Bobby nodded, but he frowned as the man pulled the box off the glass top and put it on the counter behind him. When the man lay three dollars on the counter, Bobby shoved the bills into his pocket and left. He didn't like how he felt inside, and he didn't know how to repair it.

Bobby decided he'd wait until Saturday evening to leave. Since the café was closed on Sunday, Herb would at least have a day to make other arrangements for a cook. He planned to tell Herb when he got his week's pay, but when Bobby stood in front of Herb on Saturday night, he couldn't work up the nerve. He received his wages and mumbled, "Good night."

That evening, he gathered up his meager belongings and stepped outside. Nights had been mild for weeks until a front blew in and plummeted evening temperatures below freezing. He hunched his shoulders against the cold and started for the bridge that crossed into Juárez. When he got near it, he stopped at a place the streetlamp didn't reach. He stood in the midnight shadows for a long time and studied the empty bridge. Light spilled from the customs booth closest to him on the American side of the river. Two hundred yards away, a bare incandescent bulb glowed in a booth on the Mexican side.

Slow and casual, he told himself, and approached the bridge. He turned up his collar as if to block the chill wind, but mostly to keep his face hidden from the customs officer sitting behind the glass of the stateside cubicle. He kept moving. He wasn't required to stop on this side.

He was halfway across the Rio Grande when headlamps from a car behind him lit up the bridge. In the beams, his silhouette stretched and wavered toward the Mexican customs booth. Brakes whined faintly as the motor rig slowed to his pace, but he continued walking and kept his face forward. The car advanced into his sidelong view. Lamps like chrome cones rested on wide fenders that curved gracefully down to become running boards. A gold star was painted on the side, encircled with the words "City of El Paso Police Department."

Through the rolled-down window, a man in a Stetson spoke in an easy drawl. "It's a mighty cold night for a stroll."

Bobby continued toward the Mexican side of the bridge. "Yes, sir. Hoping to find a warm cantina."

The laid-back act from the man in the car continued. "Well, hold up a bit and let's talk about that."

The man put the car in park and let the engine idle as he stepped out. He was in plain clothes, but Bobby knew a detective when he saw one.

As the man approached, Bobby could think of no other option than to stand still.

The detective asked, "You got some ID?"

"Lost my wallet months ago. All I got is some folding money."

"What are you holding in your coat pockets?"

Bobby removed his hands. "Just keeping my hands warm."

The man reached for Bobby and patted the pockets. "Well, now." He pulled out the .38. "This is a special kind of hand warmer."

"No telling what I'll run into across the border."

"I expect that's right. Still, why don't you come along with me for a while?"

"You arresting me for something?"

"You're leaving your homeland with no ID and a pistol you wouldn't tell me you had. Let's just say that bears looking into." He gave Bobby a reassuring smile. "All this will be cleared up quick. At least the car's warm." The lawman tucked Bobby's pistol into his own coat pocket and led him by the elbow.

They drove to the police station. At the counter, he gave his name as Bobby Davis, and the clerk put an ink pad in front of him.

"Give me your left hand."

Bobby hesitated. "You know I work at a diner here in town. My boss is going to need me in a few hours."

The detective who had brought him in stood close behind him. "Well, in a few hours, we'll have you back there." He was still using that friendly tone. "I'll drive you myself."

When the fingerprinting was finished, Bobby was put in a holding cell in the corner of a room where the detectives had their desks.

THE NIGHT CAME and went, and by late morning, the investigator who had detained him was back in front of the cell. He concentrated on tamping tobacco into his pipe and spoke casually, like he was reporting the time.

"Robert M. Hill."

Bobby remained on the bench and didn't say anything.

The detective struck a match and put it to the pipe, sucking the flame into the bowl until the tobacco glowed red. Two uniformed officers joined him at the cage, and he said, "Boys, this man here escaped a ninety-nine-year sentence nearly a year and a half ago. You remember that account of thirteen men tunneling out of one of the work farms? This is the last of them right here."

The two officers nodded, and they narrowed their eyes at Bobby, as if noticing a menace about him that they had missed before. Bobby dropped his gaze to a spot on the floor between his feet.

"Mr. Hill, the Eastland County sheriff is coming down himself. Seems they have a warrant for your arrest on two counts of murder. The murder of two lawmen, no less."

Bobby continued to stare at the spot on the floor. "I didn't kill no one. I didn't even shoot no one."

"Well, that's for a jury to decide now."

Bobby raised his head to face the investigator. "What made you think to stop me on the bridge?"

The man pulled on his pipe and then released a cloud of smoke that hovered around his head. "Experience, I suppose. You looked nervous in a guilty sort of way."

"You weren't watching for me?"

"Watching for you? Son, I had to sift pretty deep in our stack of dispatches till I found a photo with your big ears. I had about decided to let you go before I came across your mug shot." The detective chuckled. "You should of stayed on at that diner you say you work at. No one ever would of found you if you hadn't been so afraid of being found."

The detective sat at his desk and scratched answers on a form with a pencil. On the wall beside the desk hung a large calendar with a painting of a cattle drive. In the foreground, a steer was breaking away from the herd. In the background, a cowboy was cutting his horse in the direction of the escaping beast, his reins in one hand while his other hand reached for a lasso.

Bobby leaned back and let a long sighing breath out through his nose.

ONCE IN EASTLAND, Bobby was indicted for murder, to which he pled not guilty. He was assigned the same court-appointed lawyer from his first trial, L. H. Flewellen. As they sat together to plan the defense, the attorney asked him for details on his time at the Walls and on the prison farms, and what he had done during his sixteen months in the free world.

When Bobby told him about the City Diner in El Paso, Flewellen raised an eyebrow. "You had steady work for a stretch?"

"Nearabout eight months, I reckon."

"Did you have a good relationship with your boss? Meaning, you never stole anything, showed up on time, got along with the customers and other employees?"

"I liked him, and I'd say he felt the same about me while I was there. I don't know if things have changed now that the newspapers have reported on my past."

"Well, I'm going to call him and see if he'll come speak on your behalf. That gun you were caught with isn't going to help us, but a record of steady work might offset things."

The attorney paused. "This is beyond the scope of my duties with you, but I just got to say it. The jury took to your story back in '28. They gave you a chance the other juries didn't give to Mr. Helms and Mr. Ratliff. I don't understand you running away from that kindness."

When Bobby didn't reply, Flewellen pulled a manila folder from his briefcase and began to read the papers inside it. Bobby had never really considered the jury's life sentence as a kindness he had run from. But then his thoughts went to Willie at Wynne and to Herb in El Paso. Maybe he did run from kindness.

He slouched back in the chair. "You still think I'm like that Sean character?"

Flewellen looked up from his reading. "Hmm? What's that?"

"In my trial, you told the jury I was like the orphan in that novel. The one who was shown mercy and he grew up and did something with his life."

"Ah, Jean Valjean." The attorney smiled, a distant look in his eyes. "I did use that reference with the jury, didn't I?"

"I've done run two times now. Well, three times, come to think of it. I guess I ain't your Jean Valjean after all."

"He still has you beat."

"What do you mean?"

"In the story, Valjean escaped from prison four times. I don't recommend you try to match his record, but there it is. I'd say you still got time to be the Valjean of your own story."

ON THE DAY before the trial, boots echoed on the iron stairs and Pack Kilborn entered the west side of the Eastland County prison where Bobby was stationed. He was escorting Herb Lashee.

Pack pointed Herb to the long, narrow table and bench that served as the visitors' area. "Sit here and I'll get him."

Bobby never had a visitor other than his court-appointed lawyer. Three years ago, Bobby got melancholy whenever Marshall and Henry sat there with family members. Now he had a visitor of his own, but the thought of this encounter made his insides knot. Herb appeared no more comfortable than Bobby felt. He was taking in the dim surroundings as he rubbed his hands nervously on his knees.

Pack handcuffed Bobby and escorted him to the table, where he freed one of the wrists to attach the cuff to a bar. "I'll be back in ten minutes unless one of you calls for me first."

Bobby lit a cigarette to calm his nerves. "I wasn't sure you'd come."

"Of course, I was going to come, Bobby."

Bobby flicked ash on the floor and hesitated. He wanted to say it, to confess it, but why? To repair things? To end things? He had to blurt it out before he lost his courage. "I pawned the pocketknife you gave me for Christmas. I took three dollars for it. I had enough money, but I pawned it anyway."

A brief flicker of disappointment crossed Herb's face, and Bobby waited for it. He waited for the man to stand and walk out. Bobby was eight years old again, his little hands pressed to the window in the administrator's office in Gatesville as he watched the man whose name he bore get in a car and drive away.

Herb spoke quietly. "Well, son. It was yours to do with what you wanted."

The man wasn't driving away.

Bobby swallowed a lump that had formed in his throat. "I regret it." The cigarette trembled in his fingers as he raised it to his lips, and he blew out the smoke in a faint whistle. He continued. "Someone told me I run from kindness." He fidgeted with the cigarette. "Maybe I don't trust it."

"Maybe you don't feel like you deserve it."

Bobby hadn't thought about things from that angle, but it rang true.

He said, "I don't deserve it."

Herb frowned and seemed to be assembling the right words in his mind. "Well"—he paused and cleared his throat—"I don't suppose kindness is for those that's deserving, Bobby. It's for those that's loved."

WHEN THE MURDER trial began, Joe Frank Sparks called the same witnesses that had testified in the trials held three years earlier. Some of the witnesses had moved away from the county and were subpoenaed back. Once again, Flewellen's defense strategy was to highlight the fact that not one witness could recall Bobby shooting anyone, and he had Bobby share his life of hardship as he had done in the first trial. Bobby swore he had gone straight while on the run. In his witness testimony, Herb Lashee reinforced this portrayal, testifying that Bobby had been a reliable and trustworthy employee.

The jury recessed to decide their verdict, and several hours later, they returned to the courtroom to report they were unable to come to a unanimous decision. While ten jurors had voted for the death penalty, two refused to agree with the rest, despite multiple ballots. The judge declared a mistrial, overruling the objection of Joe Frank Sparks. Bobby would serve out his original ninety-nine-year sentence.

THEY SENT HIM to the Eastham Farm, and here most men wore the same stripes he was wearing, because Eastham was where they put those deemed incorrigible. He was placed on a chain gang assigned to dig out the sides and bottoms of ditches, repairing the erosion from the winter rains. Before dawn, the men started a mile-long lope on foot to the work site. Though the leg chains reduced their strides to a short pigeon-toed shuffle, the high riders on horseback pushed them into a trot, and they were in the ditches by the time the sun rose above the low trees. Over and over, they sliced their shovels into the heavy, damp soil and flung it high enough to clear the ditch. As the sun reached the treetops in the west, the men made the weary jog back to the unit. Right after supper, Bobby dropped his exhausted body into bed, only to wake up stiff and aching. Over the weeks of this daily routine, his muscles grew hard, and his hands formed tough callouses.

In August, his crew was transferred to the fields to get the cotton in. Back in the Wynne Unit, life moved slow among the old and frail, but it wasn't like that in the Ham, as convicts dubbed Eastham. Here the bosses drove the men to work faster, with no mercy for those who fell behind. One afternoon, Bobby saw a man collapse from the heat and exhaustion, and a high rider brought his horse between the rows of cotton and guided a heavy hoof to come down on the prone form to make sure he wasn't faking it. The man didn't respond to the crushing weight, and the high rider commanded the crew to bring him to the infirmary in a donkey-drawn cart.

Those who didn't collapse were punished if they didn't work at a speed that satisfied the bosses. The forms of punishment were as diverse as a guard's imagination. Men were whipped with rope that had been soaked in water and dragged through the sand to make it heavy and gritty when it came down on bare skin. One convict in the bunkhouse was made to straddle a tall sawhorse until his crotch went numb and the man waddled bowlegged for days after. Men were left for hours hanging on a pulley by the wrist chains, their toes raking the floorboards of the bunkhouse. Other men were made to stand on the narrow top of a barrel throughout the night while the others slept. The next morning, they would be allowed to step down in time to join the crew for a quick breakfast before loping out to the fields.

The worst Bobby could imagine, though, was being isolated in the "hot box." It was a small concrete closet off the corridor that led from the dormitory to the dining hall. He and the other convicts had to pass the iron door of the hot box every day to get their meals, and the air around it stank. He didn't want to imagine what it was like to spend day upon day in the unventilated hole, curled up on the bare floor with nothing to do but slap mosquitoes or wave off the cloud of flies drawn to the open bucket of his own filth.

Bobby was spared the punishments he saw inflicted on others. While he had no ambition to be the pacesetter for the cotton pickers, he made sure not to fall behind the pacesetter, either. His attention narrowed down to three things each day. He watched the speed of the slowest pickers so he could stay ahead of them, he watched for the arrival of the John Henry, and he watched the spot above the tree line that the sun would have to reach before they would be ordered to stop for the day.

THE BELL RANG from the dinner wagon, and a guard said, "Alright, boys, John Henry's calling. Go get your meal."

Bobby shrugged off the strap of his long, narrow picker's sack, straightened in a stretch, and walked stiffly to the turn row. Two lines of tin plates and cups lay on the gravel, and servers were filling the plates with beans and cornbread and molasses. His crew sat along one line, and across the turn row, another crew emerged from the cotton and sat along the other line of plates. Servers filled the plates and the men tucked in. A high rider sat in the saddle watching them. He held the reins in one hand and a shotgun in the other, the butt of the stock resting on his thigh and the barrel pointing to the sky. Behind him, heat waves shimmered on the edges of the field, and cicadas spun up a long, droning buzz in the ash tree where the other bosses sat under the shade.

A man on the other crew stared at him through the meal. Finally, he pointed at Bobby with his remaining nub of cornbread. "I know you." He swallowed and smacked. "You're Bobby Hill, ain't you? From the Wynne Farm."

"I was at Wynne, yeah."

"Me too." He gestured at one of his brogans crossed in front of him. "Till my foot got better and I got sent back to the Ham."

Bobby nodded. He had known the same men at Wynne. Heel stringers. Convicts who deliberately damaged their Achilles tendon to get out of the fields for a month or two in the hospital.

The man took a swig of water from his tin cup and wiped his chin. He glanced at the bosses and lowered his voice. "That escape tunnel was something else. You know they caught ever'one but you in a few weeks. After all this time, we figured you was gone for good."

Bobby shrugged and took a bite of cornbread.

The man continued: "Wasn't you in the kitchen with all those white boys taking orders from the darkie—what was his name?"

"Willie."

"You know he's gone."

"What farm did the captain bring him to?"

"No, brother. Gone. He's dead."

A chill crawled up Bobby's sweat-streaked spine. "Dead?"

"The captain lost his position at Wynne after the escape. No word whether they fired him or demoted him to another spot in the system. All anyone knew was he wasn't captain on none of the farms after that. It wasn't too many days later the guards found old Willie laid out behind the kitchen one morning. They figured it had to be two or three as ganged up on him with shivs, on account of he was stabbed all in the gut and chest and neck."

The man reported all this like he expected Bobby to be glad to hear it for having suffered the humiliation of taking orders on Willie's crew. Bobby didn't give him any reason to think otherwise, but throughout the afternoon, the old man was on his mind. He thought of their smoke breaks together on the back steps. He remembered the shouts of triumph from Willie's preaching that carried through the open windows. Mostly, though, it was his confident and serene face that played before Bobby's mind. Willie had lived for the proud smile of the daddy he was always talking about.

"Quittin' time."

The announcement from the high rider surprised Bobby, and he scanned the sky for the location of the sun. With all his memories of Willie occupying the afternoon hours, the sun had sunk to the tree line without Bobby once measuring its progress. He trotted with his crew down the long road back to the prison dorm, their leg chains tinkling across the gravel.

BEFORE THE LIGHTS-OUT signal, two guards entered the bunkhouse. They talked with one of the convicts, who stiffened and then shook his head in protest. Bobby couldn't hear the first part of their conversation, but when the rest of the men in the bunkhouse noticed the argument, the noise died down enough for everyone to hear.

"I kept up, boss, I kept up as best I could."

"That ain't the way Boss Heim here tells it."

"I had the trots all last night, boss. You ask the building tender right there. Even so, I did my best in the fields. I did."

"You didn't keep up, so you get the box. Now come on."

"I . . . I—hold on, now," he said, as each guard took him by an elbow. "This ain't right. I want to talk to who's in charge here."

The guards ignored him as they escorted him out. He whined again, "Who's in charge here?"

The building tender ordered everyone to their bunks, and they lay in silence, listening to the man's useless protests. Even as the guards shut the man in the hot box, he kept up his objections. The cry came muffled from behind the door, but Bobby could still hear it. "Who's in charge here?"

A pause. "Tell me!"

A kick thudded against the thick door, followed by frustrated sobs.

Bobby lay in his bunk thinking about the man's question. He wanted to know who was in charge here, too. If the only answer was the bosses and their random sadistic authority, he may as well get it over with. Just find something sharp enough and be done with this life sentence.

Phrases of conversations from the past swirled together in his mind like the confluence of storm-swollen streams.

When my father and my mother forsake me, then the Lord will take me up.

I don't suppose kindness is for those that's deserving. It's for those that's loved.

Ye shall be my sons and daughters, saith the Lord Almighty.

You still got time to be the Valjean of your own story.

Who's in charge here?

Who? Who-o-o?

Bobby laced his fingers over his chest and whispered in the dark, "Alright, Willie. I'll try it your way."

17

ALL THROUGH THE NIGHT

Ten years. March 1941 marked ten years in the Ham. Bobby made the calculation as he lay in his bunk, the middle one in a stack of beds three high. He had awakened to sunlight instead of the predawn shout of the building tender because the work camp was given Sundays off. He rolled over on his stomach and stared through the window screen. Out in the yard, sunlight streamed across from the east at a sharp angle, turning the dew on the perimeter fence to diamonds.

The prison chaplain had come last week to lead a service, and his circuit wouldn't return him to Eastham again for another month. Instead, Bobby joined a small circle of men around two convicts who were passable with a guitar and a harmonica. The same musicians were known for belting out bawdy ballads all during the week, but on Sundays, Bobby had learned several hymns led by these improbable church choristers. He had even grown confident enough to sing along, and he joined them today.

He tended to lose track of which day it was during the week, but Sundays helped him mark the time. And Sundays continued to carry him through the seasons of the eleventh year of his life sentence. The springtime Sundays gave way to summer Sundays and then autumn Sundays.

THE FIRST SUNDAY afternoon in December, Bobby stood on the porch and smoked as the men fell into their various weekend routines. Some sat on picnic benches with visiting family members near the front gate. Some formed a circle and shouted encouragement at two men swinging at each other with fat boxing gloves. Others played checkers.

He flicked the nub of his cigarette into the yard and went back into the bunkhouse, where men gathered around the radio of a man everyone called Beanpole.

Bobby liked Beanpole, a tall, rail-thin man in his mid-thirties. He had been sent to prison for carjacking, but the longer Bobby got to know him, the more he suspected Beanpole's own account was the truth. The lanky man had been hitchhiking to find work in Houston and caught a ride. Beanpole didn't know the car was hot until the police arrested him and the driver right in the booth of a roadside diner. The thief claimed he had been the hitchhiker picked up by Beanpole, and the jury believed him. It was Beanpole who ended up at the Eastham farm, and he was only two years into a five-year sentence.

Despite his hard luck, his prominent buck teeth were often on display because so much amused him. Beanpole was laughing now as he turned up the volume on a Roy Acuff tune.

The building tender burst into the bunkhouse. "Change the station."

"Aw, no, BT," Beanpole protested. "This is my favorite song."

"Do it now. You're missing it. Hurry."

The building tender didn't need to explain which station to turn to. Only two signals reached this stretch of the Trinity River bottoms, and only when the conditions were right. Beanpole rolled the dial to the second station until an announcer's voice came through the intermittent crackle of static.

". . . this morning. We will report more details as we receive them. Again, the Japanese have attacked the naval base of Pearl Harbor in

Hawaii by air. It is reported that hundreds of servicemen have lost their lives. It has just been announced that President Roosevelt will address Congress tomorrow."

The station returned to its music program, but Beanpole switched it off, and the room descended into stunned silence.

Bobby could hear cheers from the spectators out in the yard where the boxing match ended. A few men entered the bunkhouse, and one of them was laughing loudly as he collected his winnings and arranged the dollars into a fan, which he waved playfully under the noses of the losers. The noise of the newcomers stopped when they saw the somber faces of the men still circling the mute radio.

The man holding up his dollar fan asked, "What's going on?"

Beanpole's constant grin was gone. "They attacked Pearl Harbor."

The fan was folded up and put away. "I have a brother in the navy."

"You think he was there?"

"He's somewhere in the Pacific. I don't know where he's stationed."

The building tender said, "America's in it now, boys."

OVER THE NEXT few months, rumors spread through Bobby's bunk-house of a growing need for new laborers in the factories and farms. Some convicts claimed that parole boards in every state were swamped with requests to fast-track clemency decisions so deserving men would be available to work. Bobby figured the rumors made sense. If hundreds of thousands of free men were enlisted in the war effort, there would be shortages in manpower at home.

IN JUNE, THE picket boss shouted Beanpole's name during mail call. The man retrieved his letter and returned to his bunk staring at the return address. He looked at Bobby in the bed above his. "It's from the parole board."

"Well, open it, Pole."

"What if they've turned me down?" Beanpole tapped the envelope gently on his leg a moment, then handed it up to Bobby. "Here. Read it for me."

"Aw, come on, now. It's addressed to you."

"Just tell me what it says."

Bobby pulled the stationary from the envelope and read the three-sentence form letter. He broke into a wide smile and leapt down to the floor. "It says you're getting out of here, Pole. You're getting out of here!"

Beanpole took the letter from Bobby's hand and read it for himself. He laughed, displaying his prominent buck teeth. "I'm getting out of here!"

Other men surrounded the bunk and slapped him on the back and congratulated him.

WHEN HIS RELEASE date came, Beanpole had his bedsheets stripped and his mattress folded in half as he waited to be carried to the Walls Unit.

He and Bobby faced each other, grinning self-consciously. Bobby finally spoke. "I guess I never asked where home is for you."

"Henderson. North of here about a hunnerd miles."

"What do you plan to do first?"

"Eat my momma's cooking till I'm near to bursting and take a long soak in my tub. Then I become a working man again, Bobby. The supervisor at the public works is expecting me in two days." He shook his head and grinned. "I ain't never looked forward to an old square john job like I'm looking forward to that one."

"Well, we're going to miss your radio around here."

"No, you're not, because I'm giving it to you."

"Aw, Pole, now that's too—"

Beanpole interrupted him. "My mind's made up on this point. It's yours. On one condition."

"Name it."

"That you pass it on to someone when you leave here."

"Then I guess it'll be mine for a long, long time, Pole. I figure I got nearly twenty more years till I'm eligible to apply for parole."

"Bobby, they got need of workers out there in the free world. This war's changed everything." Beanpole poked him in the chest. "And you've changed, too." His buck teeth jutted out from his wide grin. "I'm going to tell them about you at the public works, Bobby, and you can join me. So, you go ahead and be thinking about who you want to give that radio to."

He laughed and shook hands with Bobby and the other men as he headed out the door.

THAT NIGHT, BOBBY lay in bed thinking about Beanpole's words. He couldn't apply for parole. He had no momma to advocate on his behalf, and no wife to tell the board how hard life was without her breadwinner beside her. His escapes had been all over the newspapers. He had a long record of good behavior now, but what did that count against a ninety-nine-year sentence? Beanpole was wrong to think there was nothing to lose in taking a shot. There was a lot to lose. If the board threw the application back in his face, Bobby couldn't endure Eastham after that. Better to assume he had no hope of getting out than to have it formally confirmed.

Bobby got a letter from his friend in September of 1942 that changed his mind. It was the first news he had heard from Beanpole since the man left Eastham. The letter was scrawled in pencil by a hand unfamiliar with writing.

Hello, Bobby. How are you? I am fine. I am still skinny, but Momma dose her best to faten me. I like my job. I tole the boss about you. If you apply for parole, he will rite the board and say he needs you. So who will you give the radio to. Hope it still works good. Well I got to go.

Beanpole.

Everone calls me Lloyd here but when you come you can stil call me Beanpole.

Bobby put the letter down, wondering if he should risk getting his hopes up after all. But it was too late to close the gate now that the horse was out of the corral and kicking up its heels.

The next day, he made his application for parole. He still exchanged letters with Herb Lashee in El Paso now and then, and he asked him to send a reference to the board on his behalf. The Eastham captain agreed to write the board about his record of good behavior. Beanpole's boss sent a letter saying a job was waiting in Henderson if the board found Bobby deserving of clemency.

THE AUTUMN PASSED, then winter gave way to spring, and spring evaporated in the onset of summer heat, all without a word from the parole board.

In June, it rained for days, so the men weren't called out to the fields. It felt like a holiday at first, but by the fourth day, the men were bored with card games and tall tales, and the bunkhouse was silent. Electric fans moved the humid air around but didn't cool anything down, and shirtless torsos glistened.

Bobby lay on his stomach in his bunk and watched the rain fall in a steady drizzle outside. Movement closer to him caught his attention. A fly flitted back and forth inside the window, and Bobby's eyes followed its flight path until it landed vertically on the screen. It walked in tiny herky-jerky steps, and then it lifted into the air to again bump repeatedly against the mesh.

Bobby sighed. He had been a fool to ask the parole board for anything.

A MONTH LATER, as the picket guard called out the names of men who had mail, Bobby heard his own. He took the envelope that the guard extended between the bars.

It was from the board.

He pressed his lips together and pulled out the stationery. The paper shook as he unfolded it and read the words.

Mr. Hill, we received your request for clemency, and we have considered the letters of reference that were sent to us on your behalf. We have decided to grant you a six-month reprieve on your sentence to see how you conduct yourself in the free world. Your farm manager will give you more information, including the Parolee General Rules and Conditions. You have requested to be released to Henderson, Texas, and so you must report to the Rusk County parole supervisor when you arrive. We will reevaluate your case after six months.

He read the sentences again to make sure. They were going to give Bobby Hill a try at being a free man.

BOBBY WAS TAKEN to the Walls to be processed out. He took off the duck-cloth shirt and trousers and traded them for a dress shirt and a pair of slacks more like what men wore in the free world. He was also given a new pair of prison-made brogans, which seemed clunky and unnaturally orange jutting from the legs of the dress pants. He was handed fifty dollars in folding money to start his new life, and he walked out the front door of the administration building.

People waited under the trees in a park across the street. Every face turned toward him expectantly, and then their eyes looked past him to the door he had come through. They were alone or in little clusters. A black mother handed out homemade sandwiches from a paper bag to her children. A gray-haired couple talked together. A young and shapely woman stood unaccompanied. Their faces disclosed the hope or apprehension or weary resignation they carried for the men they were here to pick up.

Bobby lingered for a moment on the porch and drew in a breath. The air seemed fresher on this side of the walls. He descended the stairs and walked two blocks to a store where the Greyhound stopped. The prison office had arranged a one-way bus ticket for him to Henderson. He bought an RC Cola and a MoonPie and sat down on a bench in the shade of the store awning. A plump older woman in a flower-print dress sat on the other end of the bench. Her unfriendly eyes scanned his new outfit and clunky brogans, and she snugged her purse closer to her ample bosom.

The bus wasn't crowded. A few black passengers were in the back, and whites were scattered out by themselves in the rest of the seats. Bobby had his row to himself, and he stared out the window. This was the first vehicle in over fifteen years where he could watch the passing countryside through windows made of glass instead of wooden slats covered in galvanized screen.

When they reached Henderson in the late afternoon, he was the only one to disembark at the filling station that served as a Greyhound stop. He watched the bus roar away in a cloud of dust and diesel fumes, and he turned toward the awning at the front of the station. Two old men sat on a bench in thin short-sleeved shirts and sweat-stained straw fedoras. They stared at him with quiet reserve.

He approached them and pulled out an envelope, showing the men the return address written in Beanpole's unsteady scrawl. When he asked for directions, one nodded in recognition and gave him the route to take.

The other shook his head and spat a stream of chewing tobacco as he returned to whittling a stick, sending curls of wood shavings to the dirt between his feet.

As Bobby approached the house, the aroma of fresh-baked bread drifted through the screen door. He knocked on the frame.

A boy about five years old ran down the hall toward the door while a clatter came from the back of the house like a lid being set hurriedly on a saucepan. A woman's voice called out, "Coming. Coming." The child stopped at the door, holding a crayon in his hand, and he squinted up at Bobby through the screen. A short, plump woman waddled toward the door. Bobby supposed she was in her seventies.

She wiped her hands on her apron. "Yes?"

"I'm Bobby Hill. Is this the home of Lloyd Howell?"

When her buck teeth jutted out from a welcoming smile, Bobby grinned. He had found the right place. She laughed as she opened the screen door. "Come in, come in. Bobby Hill. It's so good to finally have you here. Lloyd has told us all about you. I'm his mother, Vivian. Everyone calls me Vivy."

The child held up his crayon. "I'm drawing a cow."

Vivy put her hands on her hips. "And you're doing a wonderful job, Samuel. You go back in the kitchen and finish that up for your momma." Samuel ran back into the kitchen, holding up his crayon like a flying arrow.

Vivy chuckled as she watched the boy disappear, and she turned her attention to Bobby, looking him up and down. "Well, you aren't as skinny as my Lloyd, but I got some work to do on you both. Are you hungry?"

"I could eat something, sure."

She laughed again. "Of course, you could eat something. Supper's another hour, but let's get you some bread. I think it's cooled enough to slice and butter." She led him in a breathless waddle toward the kitchen.

As they passed the dining room table, six place settings were laid out.

"Mrs. Howell, I don't want to barge in on any company you've got coming over."

"It's Vivy," she reminded him. "I see Lloyd didn't tell you I run a boardinghouse. That boy." She shook her head, amused. She pointed to each place setting and spoke the names as if she were recalling fond stories of each of them. "That spot on the end is for Mr. Jamison. Those two chairs are for Dorothy and Samuel. That one is for Lloyd. And this one—" She patted the back of a chair with both hands. "This one's been waiting for you, Bobby, ever since we got your letter. Course now, if you've got other arrangements, that's fine, too. But I have a spot at the table here and a room for you upstairs, and I charge eight dollars a week. Washing sheets and towels is part of the rent, but I can do your own laundry for another dollar a week."

"Bean—" He corrected himself. "Lloyd, I mean to say. He told me I had a job waiting for me at the public works, and I go to see about that tomorrow. I figure if I get on there, I'd be very happy to stay here. Thank you."

She waved for him to follow her into the kitchen. "Well, now, let's go see about that bread I promised."

The five-year-old was at the kitchen table, concentrating on his drawing. He held up the paper to Bobby. "It's a cow."

"I can see that." He pointed to dots around the cow. "What are these?"

"Flies. Cows have flies."

Vivy collected stray crayons together. "You're a very good artist, Samuel. Now, let's make some space for Mr. Bobby to sit while you finish that." She pointed Bobby to the other end of the kitchen table and served him a thick slice of buttered bread and a cold glass of milk. "This'll tide you over till everyone's here for supper."

Bobby ate as he listened to Vivy talk in a constant stream. She told him how she and Mr. Howell found each other in their thirties after thinking marriage wasn't in the cards for either of them, and then how they had given up on any children until she found she was expecting Lloyd, and then how they saw early on he was a little simple but still so sweet, and then how her husband had been an assistant bank manager until a heart attack took him, and then how she took in boarders to pay expenses as a widow, and then how unfair the trial was for her Lloyd, and then how proud she was of his county job. It all tumbled out as she bustled around the kitchen, waving Bobby off whenever he offered to help with the pots and pans.

There was a gentle slap of the front door screen against the frame. Samuel gave Vivy a look of exaggerated surprise and said, "Momma's home!"

"Your momma's home!" she repeated, matching his excited face.

Samuel picked up his drawing and held it up like he was sailing a kite as he ran from the kitchen. The child's voice echoed down the hallway: "I made this for you."

A woman's voice replied, "You did? It's beautiful. I like the cow."

"And the flies."

"Yes, and the flies."

A woman walked into the kitchen holding the sketch. Bobby guessed her to be in her late twenties, and she wore a post office uniform. Samuel wrapped his arms around her legs, and she drew his head to her hip, smiling.

"How was he today, Vivy?"

"A joy, as always, Dorothy. He was a big helper in the garden, weren't you, Samuel?"

The child nodded proudly at his mother.

"Long day?" Vivy asked.

The woman exhaled wearily. "Long day."

"Well, honey, you're done for tonight."

Dorothy looked past Vivy to Bobby, and Vivy threw up her hands. "Goodness, now. I've been talking with Bobby so long this afternoon, I've already figured him part of the family. This is Bobby Hill. Bobby, this is Dorothy Allen."

Bobby stood, self-consciously brushing bread crumbs off his shirt. He nodded, and she gave him a polite smile.

The front screen slapped again. Samuel let go of his mother's legs and ran out the kitchen door, shouting, "Your friend's here."

"My friend?" It was Beanpole's voice.

The lanky man appeared in the kitchen doorway, and his buck-toothed grin spread across his face. "Bobby!" In two steps, he crossed the kitchen and gave Bobby a hug, slapping his back. "Everybody, this is my old buddy, Bobby."

His mother chuckled, her grin a mirror image of her son's. "We've all met him, Lloyd. We're so glad he's here!"

"We're so glad he's here!" Samuel echoed in a silly mimic of Vivy's voice and face, and everyone laughed. Bobby joined in, too, despite himself.

At supper that evening, Bobby met the other boarder, Mr. Jamison, a man in his nineties. He was employed at the hardware store, though Bobby wondered if his job wasn't mostly for charity. At the table, he kept cupping his hand to his ear and asking people to repeat their questions, and he would often lose his train of thought when answering.

But Bobby was glad Dorothy was asking most of the questions of Mr. Jamison because it gave him a chance to watch her. He suspected she was shapelier than the baggy post office uniform publicized. Her auburn hair was tied up in a bun, revealing her neck and face. She had a fair complexion, lightly freckled, and her gray eyes crinkled at the edges when she smiled at the old man's rambling answers to her questions.

After supper, Bobby and Beanpole sat on the front porch to smoke.

"So, you're Lloyd here."

"You can still call me Beanpole."

"No, those days are behind us. You're Lloyd to me, like you are to everyone else here."

Lloyd asked him about his last year in the Ham, but Bobby kept that topic short. He had another subject he wanted to talk about.

"Tell me about your girlfriend."

"My girlfriend?"

"Your girlfriend, Dorothy."

Lloyd broke into a shy grin and wagged his finger at him. "Aw, now, Bobby, you're teasing me. You know she ain't my girlfriend." He shook another cigarette from the pack. "I admit I'm a little sweet on her, but these teeth of mine ain't my best calling card."

"And that's just the start of your liabilities." Bobby winked at him and grinned.

Lloyd laughed. He flicked the flint wheel of his Zippo and got his cigarette going and snapped the lid of the lighter to extinguish the flame. "Dorothy and her boy come to live with Momma maybe three years ago, just after I was sent up. Her husband was a delivery truck driver and lost his life in a highway accident, and she had no family to move in with. She got on with the post office when the war started. She pays Momma a little extra on top of the room and board to watch Sammy during the day. Momma says he's her grandson on loan."

"Dorothy have anyone call on her?"

"With the war on, no one's left in Henderson but men twice her age and a few 4-F's like me." He gave Bobby a knowing grin. "The road's wide open for you, brother."

Bobby changed the subject. "Tell me about this job you've talked me into."

They chatted and smoked for another half hour, and Lloyd took Bobby upstairs to show him his room. The smell of soap drifted on the humid air coming from the open door of a darkened bathroom, and a trail of

Samuel's wet footprints led from the bathroom to a bedroom door with light coming from under it.

Lloyd spoke in a whisper. "The bathroom at the end of the hallway serves the four bedrooms up here. Momma's room is downstairs." He pointed to each door as he continued. "Mr. Jamison's in that room to the left. Probably already asleep. My room's next to his. That's Dorothy and Sammy's room on the right. Yours is next to theirs." He gestured for Bobby to follow him into an open room, and he flicked the wall switch to light the space.

Inside was a single bed, a desk with a chair, and a chest of drawers. In the open closet, empty hangers hung on a rod. Bobby imagined Vivy and her husband as newlyweds years ago, buying this place on his assistant bank manager's salary to fill with a large family.

Lloyd moved to the door. "Well, good night, Bobby. I'll introduce you to my supervisor tomorrow."

"Good night, Beanpole—I mean, Lloyd." Bobby grinned, but then nodded with conviction. "You got a good momma. I'm sure glad to be here."

Lloyd smiled and nodded as he closed Bobby's door.

Bobby turned off the lights, undressed, and crawled into bed. He heard Samuel's voice through the wall. It was too muffled to make out the words, but the child was whining about something.

Dorothy's soft voice began a lullaby. Bobby could only hear the tune through the wall, but he knew the words.

> *Sleep, my child, and peace attend thee,*
> *All through the night.*

Bobby was five years old again, yawning widely as his mother sat on the bed. She swept her fingers through his locks of hair and continued the song he asked for every night.

> *Guardian angels God will send thee*
> *All through the night.*

In the next room, Dorothy's muffled singing rose to reach the higher notes of the next line, drawing up more lyrics from the murky depths of Bobby's memory.

> *Though our hearts be wrapped in sorrow,*
> *From the home of dawn we borrow*
> *Promise of a glad tomorrow*
> *All through the night.*

Thirty-five-year-old Bobby Hill yawned contentedly, and he fell into the best sleep he had ever known.

18

SUNNY SIDE

Bobby considered the steady drizzle outside Vivy's car and calculated the distance to the church building. He turned to his passengers. Lloyd sat next to him. In the back, Vivy, Mr. Jamison, and Dorothy were assembled side by side, with Samuel on Dorothy's lap. They were all dressed for the Easter service.

"What do you think?" he asked. "Do we make a run for it?"

Vivy rubbed her gloved hand on the fogged window. "I think it's letting up." It sounded more like a wish than a statement of fact.

A man and woman trotted past them toward the building, huddled together under a shared umbrella.

Bobby pointed to them. "I'm going to follow those two in and see if I can borrow their umbrella."

He opened the door and the sound of rainfall entered the compartment like a light hiss. He snugged his felt fedora firmer on his head, popped up his jacket collar, and jumped out. Slamming the door behind him, he ran with his shoulders hunched against the shower.

When he got inside the church building, he found that Lloyd had followed him, and together they returned with two umbrellas. Lloyd handed his mother one for herself and Mr. Jamison, and he darted back into the church on his own. On the other side of the car, Bobby lifted Samuel into his arms and waited for Dorothy to join them under the umbrella. As she stepped out and fumbled for the shaft, her hand went over his and she left it there.

Samuel shouted over the rain thumping on the fabric above them, "Miz Vivy says April showers bring May flowers."

Bobby grinned at Dorothy and mumbled, "Keep on the sunny side, Miz Vivy."

Samuel began to sing, "Keep on the sunny side, always on the sunny side." Bobby and Dorothy joined him in the song as they jogged toward the church building, laughing over their efforts to stay huddled under the umbrella while keeping in step with each other.

The group reassembled inside, breathless, and returned the umbrellas to their owners with thanks.

They settled into a pew, and as the preservice music played, Bobby glanced down the pew at his uncommon family. Vivy was patting Lloyd's knee affectionately; Mr. Jamison was trying to read the worship bulletin, which shook in his palsied hands; and Dorothy was pointing Samuel's attention to a stained-glass image of the crucifixion and explaining the scene to him.

Willie had once asked him who his people were. He'd like to think these were his people now.

He hoped he could stay with them.

When he had moved to Henderson in June last year, he couldn't shake the fear that the parole board had sent the wrong paperwork, and the authorities were going to pull up any day to take him back to Eastham. He got notice in November that the board had extended his reprieve a full year, but he still got nervous anytime he saw a cherry-topped police cruiser.

He flexed the hand that Dorothy had grasped in their run through the rain, and he wondered why he trusted happiness the least when he felt it the most.

While the preacher talked, Bobby's thoughts went back to Sundays on the back stoop of the kitchen at the Wynne Unit, listening to Willie's triumphant shouts coming through the windows of his bunkhouse. He thought about what that old man would say if he could see Bobby now.

Maybe he could see him now. Bobby remembered a newspaper report of the 1936 Olympics in Berlin. It had been the last Olympiad before the war interrupted the games. The newspaper had printed a photograph of the black American Jesse Owens. In the image, Owens was far ahead of the pack, running for his third gold medal against Hitler's master race. In the background of the image was a vast crowd in the Berlin stadium, each head a tiny dot in a sea of spectators. Like Owens, Willie had already succeeded in his contest down here, and maybe now he was up there in the stands, a tiny dot among a great cloud of witnesses cheering for Bobby.

They returned to the house after the service, and Mr. Jamison read the Sunday funnies to Samuel while the other four got dinner ready. It was two o'clock when they all sat down at the table, and when the plates were empty, Samuel announced, "Now it's time to hunt Easter eggs."

Vivy squinted through the windows at the drenched yard and heavy gray clouds. "Another day, honey." She collected the plates.

"But it's Easter *today*."

Lloyd tried to be helpful. "The Easter Bunny don't hide his eggs when it's raining, Sammy."

"I'm Samuel. You're always calling me Sammy, but my name's Samuel."

The voice was turning into the whine of an overwrought child in need of a nap. Dorothy spoke to him in a patient voice. "It's just a nickname, Samuel. Sammy is another way to say Samuel. It's like our friend Bobby. Everyone calls him Bobby but his real name's Robert. You know"—her eyes crinkled at the edges as she grinned—"I'm kind of partial to Robert." She turned her face to Samuel again. "What do you think? Should we call him Robert or Bobby?"

Samuel crossed his arms, still frustrated about the Easter eggs. "He's Bobby and I'm Samuel."

Bobby put his arm around Lloyd's chair. "I bet you didn't know Lloyd has a nickname." Bobby waited until Samuel's scowl converted into curiosity. Then he said, "We used to call him Beanpole."

Samuel's face scrunched up, incredulous. "Beanpole?"

"Well, don't he look like a tall, skinny beanpole sticking up in Miz Vivy's garden?"

Lloyd straightened in the chair like a pole and made a comical face.

Samuel cackled, and the table joined him in the laughter.

Vivy stood with her stack of plates. "Tell you what, Mr. Samuel, sir. You lay down upstairs—" Samuel opened his mouth to protest, but Vivy continued, "Hear me out. You lay down upstairs for just a little nap, and we'll see if we can't find the Easter Bunny and persuade him to come in the house and hide his eggs inside."

Samuel brightened at this idea. When Dorothy began collecting the silverware off the table, Vivy said, "No, honey. You go get him settled in. I got three strong men to help me clear the table."

She had two strong men, anyway. At Mr. Jamison's unsteady handling of her china, Vivy sent him to the living room to lay on the couch, where he was soon snoring.

After all the washing was done, Bobby and Lloyd went out on the front porch to smoke. Dorothy joined them and sat on the wicker two-seater next to Bobby. The three had not talked long before Vivy stepped out on the porch. "Lloyd, I need your help in here."

Bobby started to stand. "You need me, too?"

She waved him back down. "No, Bobby. You sit, you sit. Lloyd can do this for me."

When Lloyd was back in the house with his mother, Bobby grinned at Dorothy. "I think she figures maybe we want to talk alone."

"Do you?"

"Do I what?"

She turned her gray eyes to Bobby. "Do you want to talk alone with me?"

He gave her a shy grin, and then concentrated on shaking out another cigarette from his pack. After a moment, he asked, "You ever thought about marrying again?"

"Yes. Yes, I have."

He nodded, thoughtful, tapping the end of the cigarette on his knee.

She stared at him like she was expecting him to say more. Finally, she looked away. "I've begun to think—" She began, then hesitated, serious and uncertain. A mild, humid breeze crossed the porch, and Dorothy hugged her bare arms to herself as she gazed out into the yard. "I've begun to think no one would want to take on Samuel, though. I expect lots of men wouldn't want to raise another man's son." Her face turned toward his again. "You think a man might feel that way?"

Sure, a man might feel that way, he thought, remembering his abandonment by his mother's husband. But for his part, Bobby wasn't reluctant to be saddled with Samuel. Bobby just didn't want the boy to be saddled with him.

"I think any good man would love that boy right away, Dorothy."

He couldn't think about any more to say, and he occupied himself with fishing in his shirt pocket for the lighter.

She opened her mouth to say something, but Samuel came out the door holding an Easter basket.

"Well, that was a short nap," Dorothy said to him.

"Miz Vivy said the Easter Bunny's come and hid the eggs all inside! Help me find them!"

Bobby returned the unlit cigarette to the pack, and together he and Dorothy followed Samuel. Vivy put her arm through the crook of Dorothy's folded arms and gave her a questioning look. Dorothy returned a slight shrug.

Samuel skipped around the room, shouting in triumph as he held up each decorated hard-boiled egg he found, and all the adults cheered his success.

Vivy's eyes followed Samuel as she spoke in a low voice to Bobby and Dorothy. "I hope Lloyd didn't forget where he put them all." She giggled. "Can you imagine what this house will smell like in a week if we leave any behind?"

A SONOROUS VOICE came through the radio. "Ladies and Gentlemen, the president of the United States."

Vivy waved Samuel down. "Shush now, honey. Sit down. It's starting."

Samuel settled cross-legged in front of the radio console and spun the propeller of a toy fighter plane. Lloyd and Bobby were on the couch with Dorothy between them, and Vivy and Mr. Jamison sat in armchairs under the front window.

A voice came through the speaker, somehow patrician and populist at the same time, the voice of President Roosevelt addressing the nation on the evening of June 6, 1944.

"My fellow Americans: Last night, when I spoke with you about the fall of Rome, I knew at that moment that troops of the United States and our allies were crossing the English Channel in another and greater operation. It has come to pass with success thus far. And so, in this poignant hour, I ask you to join with me in prayer."

There was a dramatic pause in the radio address, and the prayer began.

"Almighty God: Our sons, pride of our nation, this day have set upon a mighty endeavor, a struggle to preserve our republic, our religion, and our civilization, and to set free a suffering humanity."

Mr. Jamison leaned forward, his hand cupped to his ear, and since Bobby was nearest the radio, he turned the volume up for him.

"They will need thy blessings. Their road will be long and hard. For the enemy is strong. He may hurl back our forces. The darkness will be rent by noise and flame. Men's souls will be shaken with the violences of war."

Bobby had the vague image in his mind of a vast assembly of ships on the gray sea of the English Channel, and thousands of men pouring out of those ships on their way to some French coastline, pressing forward against enemy fire.

"Some will never return. Embrace these, Father, and receive them, thy heroic servants, into thy kingdom. And for us at home—fathers, mothers, children, wives, sisters, and brothers of brave men overseas— whose thoughts and prayers are ever with them, help us, Almighty God, to rededicate ourselves in renewed faith in thee in this hour of great sacrifice. Thy will be done, Almighty God. Amen."

As the president's prayer ended, Bobby lowered the volume, leaving a somber silence in the room. Vivy sniffed, and dabbed at her eyes with a handkerchief.

Samuel rolled the wheels of his airplane on the rug. "Michael's daddy is in the war."

Dorothy said, "That's right, Samuel. Lots of men are."

"They have a blue star in the window of his house. Jimmy's got a blue star at his house, too."

Bobby had seen them. He imagined hundreds of thousands of homes across the nation had service flags hanging in the front window, displaying a blue star for every family member in the fight, and a gold star for every family member who had been killed in action.

Samuel flicked the propeller of his toy. "They asked me why we don't have a star in our window." He cocked his head to Bobby. "How come you and Mr. Lloyd aren't soldiers?"

Bobby and Lloyd both had registered with the draft on getting out of prison, but the Rusk County Selective Service board deemed Lloyd as mentally 4-F, and they regarded Bobby as ineligible as long as he was temporarily reprieved and not formally paroled. He held his coffee cup between his hands and thought about how to explain this in a way a six-year-old could understand.

Dorothy spoke up. "Keeping this country running is as much a part of the war effort as fighting overseas, as I see it. Robert and Lloyd will serve overseas as soon as they're asked." She took the hand of the men on each side of her. "Until then, we're glad they're with us, aren't we?"

Samuel didn't respond to her as he raised the toy airplane to his eye, squinting into the cockpit.

LOGS POPPED AND crackled in the fireplace as Lloyd and Bobby and Dorothy drank coffee and visited together in the living room. It was three days after Christmas, and the needles of the holiday tree had gone pale and brittle underneath the glittering tinsel and baubles.

Samuel padded downstairs, his hair damp and his feet sticking out of the legs of his pajamas. Dorothy wrapped him in her arms. "Mmm. You smell so clean. That was nice of Miz Vivy to make your bath tonight and let me stay down here with the boys."

"Can't I stay up a little longer?"

Vivy waved him to her on the stair landing. "Now, honey, I said you could come down just to say good night. We're going to let the young people talk down here."

Samuel protested. "I'm young people."

Vivy chuckled. "Yes, you are, honey. Now, come along. I've got a book all picked out to read to you."

As Samuel joined Vivy on the landing, Dorothy said, "You sure you don't mind, Vivy?"

"No, indeed!" Vivy kissed Samuel's forehead. "This is my grandson on loan right here. You kids talk."

As Vivy and Samuel disappeared up the stairs, Lloyd stood and stretched. "No, *you* kids talk." He yawned. "Mr. Jamison had the right idea an hour ago. It's bedtime for me, too."

"Maybe your momma will read to you after she's tucked Samuel in," Bobby teased. "Pick out a good Archie Comics for her, Jughead."

Lloyd gave Bobby a sleepy grin and climbed the stairs.

Bobby jutted his head toward the stairs. "You see how far Samuel's limbs were sticking out of those PJs?"

Dorothy nodded and smiled. "He'll be as tall as me before you know it."

Things grew quiet between them as they stared into the fire. Bobby spoke, his voice soft. "I think my momma would have liked you."

"Tell me about her."

"I really don't remember much. I wasn't a year older than Samuel when she died." Bobby started to say his mother had the same color hair as Dorothy, but he wasn't sure she wanted to hear that. "I just think she would have liked you, is all."

She lay her head on his shoulder. After a moment, Bobby continued. "I guess it ain't no secret how I feel about you. A blind man could see it easy as anyone." He paused. "But it scares me, too."

"I scare you," she stated flatly.

"No, not you."

She sat up and crossed her arms. "Samuel scares you."

"I scare me, Dorothy. I scare me."

He stared into the fire again, trying to find his words. "I never told you, but it wasn't too much after my momma died that I was packed off to the Gatesville State School."

"Your daddy sent you away?"

"No, no. I never knew my daddy. He died when I was a baby and my momma remarried. It was her second husband what sent me off." A bead of coffee rested on the lip of his cup, and Bobby rubbed it off with his thumb. "He never came back for me."

"That's awful."

He nodded as images of childhood heartbreak rolled through his mind. "I aged out at sixteen and right away got pinched for the tailor shop break-in. You know the rest of my story."

Bobby put down the coffee cup. "They gave me the name Hill in Gatesville. It was the family name of the man who brought me there, so they just assumed it was mine, I guess. All my life, I've had to carry the name of the man who abandoned me."

He wrung his hands together nervously. "I guess I'm saying I don't know nothing about how to be a husband or a daddy to no one."

Dorothy didn't say anything, and he knew she was letting him set the pace.

"I got a letter from the parole board today."

"I saw the envelope come through the post office," Dorothy said.

"They've extended my reprieve for another year."

"That's wonderful news," she said, and waited.

"I figure it's time I applied for parole."

"Maybe even a pardon," she added.

He forged ahead, fearful that if he paused now, he'd never say it. "Dorothy, if you'll have me, I'd like to try to be what you and Samuel need me to be."

She put her hand on his cheek and turned his face toward hers. "Robert Hill, you've carried that name long enough by yourself." She kissed him. "Mrs. Dorothy Hill. I like the sound of it."

Vivy burst down the stairs. "Oh, you kids!" She waddled over to Dorothy and hugged her, rocking her from side to side, and then whispered conspiratorially, "I like the sound of it, too, honey."

She turned to Bobby. "And you. If I'd of sat waiting on that top stair any longer, I would have come down and done the proposing for you!" She laughed, her buck teeth jutting out of her wide smile, and pulled him into an embrace.

WHEN THEY MADE the announcement over dinner the next evening, Mr. Jamison and Lloyd congratulated them, while teasing Bobby about taking so long.

As the adults celebrated, a solemn, anxious expression fell over Samuel's face. Dorothy asked him, "What do you think of our news, Samuel?"

"Will we have to leave Miz Vivy's house?"

Bobby pulled at his lip, pretending to be in deep deliberation. "I've been giving that some serious thought." He put both hands down on the table like he had just made a decision. "I think we should stay. What do you think?"

Samuel nodded hard, a relieved smile on his face.

Bobby continued. "But I got to ask you something, man to man."

Samuel straightened up to the challenge. "What?"

"When your momma and me get married, you and me should plan on switching rooms."

"Well, we only got the one bed in there," Samuel informed him. "You'll have to share it with Momma."

"That's what I'm counting on." Bobby winked at Dorothy, who blushed, and the table laughed.

THEY WERE MARRIED the first week of February at a small ceremony, and Vivy loaned her car to them so they could honeymoon in Tyler for a couple of nights. Vivy prepared a special meal for the boardinghouse to celebrate their first night back as a married couple. Upstairs, they found that while they were away, Lloyd and Vivy had helped Samuel move into Bobby's room and they had relocated Bobby's few belongings into Dorothy's room. Samuel was excited to show his mother and Bobby how he had arranged his toys and clothes in the new space, and when they tucked him in for the night, he displayed no anxiety about sleeping in the room by himself.

Bobby and Dorothy got ready for bed, and as they settled in, she laid her head on his chest.

He stroked her hair. "Did you ever read *Les Misérables*?"

"Back in high school," she said, her voice sleepy.

"I read it while I was in prison."

She propped her chin on her hand so she could face him. "You're always full of surprises, Robert Hill. What made you choose a book like that?"

"In the trial, my lawyer told the jury I was Jean Valjean. You remember him?"

"Of course."

"I had no idea what he was talking about. So, when a ladies' society donated a bunch of books to the prison, I saw the book in the stack and decided to read it."

"Did you enjoy it?"

"The main line of it, sure. Now, the French names weren't easy for me. I asked a Cajun to help me figure out how to pronounce them all. And I got tired of the rabbit-chasing." He chuckled. "I learned more about Paris sewers than I ever wanted to."

She smiled. "Most of us skipped over that part in high school."

"Not me. I wanted to know what the lawyer saw in the story that reminded him of me." He gave her a rueful smile and added, "I figured I had enough time on my hands to work through the whole thing, anyway."

She lay back down on his chest, and he stroked her hair.

"My lawyer told me I had time to become the Valjean of my own story."

"I like that. I think you have."

He rubbed her back. "No, the lawyer compared me to the wrong man in the story. I'm that Pontmercy fella."

"Oh? And why is that?"

Bobby pulled her into an embrace. "I finally got my Cosette."

THE SECOND EXTENSION of his reprieve would be up in December of 1945, and with Dorothy's help, Bobby filed an appeal for the parole board to grant him a pardon. She wrote a letter about their marriage and Bobby's attentive care of her and her son. Vivy also sent a letter, as well as Bobby's supervisor and pastor and local parole officer.

They didn't expect to hear anything in the spring, but as the summer passed, they watched the incoming mail with growing anxiousness.

ONE AFTERNOON IN late September, Bobby and Lloyd broke for lunch in the county garage. The wooden panels of the bay doors were rolled open, and they dragged chairs to a spot where they could catch the mild air of an early-autumn front.

They unpacked their lunch kits. "Let's see what your momma put in here for us today," Bobby said. "It's always good."

A shout came from behind them: "Well, it ain't right. It just ain't right."

They turned around. In the office, an angry man was jutting his finger at their boss, who replied calmly to the man, "I understand, I do."

The new man was a stranger to Bobby, but Lloyd said in a low whisper, "That's Newt Searcy. He was in high school with me. Been off in the Pacific since the war started. Heard he had it rough over there."

Newt stepped out into the garage, shouting back into the office at their boss, "I ain't going to be the only veteran coming in here looking for work."

He was the third veteran Bobby had seen at the garage just that week. The fighting in Europe had ended in May, and the war in the Pacific had ended in August. Newspapers reported the challenges that returning soldiers all around the nation were facing in finding work.

Newt scowled when he saw Bobby and Lloyd, and he strode up to them. "No, sir. It ain't right for felons like you to be taking up jobs that should be going to us as fought for our country. Maybe I'll see what the parole board feels about this." He stormed out.

A newspaper photo from a year ago came to Bobby's mind. In the picture, sailors were throwing tomatoes at a colossal image of Frank Sinatra above the marquee of the Paramount in New York City. During the war, veterans had always been suspicious of the crooner's 4-F status, which kept him stateside, getting rich making women swoon while their boyfriends and husbands were overseas. If feelings could run so high like that against someone famous, Bobby had no doubt Newt would make good on his threat to write the board in Austin over someone like him.

Lloyd's parole wasn't likely to be reversed, but Bobby feared what might happen to his own pardon application. Maybe the board would decide it was too politically inconvenient to grant it. Maybe the board would even let his reprieve run out in December and he'd find himself back in Eastham.

THAT NIGHT HE lay awake in bed, and for the first time in fifteen years, he considered running. He could get Dorothy and Samuel packed up and they'd slip out of town before his reprieve ran out. They'd head to Montana. His mother had told him he was born there, and he was always curious about what it was like. He and Dorothy would get jobs, and the three of them could live under assumed names.

Bobby sighed. Why do that to Dorothy and Samuel? He should leave them with Vivy in Henderson and disappear. They'd cry for a while, but they'd realize he had done them a favor. He should cut them free from all his baggage before they got pulled under with him. Dorothy would be taken care of. She was young and pretty. With all these men coming back, she'd eventually find a war hero to marry.

He put his forearm over his eyes and eventually fell asleep, but fitfully, and he left the bed before dawn. The floor creaked as he dressed, and Dorothy murmured something indecipherable before falling back into long, slow breaths. Bobby went into the kitchen and collected the ingredients to make biscuits like he used to do at the Wynne Farm.

He was kneading the dough when Vivy entered in a sleepy shuffle. She filled the percolator with water and coffee grounds and set it over a low flame on the back burner. It began to gurgle, sending splashes of water into the glass knob on the top.

She yawned. "That reserve has come back."

"Ma'am?"

"I saw it last night. You've got that reserve you had when you first came here. Like you don't quite trust a chair to hold you up."

He set the tray of biscuits in the oven. "I've just got things on my mind."

"You've got that pardon on your mind. We all do." She patted his arm as she passed him to the dish strainer. She turned up two cups and filled them with coffee. "We'll hear soon enough."

"And what if we don't like what we hear? You're the most positive person I know, Vivy, but things don't always work out the way we want."

She gestured to the table, and they sat with their cups. "I never said they did, and I surely know they don't. Not much of my life has gone the way I thought it would."

He frowned, regretting his statement.

She put a hand on his forearm. "You don't get to call the tune, honey. You just got to find a way to dance to it."

He slumped back in the chair. "Well, if they send me back, I can tell you that's no tune to dance to."

"They aren't going to send you back, Bobby."

"But what if they do?"

"Then maybe you're meant to be a Lloyd to someone."

"You're going to have to draw a better map because I'm not following."

"Do you think it was right what they did to Lloyd, sending him off to prison like they did?"

He shook his head. "That wasn't right."

"And yet if Lloyd hadn't been sent to prison on that setup, you two would have never met. If you two had never met, you would have never come to Henderson. And then, you would have never married Dorothy. Things aren't always pretty, but they're always *meant*."

She took his hand, rubbing her thumb fondly across his wedding band. "They aren't going to send you back. But if they do, well, then, you get to be Lloyd to someone there like Lloyd was to you."

He stared in speechless marvel at Vivy. He had indulged her as a naïve optimist with a fragile wish that the world would just turn out to be the way she wanted it to be. Now he saw her perspective on life was something more rugged, more durable. Her one son, the last thread that remained of the fabric of her life plan, had been unjustly taken from her and put in the hellhole that was Eastham. Even so, here she was looking upon everything that had happened to Lloyd as part of a much larger story. Not Bobby's story, because everything that happened to Bobby, too, would be seen by her as part of a much bigger tale. Bobby and Lloyd and Vivy and Dorothy and Samuel—all their joys and sorrows were precious scenes woven together in a tapestry far larger than any one solitary life.

Bobby kissed her on the cheek. "I like that angle on things, Vivy. It reminds me of someone I knew once. He would have told me the same thing—and then quoted me a scripture to back it up." He stood and went to the refrigerator. "Now, what do you want me to cook this morning? We got bacon or sausage links. You pick."

BOBBY THOUGHT NO more of running, and he even did his best to break out of the reserve that Vivy said he had fallen into. If the parole board was going to let his reprieve expire in December, well, he wasn't going to let that ruin his last remaining months with Dorothy and Samuel.

Still, every day after coming home from work, he would stop at the kitchen counter where Vivy put the mail to see if anything had come for him.

One November afternoon, he found an oversized brown envelope addressed to him from the office of the governor. Vivy gave him a significant look, and then turned back to the frying pan where chicken spattered in the grease. No one else but Vivy had seen him pick it up from the counter. Dorothy had not come home yet; Samuel was at the kitchen table, concentrating on a new drawing to give his mother; and Lloyd and Mr. Jamison were in the living room discussing the news.

Bobby wanted somewhere to be alone when he opened the envelope. He stepped out the back door and sat on the stoop. He remembered the chats with Willie on the kitchen steps at Wynne. It seemed like a fitting place to sit as he read news that would change his life.

The letter trembled, and he turned it to the back and front to occupy his nervous hands. Finally, he pressed his lips grimly, and ripped open the top of the envelope. As he pulled up the single sheet inside, he saw the word "PROCLAMATION" printed at the top of the page in large, bold letters.

Bobby slid out the rest of the document and read it. "*I, Coke R. Stevenson, Governor of the State of Texas, by virtue of the authority vested in me under the Constitution and the laws of this State, and upon the recommendation of the Board of Pardons and Paroles, do hereby grant unto ROBERT M. HILL pardon, conditioned that he will continue to observe the rules of the clemency previously granted him.*"

A pardon. Not just another extension of his reprieve, but a pardon. The parole board had recommended it and the governor had granted it. He wasn't going back to Eastham. He could stay with Dorothy and Samuel.

The doorknob rattled behind him, and the spring on the screen door twanged.

"Ah," Dorothy said, and sat down beside him, wrapping her post office jacket tightly around her. "Found you."

What did Valjean say about Cosette at the end? The proof that God is good is that she is here.

He smiled at her. "You found me."

AUTHOR'S NOTE—FACT AND FICTION

You're in a diner in the late 1920s. The waitress refills your coffee cup and takes away your empty breakfast plate, and you riffle through the pages of the newspaper to find the continuation of the article that began on the front page above the fold.

It's the story everyone's calling The Santa Claus Bank Robbery. Every day the paper provides updates on the manhunt, the trials, the execution of Henry Helms, the escapes of Robert Hill, and the lynching of the Santa Claus bank robber himself.

You put down your cup, now faintly smudged with newsprint ink, and you start forming an opinion of the individuals behind the names: their character, their upbringing, their motivations, and whether they got what they deserved in the end. It requires a certain measure of supposition on your part, which makes for interesting conversation with anyone in the diner who has drawn different conclusions from reading the same daily articles.

The Last Man was written from my suppositions after reading those very accounts nearly a hundred years later. I had to devise the dialogue and motivations of the characters, but the robbery, the manhunt, the execution, the escapes, and the lynching follow the newspaper record. These details were first gathered into a single story by legendary journalist Boyce House. *Startling Detective Adventures* magazine published his piece in March 1930. Hill was still on the lam when that article came out. In 1958, the Cisco newspaperman and historian, J. W. Sitton, released the first book on the robbery, titled *The Santa Claus Bank Robbery*. For decades, the First National Bank of Cisco distributed Sitton's thirty-two-page publication. It was my first introduction to the event when I lived in Eastland County in the 1990s. When I wanted more information, I was given a copy of A. C. Greene's 1972 book, also called *The Santa Claus Bank Robbery*.

Anyone who researches this true crime and its aftermath is largely dependent on the old newspapers because there are few other historical records. I was able to glean some information about the bandits from the handwritten prison reports. I pieced together a little of what happened at the trials from reading the summaries presented to the Court of Criminal Appeals. I found the formal proclamations of Hill's two pardons from the archives of two Texas governors—a conditional pardon in 1945 by Coke Stevenson and a full pardon by John Connally in 1964. But the actual transcripts of courtroom testimony no longer exist, and the Board of Pardons and Paroles tells me that they have no remaining paperwork to explain why they recommended pardons for Hill.

In my novel, Ratliff ascends stairs to a second-floor closet in the bank. No newspaper or book has previously mentioned that detail, but I climbed those stairs. The building was an auto parts store in the 1990s. Since it was a slow day, the manager gave me a tour of the stairs that led to a single door and closet. He insisted it was there when the building housed the First National Bank. Chalk that up to a previously unreported detail, or as evidence that a notorious event expands in the retelling.

There is stronger evidence for my novel's account of the gawkers who lined up at Louis Davis's hospital window. No previous printed account of the Santa Claus Bank Robbery mentions it, but I was told about it by those who remembered. You can find an old video online from Abilene's KTAB-TV, where an eyewitness recounts that scene. In my story, Davis died in Eastland on Christmas Eve. In the historical record, authorities transferred him to a Fort Worth hospital for fear of mob violence. He died there on Christmas Day.

For the three who went to trial, the defense strategy depended in part on stoking discomfort over the reward for dead bank robbers. It was worth over $85,000 in today's currency. In that period, an average of four banks were hit each day in Texas, and bankers hoped the reward would stem the tide. Their incentive was a controversial measure from the start, but it lasted four decades until it was quietly discontinued in 1964.

The Texas Bankers Association never paid anyone the reward for Louis Davis's death.

Since transcripts of the court testimony no longer exist, I depended on two sources for writing the courtroom scenes: newspaper reports and summaries of the trials submitted by the prosecution and the defense to the Court of Criminal Appeals. These summaries are preserved at the Texas State Library and Archives in Austin. Based on those court documents, the prosecutor, Joe Frank Sparks, pointed an empty gun at the jury in Abilene and yelled, "Bam!" And in his closing arguments, he referenced the hanging of horse thieves as an admirable model for what should happen to Marshall Ratliff.

I did, however, try to simplify the legal details of the story. I presented only one defense attorney for Ratliff and Helms. In the historical record, as in the novel, J. Lee Cearley represented both men in their separate trials. In the real trials, he was joined at the defense table by a former judge J. K. Baker. Also, Cearley did not represent Ratliff or Helms during their insanity claims. The men each had different attorneys by this point. It is not clear in the newspapers if the lawyers who served the men at this stage were working for Cearley's firm, or if the families had to go out and find other representation. Either way, I decided for the novel that Cearley would represent them from beginning to end. In the historical record and in the novel, L. H. Flewellen was the only attorney for Hill. He was appointed by the court to represent Hill without cost to the defendant at both his 1928 and 1931 trials. Joe Frank Sparks was no longer the county attorney for Bobby's last trial in 1931, but in my tale, I have him still unsuccessfully pursuing a capital sentence against Bobby.

The little hostages, Emma Mae Robinson and Laverne Comer, testified at all the trials, and it is true they had to repeat the fourth grade for missing so many class days. However, the newspapers covering Ratliff's trial featured Emma Mae's testimony, and I presented her words as coming from Laverne. Laverne had met Ratliff previously. Her parents bought the Cisco café from Ratliff's mother, as I referenced in the novel.

According to the newspapers, Helms ripped out the pages of a Bible during his insanity trial, and on the night of his execution, he refused to see his father, who was a pastor. The newsmen also reported how he fought the guards on his way to the chair. It was uncharacteristic of death row inmates, who put much stock in facing their peers and their guards with defiant fortitude.

Henry's family let the state bury his body. Did they run out of money after the long, costly defense, or had they simply given up on Henry? I asked myself this question while visiting his lichen-covered tombstone in the Captain Joe Byrd Cemetery (a.k.a., Peckerwood Hill) in Huntsville. I decided not to settle on an answer in the novel.

In the 1920s, men were held in the jail of the county that sentenced them to die, and then they were transferred to the death row a few weeks or months before their execution. So, Ratliff had an uncharacteristically long stay there. In the novel, the men with whom he interacts in the death house are historical. This includes Harry Leahy, whose insanity ploy led to several copycat attempts. Ratliff's habit of playing "When the Roll Is Called Up Yonder" was reported by journalists covering Texas executions in 1928 and 1929. Until his transfer from the death house, Ratliff played it for every man who walked to the chair except one. We don't know why he didn't play it for Henry Helms.

Anyone who schedules a tour of the historic Eastland jail will see how the second floor splits into two sides at the top of the iron stairway. Cells are clustered in an east-side section to the right of the stairway, and in a west-side section to the left. What you won't see on a tour of the Eastland jail is an exterior window in any of the jail cells. I presented Ratliff as looking out a southern window above the entrance to the jailer's apartment on the night of his lynching, and that decision was based on an old photograph. In the image, the jailer and his family sit in front of the jailhouse entrance facing the east. In the shadows, you can make out a man looking through a barred window above them. The photograph likely predates the Santa Claus Bank Robbery by some years, considering the clothing styles of the jailer and his family. Still, I decided to have Marshall Ratliff at a window over the entrance to the jailer's apartment, watching in horror as a lynching party stormed in the door beneath him.

In history and in the novel, Ratliff's life was spared (for one more day, at least), because he loaded only five bullets in the pistol that he used in his attempted escape from the Eastland County Jail. Also, the assistant jailer, Tom Jones, would not have suffered the fatal shots from that pistol had he retired a few days earlier, as he was scheduled to.

And during Ratliff's funeral, a department store Christmas parade really did pass by.

There are some differences of opinion on Bobby Hill's age. He is listed in a 1920 census as a twelve-year-old living in the Gatesville facility, which would mean he was a nineteen-year-old at the time of the robbery. A copy of his draft card online lists his birth year as 1905, which would put him at the bank as a twenty-two-year-old. Hill himself probably never knew his actual birth year. In the novel, I stuck with the 1920 census.

I found no public record explaining why little Bobby was delivered to the Gatesville School after his mother died. In the newspaper reports of Hill's trial, the school's administrator testified that it was not on account of any crime committed. The Gatesville School did house some foster children at that time. The record shows that, on one occasion, Hill escaped from Gatesville and made his way home, only to be immediately returned to Gatesville. It does not appear he was ever adopted by the man whose last name he bore. Newspaper reporters said he sometimes introduced himself as a Foster and sometimes as a Catcher, his mother's maiden name.

In the chapter on Hill's trial, I wrote about a boy who was whipped to death by a captain at the Gatesville School in 1917. I don't know if this detail was raised in the actual trial, but it happened, and it must have been traumatic for Hill. He would have been a resident at the Gatesville School at the time, assuming the 1920 census has his correct age.

Hill was indeed presented to the public as "the Jean Valjean of the Santa Claus robbery." It was a reporter for the Associated Press who said this and not his attorney, as I presented it in the novel. To me, this Texas Jean Valjean has always been the most intriguing character of the four bank robbers. Why hasn't there been more written about him over the years? The story of the Santa Claus Bank Robbery continues to appear in various media to this day, usually around Christmastime, but the accounts all end at the lynching. Hill's escapes and pardon deserve to be part of the story and not just a footnote or an afterword.

We have a lot of newspaper coverage of Hill's first escape from the Wynne Unit because it was led by Bob Silver. Reporters called him "the Kansas City crooner," and his escapades captured the public's attention. Just as the novel depicts, the four escapees did steal Haydon Malone's vehicle from the front of the Sam Houston State Teachers College (now Sam Houston State University), and Malone and his girlfriend were taken against their will to Houston. One newspaper report even included the titles of two songs the crooner sang during the escape. He must have found a song for any occasion. The four desperados were all captured, but they were not captured together, as presented in the novel.

The second breakout from Wynne that Hill joined was spectacular, too, and widely covered by the newspapers. Hill's several escapes were part of a record-setting year for the Texas prison system. Over three hundred men were involved in breakouts in 1929 alone.

Much of the novel after Ratliff's lynching had to become more speculative. In Hill's 1931 murder trial, an H. B. Lashee appears in the record as Hill's former employer in El Paso and a character witness. Other than the fact that Lashee owned a diner, I found no further information about him. There must have been a bond between the two men strong enough to bring Lashee all the way from El Paso to Eastland to testify on Hill's behalf. Inferring this, I took the liberty of creating the details of their relationship.

After Hill's 1931 trial, the handwritten prison record shows he was moved around to different work camps every few years and was eventually returned to the Wynne Unit before his release. For simplicity, I kept him in just one of his camps following the 1931 trial: the infamous Eastham. The horrific conditions of the work farms were described in several books by ex-offenders preserved in the Texas State Library and Archives. The rumors of farmers and factory owners begging parole boards to fast-track paroles can be seen in archived correspondence to and from the Texas governor of the time, Coke Stevenson.

The earliest newspaper reference to Bobby's release shows up in a story commemorating the twentieth anniversary of the robbery in 1947. In the *Fort Worth Star-Telegram*, Presley Bryant reported that Hill had been released to the Rusk County parole board, was married, had a stepson, and had joined a church.

With his book *The Santa Claus Bank Robbery*, the late journalist A. C. Greene did more than anyone else to make this story widely known, at least to the point of the lynching. Like other accounts, his book doesn't provide much on Hill's life in prison or his famous escapes, and no word on his life after prison. In a phone conversation with Greene in the 1990s, he told me that Hill connected with him after his book came out and they corresponded on and off through the 1980s. Back then, Greene told me that Hill had recently moved to Oklahoma after spending a few decades living in the West Texas town of Carlsbad with a wife named Gladys, who worked for the post office. The prison records show that in 1950 the supervision of Hill's conditional pardon was moved from Rusk County to Tom Green County, where Carlsbad, Texas, is located. Do a search of the US Post Office website and you'll see Gladys L. Hill served as postmaster in Carlsbad in the 1970s. Greene also told me that, though the Hills had no children of their own, Gladys had brought a son named Max into the marriage, and through Max they had grandchildren.

At the time I talked with Greene, I wasn't serious about writing a book. So, when he told me that Robert and Gladys Hill had moved from Texas to Oklahoma, I didn't try to find them.

Let's return to that Presley Bryant dispatch in the *Star-Telegram*, though. If you read in 1947 that Hill was released to the Rusk County parole board and got married and had a stepson, you'd likely have some questions. Why did they release him only fifteen years into his life sentence? Once he was released, how did he and his wife meet? What did Bobby think about becoming a stepfather after being abandoned by one himself? Why did the journalist regard it as important to tell his readers that Hill had "joined a church"?

The Last Man is my fictional answer to these questions. The actual names of Hill's wife and stepson do not appear in the 1947 newspaper report, or any newspaper report since. So, I decided not to use their names. In writing the novel, I called them Dorothy and Samuel. The stories of Dorothy's widowhood and how she and Bobby met are fictional. Beanpole and Vivy are fictional characters, and so is Willie.

When I think of Robert Hill, the last man of the Santa Claus Bank Robbery, I see someone who finally found happiness in faith and family after years of bad luck and bad choices. Go read the old newspaper articles online, too. If you come to different conclusions, let's meet at some small-town Texas diner to discuss it over breakfast.

Please leave a review!

Independent authors depend on reviews from readers like you to help others find their books. So, please comment about *The Last Man* on your favorite review site and your favorite place to buy books online.

Want to see photos of the characters and places in this novel?

Go to www.thomasgoodmanwrites.com

ACKNOWLEDGMENTS

My thanks to those who offered advice and help during the research: the late A. C. Greene; Duane Hale, professor of history at Cisco College; Johnnie Jo Dickerson, genealogist of Huntsville, Texas; Barbara Kievit-Mason, university archivist for Sam Houston State University; Rebecca Shelton, archaeologist for the state of Texas; the staff of the Austin Public Library; Sandy Rogers and other staff at the Texas Prison Museum; the staff at the University of Texas at Arlington Library and Archives, where correspondence between A. C. Greene and the Hills was found; Wayne Bradford, the former Eastland County sheriff who gave me a tour of the old jail; Cathy Jentho and the staff the Eastland County Clerk's Office; the staff at the Texas State Library and Archives; Brian McNerney and the staff at the Lyndon B. Johnson Presidential Library and Museum for help researching the pardons of Texas Governor John Connally; and the staff of the Texas Board of Pardons and Paroles.

I'm also grateful to Brian Perry for insights about Eastland County history, to Terry Slavens for promotion in Eastland, and to Tammy Loran for promotion in Cisco. John Messinger verified my presentation of the criminal justice proceedings with Texas legal practices of the early twentieth century. Carrie Messinger designed the logo for the Mainstay Books imprint, and Courtney Platt provided my author headshot. Thanks to the many who read portions of the manuscript and offered comments, and a special thanks to those who read through every new draft from the beginning to the end of the process: my monthly writers group consisting of

Amy Koch, Mark Scovil, and Kim Nixon; and especially my wife, Diane, who believed in this project from the start.

A WORD ABOUT RACIAL TITLES

For the racial titles in this book, I used lower-case letters. As this novel was being written, the latest print version of The Chicago Manual of Style recommended lowercase letters for terms such as "black" and "white" when referring to a person's race or ethnicity. In 2020, the editors of the CMOS announced that in the next print edition they will advocate for capitalizing the first letter in racial titles. They acknowledged, however, that "usage is far from settled," and "if an author has a conscious and consistently applied preference regarding capitalization, punctuation, or the like that differs from what the Manual recommends, we will respect that preference" (https://cmosshoptalk.com/2020/06/22/black-and-white-a-matter-of-capitalization). There may be legitimate value in capitalizing the first letter of racial titles in contemporary usage, but this choice did not seem to fit in a story set a hundred years in the past. Should the capitalization of racial titles in historical fiction become standard in the future, I will reflect that in a later edition of this novel.

Printed in the USA
CPSIA information can be obtained
at www.ICGtesting.com
LVHW090716150923
758078LV00003B/131